THE KING'S ORACLE

SHERRY TORGENT

BLUE INK
PRESS

Published in the United States by Blue Ink Press

ISBN: 978-1-948449-06-9

Library of Congress Control Number: 2020933033

Printed in the United States of America

www.sherrytorgent.com

Cover by Cassie Torgent

Cover illustration and map design by Gavin Churchill

Instagram: @gavindrawstheworld

— F E R R A N —
WHITE
MOUNTAINS
Gorge
AREA OF
DESOLATION
NORTHERN
FOREST
ULUN TERRITORY
ALRENIAN TERRITORY
Glasser River
MIDDLE
FOREST
SOUTHERN
FOREST
N
W
E
S

The lips of a king speak as an oracle, and his mouth should not
betray justice

Proverbs 16:10

PROLOGUE

MANY YEARS EARLIER

I am Rodolf, King of Ferran, and this is my final oracle for a time that is yet to come. My death will bring war—a fight for the throne. There will be a great battle between the eagle and the wolf. But the Destroyer will come and rain down fire from the heavens, poisoning our land. Divided by war and calamity, and struggling to survive in the face of dwindling resources, the people of the eagle will flee to the safety of the trees, while the people of the wolf roam at their feet. Yet there is one hope—the promise of a new land hidden from prideful eyes. The Iron Gate to Isidor lies hidden within the White Mountains. Heed this oracle, for the time of its fulfillment will be short. Yet, he who will go forward with his whole heart will obtain what he seeks. Only do not be of two minds, for the two rings of Ferran are the key to your salvation.

1

GIDEON

Gideon sat up and gasped, digging his fingers into his sheepskin pallet. The cool night air pierced his sweat-soaked shirt. His heart pounded as if a foul Morbid was trapped inside, beating his rib cage with its spindly fists.

He fell back and ran a hand over his forehead, gripping his long, dark hair.

Oh wretched sleep. Why do you elude me?

The dream was coming more often now. He couldn't wait any longer. He needed to see Gotz, his father's seer.

He stuffed his feet into his boots and threw open his tent flap without bothering to dress beyond his underclothes.

The soldier guarding him came to attention. "My lord."

"I need some air," Gideon grumbled.

"I'll accompany you, my lord."

"No. Stay here. I won't be long."

"Sir." The soldier's voice faltered as he took in Gideon's lack of proper attire. "Perhaps a cloak is in order?"

"I won't be long," he repeated.

"Yes, my lord."

A full moon lit the sky, making it easy for him to find his way to Gotz's quarters. His teeth clenched against the chill spreading through his body.

Perhaps a cloak would have been a good idea.

The camp was quiet, the tents dark. He passed through the center of what felt like the eye of a storm—a sereneness that wouldn't last. Too many years they had lived like nomads on the cursed ground of Ferran, with no real place to call home. His father, King Niko, lay ill, and soon Gideon would be leading the Ulun people. Now this dream was invading his sleep, torturing his soul night after night. He needed rest if he was going to save his people. He was desperate to be rid of the nightmare, though he held little confidence in his father's seer.

He lingered outside Gotz's tent, fighting the urge to turn back. A faint voice broke the darkness.

"Well, you might as well come in, Gideon. You're here now."

Gideon shook his head. *How does he always know?*

He lifted the tent flap and ducked inside. Light flickered on as the seer lit a candle. The air smelled faintly of cloves.

"I'm sorry about the late hour," Gideon said.

Gotz hobbled over to the line of clothes that hung behind his pallet. "Bah. I was awake. I've never been much of a sleeper. Daytime is much more restful for me. Visions seem to prefer darkness." He slipped on a thick robe then used his gnarled hands to smooth back his short white hair which grew in tufts on the sides of his head. He came back and inspected Gideon with his icy blue eyes. "You've had a dream."

Gideon narrowed his eyes. "How did you—"

Gotz grinned and busied himself with pouring a drink from the water jug on his table. He took two swallows, then turned back to Gideon and held up the cup in offering.

Gideon frowned. The seer could simply be guessing he'd had a dream. The hour was late, and his underclothing was soaked through. It was a logical conclusion anyone could make.

Gotz smirked. "Still don't trust me?"

It was unnerving the way the man seemed to read his mind. Gideon opened his mouth to speak then decided against it.

The seer waved off the question. "Never mind. I already know the answer." He gestured to one of the two chairs at his eating table.

Gideon sat down—reluctantly. He bent over his knees and rubbed his hands together.

The seer sat, nursed his drink, and acted uninterested.

"There's a woman," Gideon said softly. "She's in a river." Speaking of the dream sent his heart racing.

I can't do this.

He stood. Gotz's hand shot out and grabbed him by the wrist. The seer's steely eyes held Gideon's.

"You must continue, or you will never be free from it."

The old man's grip was surprisingly strong. Gideon relented and sat back down. He focused on the flame of the candle and let it lull him back to the river.

"She's drowning." His voice cracked.

Why does this trouble me so? What is she to me?

"I dive into the water as she goes under. The water is dark and murky. I can't see." He curled his fingers, scraping the wool of his undergarment.

"I spin in circles looking for her, diving over and over. I finally find her hand, then I'm grabbing her arm and kicking to the surface." He took a deep breath. "I lift her out of the water and place her on the bank." Sweat rolled down the back of his neck. "She's cold and pale." He closed his eyes. "She's dead," he whispered. "I'm too late."

There were several minutes of awkward silence. "Who do you think she is?" Gotz finally asked.

Gideon shook his head. "I don't know. Her face is hidden from me, but she wears the medallion of the wolf around her neck—the symbol of our people."

Gotz filled another cup and slid it over to him. Gideon chugged it down.

"The Alrenian child you encountered in the woods when you were a boy, perhaps," Gotz suggested.

Gideon frowned. "The dream is not of a child."

"She would be of age now. No longer a baby."

He shook his head. The idea was ridiculous. "I'm Twenty-eight years old now, Gotz. That was a long time ago."

"Yet didn't you give the Alrenian child your wolf medallion? Ulun women don't wear the medallion, only the men. So it bears to reason, your dream is of the Alrenian girl, a woman by now."

"You're grasping, Gotz. It couldn't be the girl."

"Why not?"

"The woman was also wearing a gold ring with an eagle crest. The crest of the Alrenian queen. The child from the woods was a transporter's kid. The child of a courier is no queen."

Gotz's eyes widened.

"What?" Gideon asked.

The seer rose slowly, his face as pale as his hair.

Gideon stood. "What does it mean?"

Gotz's gaze hardened. "You must agree to receive the truth, or I cannot give it to you."

Gideon sighed. This was the seer's way. He'd seen it with his father dozens of times. Gotz would not simply interpret a dream because the king wished him to. His father was required to take an oath to accept the seer's revelation as truth and act upon it if necessary, or Gotz would refuse to make the meaning known.

Gideon's jaw tightened. He'd never made an oath he hadn't kept, but he certainly wasn't going to put his future and the future of his people into the hands of his father's seer.

"I agree to consider your interpretation."

Gotz scowled. "I see your heart is still hard."

Gideon spread his arms. "I'm not my father."

"No. You are not," Gotz snapped.

The seer stared at him, as if considering. "Very well. This is too important to simply dismiss." He placed himself in front of Gideon. "Close your eyes."

Gideon closed his eyes and took a deep breath. He'd only received a vision from Gotz once, when he was a boy. The experience had been…unpleasant. When one's own mind was lost to another, it was a frightening fall into madness.

Gotz placed his hands on Gideon's shoulders. The knowledge immediately gripped Gideon's mind. He was back on the bank of the river. The young woman, still faceless, stood on the bank and held out her hand. Her eagle-crested gold ring sparkled. *"Until the wolf unites with the eagle, there will be no peace, and we shall all perish. Come, let us begin."*

And just like that, it was over. His eyes flew open. The seer removed his hands from Gideon's shoulders.

"That's it?" Gideon barked.

Gotz's face fell in disappointment.

"You expect me to unite with our bloody enemy!" he shouted.

Gotz turned away. "You've received your answer. It is yours to refuse. I only hope you understand the consequences of ignoring it."

Gideon seethed. "I knew this was a mistake. Coming here. Visions, dreams, prophecies! What good has any of yours ever done for our people?"

The seer turned to him, but instead of angry, his eyes looked sad. "All visions lead to the one that will save us, regardless of what you think."

Gideon upended the small table, sending the water jug to the floor and extinguishing the candle. "These are a fool's words."

"No Prophet is accepted in his own country."

Gideon huffed. "Don't preach to me, seer."

"Words from the Bible offend you? Perhaps you are not ready to take your father's place."

"Try and stop me."

With those fighting words, Gideon tore out of the tent. Gotz came after him, spilling more words into the dark. "I will pray for you, young Gideon!"

He kept walking. "Do me a favor. Don't."

He fumed as he made his way back to his tent. There was no way he was uniting with the queen of the Alrenians. Everything the sons of Ulu had fought for would have been for naught. Besides, how would a union even be possible? The Uluns and Alrenians had each made a claim to the throne of Ferran and living on divided territory had been considered temporary by both sides for many years until one or the other was able to obtain the throne. The two sects couldn't be further apart from peace. But the dream came again as soon as he fell back asleep, and he woke at dawn, choking on water from the river that only existed in his dream.

2

___

WYNTER

Wynter lay on her feather-stuffed pallet and held the cool medallion that hung from a cord around her neck. The wind gently rocked the tree her home was built in, and its thick trunk creaked in protest. She closed her eyes and let her fingers graze across the small ridges and grooves of the medallion that made up the profile of the wolf—the crest of the Uluns—her people's sworn enemy. She had found it in her father's things two weeks ago, the day after he'd died from a fall while transporting food to the northern tip of the middle forest. As soon as she'd seen the necklace, she had remembered.

She had been only two years old the day she'd fallen from the trees and an Ulun boy, a person of the ground, had tied the medallion around her neck. That was twenty years ago, but she could still recall his kind, dark eyes. He should have killed her; she was Alrenian, a person of the trees. Instead, he'd returned her to her father by tying her to a rope her father had tossed to the ground below. Now, rubbing the metal between her fingers, she felt a connection to the boy all over again like it had been yesterday.

How can I remember something from so long ago?

"Wynter!" Jack called from below.

She listened to the rope ladder creak beneath her cousin's hands and feet as he climbed to her home at the top of the large sycamore. His blond hair appeared through the square hole in the floor. He frowned when he saw her still in bed. He propelled himself up and into her room and sat down cross-legged on the floor next to her. Why he had been coming by to check on her she didn't know. They weren't close, they never had been. In the past, he'd only shown up when he needed something. Jack usually only looked out for Jack.

"I got you a job," Jack said.

She rolled over, away from him. "I'm not interested," she said flatly.

"Look, I know it's been hard losing your father, but you can't stay holed up in here forever."

Couldn't she? Why couldn't she be the crazy girl who lived in the trees? She was sure that's what everyone thought anyway. She imagined the older women discussing her as they sat in their sewing circles mending their husbands frayed collars and cuffs.

"She was never the same after her father died. Poor dear."

"It's been two weeks," Jack continued. "I've given you what I can, but I can't keep supporting you." He paused to chew on a thumbnail. "If our queen wasn't so stingy with wages, we'd have it far better than we do, I can tell you that. Some days I think it would be better to be Ulun. We're practically slaves if you ask me."

Wynter sat up.

"You shouldn't talk like that, Jack. We have a duty to the queen."

He shrugged and spat a piece of his thumbnail into the corner.

"Tell me you wouldn't give your right arm to see more than trees and leaves all day. Don't you ever think of what it would be like to live on the ground and ride a horse, or eat pork fat?"

Jack had always been outspoken about the fact that the

Alrenian queen was too soft when it came to the Uluns. He wanted a powerful queen, a queen that would rise up and fight the Uluns. Jack dreamed of returning to the ground. That was a dangerous thought and one that should never be spoken of. The truth was, she needed to distance herself from Jack. Her father had helped him from time to time, yes, but he'd also warned Wynter to keep her distance from him. Her father never said why.

Her stomach twisted into a knot. She had no other living relatives besides Jack, and he wasn't someone she felt she could count on. She was alone. It was time to return to her duties.

"Okay," she said. "I'll go back to work."

His eyes widened. "Okay?" he asked, brightening.

She nodded. "You're right. I have to earn my own way."

Relief flooded his freckled face. "Thank goodness," he said, sighing.

He reached in his pocket and pulled out a handful of juniper berries and held them out to her. She popped them into her mouth. She tried to ignore the bitterness by swallowing quickly.

"You'll be able to get better food once you're working again," Jack said.

"I know."

Wynter stood and rummaged around for her soft leather shoes. "What's the job?"

No response. *Great. It's probably something horrible like transporting bird carcasses.*

She found her shoes and turned to him. "Well?"

"Queen's escort detail."

She stared at him like a deer catching the sight of a hunter's bow. Being a transporter on a queen's escort was risky business.

"You need this, Wynter. The credits you'll earn are premium."

"Because it's dangerous!" She flopped down on the floor, dropping her shoes next to her.

"You know the odds of being picked for the queen's transporter?" He smiled.

He was clearly trying to spin the job in a positive light.

She narrowed her eyes. "It's a lottery, hardly an honor."

"Still," he said, raising an eyebrow.

Wynter took a deep breath. The Alrenian queen was a high-risk target. In the past, there had been attempts on her life. The Uluns had been trying to kill their queen for years without success. "Kill the queen, bury the Alrenians" appeared to be their battle plan.

And there was always the Morbids, the vile creatures, half-human, half-animal, that seemed to have a strange obsession with hunting the queen. Legend said they had fallen to earth during the Great Destruction. People claimed they were demons.

She shuddered and slipped her feet into the smooth leather shoes and tightened the laces around her ankles. The danger was a moot point now that her mother and father were dead.

What difference would it make if I died? I'm twenty-two and I have nothing left.

"You might be with one of the six decoy queens. It probably won't even be the real queen," Jack said. "Plus, there hasn't been an Ulun attack in a *long* time."

He had a point. The queen rarely traveled, and there hadn't been any real battles with the Uluns and their current king, Niko, in a long time. Both the Alrenians and the Uluns had made claim to the throne of Ferran, but neither had successfully taken it. Even if both sides wanted to continue their fight for the throne, basic survival left little time for either side to continue their civil war. Since the Great Destruction, the land of Ferran was not what it used to be, and a big part was still uninhabitable. So, the Uluns sent soldiers to fight in other countries in exchange for supplies, and the Alrenians lived in the remaining forests above the contaminated ground, using frugality and ingenuity as the key to their survival. Both sides governed their own people in their own way, each claiming that their leader was the true heir to the throne of Ferran.

However unlikely an Ulun attack was, the thought did nothing to allay her fears. The job was dangerous. But the extra credits would put her back on her feet again and past Jack's paltry juniper berries and flat cakes.

She slipped on a beige tunic and tightened one of her father's leather belts around it. She needed a little piece of him with her today.

"There's one little thing I forgot to mention," Jack said hesitantly.

She glared down at him.

"My transporter alias was actually chosen from the queen escort lottery."

"Your alias?"

"I have a fake name I use sometimes to get extra jobs."

She put her hands on her hips. "Then why in Alrenia's name am *I* doing this?"

He shrugged. "Because I have another job already?"

He grinned. "Unless you want to transport bird carcasses."

"You…" Her fists clinched at her sides. The real reason he'd been checking in on her was clear. He needed her for his dumb scheme.

He scrambled to his feet and took her by the arms. "It will be fine. We do what we have to do to survive. Right?"

His words almost sounded like some kind of apology, but Jack wasn't one to apologize for anything.

She jerked out of his grip and swatted at her long brown hair. "But I'm a girl!"

He eyed her up and down. "Who could easily pass for a young gentleman."

She huffed. It was true her figure lacked *curves*, but the words stung just the same.

"Don't worry," he said.

"Said the idiot who created the alias." Wynter picked up a

wooden bowl from the table and threw it at him. He easily ducked out of the way and the bowl slammed into the wall with a thud. She stormed over to the storage chest and grabbed one of her father's woven caps and stuffed her hair up into it. Maybe she'd been manipulated into the job, but she still needed it regardless of Jack's real intentions.

"There," she said, spreading her arms for his approval.

"Perfect," he grinned. "Just don't flash those blues eyes at anyone and you should be fine."

She kept the scowl on her face.

"Chin up and all that," he said cheerfully.

"Who am I supposed to be?"

His lips curved into a mischievous grin. "Beamus Trout."

Her mouth went agape.

"What?" he asked, shrugging his shoulders. "It has flair."

"It's ridiculous!"

He gave her a friendly slap on the back. "Good luck. Post 21."

She made a quick exit before she changed her mind and throttled Jack instead. The ramifications of what she was about to do checked off in her head. *Dangerous queen escort. Illegal use of an alias. Disguised as a boy.* All set up by her scheming unreliable cousin.

What could go wrong?

3

GIDEON

Gideon sat in his tent, drumming his fingers next to his untouched breakfast. Last night's visit with the seer had done nothing more than add to his looming problems. The seer had interpreted his dream with a vision. The image of the faceless woman with the gold ring of the eagle played over again in his head. No. Not a faceless woman exactly. The Alrenian queen.

Until the wolf unites with the eagle, there will be no peace, and we shall all perish. Come, let us begin.

Thirty years of conflict between the Uluns and the Alrenians and this was the vision the seer gave him? Unite with the Alrenian queen? Gideon may have decided to put his hope in the oracle of the late King Rodolf, but he certainly wasn't going as far as buying in to Gotz's vision that he needed to unite with the Alrenian queen in order to save his people.

A shadow darkened his doorway. His brother, younger by two years, stood patiently in the shaft of morning light spilling between the tent flaps. Was he bringing news of their ill father, the king? Every day brought Gideon closer to inheriting the throne. A throne he'd never wanted. A throne that should have been his older brother's.

15

"What do you want Lark?" Gideon asked.

"I have some good news," he said, grinning like a wildcat.

Gideon stopped his obsessive thrumming and looked up. He straightened in his chair. He could use some good news.

Lark ducked inside. "I have it on good word that the Alrenian queen is preparing to leave for the southern forest," Lark said.

Gideon's day was brightening. The queen rarely moved about. And when she did, her movements were a highly guarded secret. An opportunity like this couldn't be ignored. All his father's past attempts to assassinate the queen had failed. But this… This could be the break he needed to save his people.

"How good is the source?" he asked.

Lark scratched his dark beard. "The Alrenian kid has been smuggling us medicine for over a year and his stomach is full of our pork fat."

Gideon stood and paced, exchanging measured looks with Lark. "This could be exactly the moment to strike. If we take the queen, it would ensure safe passage through the northern Alerenian territory," he said. "And with her ring—"

Lark grinned. "Our chance to unlock the Iron Gate of Isidor."

Gideon's heart filled with hope for the first time in months. The king lay dying. The Ulun resources were depleting. The enemy queen was knocking at their door. It had to be fate. If they found the hidden land of Isidor, they would find a land untouched by the great destruction and fulfill the late King Rodolf's oracle.

"Prepare a scouting party," Gideon said.

Lark grasped Gideon's shoulder. "If we capture the Alrenian queen, this will be the first time in thirty years that we've held the key to Isidor."

Gideon clasped Lark's shoulder in return. "Go in peace, brother," Gideon said. "Bring her to me unharmed."

Lark nodded. "On my life."

"Let's hope it doesn't come to that."

Lark drew back, made a low bow, and hurried from the tent.

Gideon's heart soared. The seer's great revelation couldn't have been more wrong. There would be no uniting with the queen to save his people. The meaning of his dream was clear now. The Alreniain queen's drowning meant that Gideon and his people would come out the victors. A new era was here, and Gideon would lead his people into the future on his own terms, not by Gotz's vision. He'd take the Uluns to a world where the wolf would rule once again—the hidden land of Isidor. All he needed was the two rings of Ferran to open the gate—his father's ring and the Alrenian queen's.

4
———

WYNTER

Post 21 was fifteen minutes north of her home. The trip through the tree canopy was mostly slat bridges, with a few rope bridges in between. She passed a western passage with a large M carved into the tree. The M was a notice that the way led to something she'd never had to use—a Morbid pit. The creatures were something she'd never encountered, but she'd heard the stories and seen pictures drawn by other transporters. They were small, human-like creatures with spindly bodies like monkeys. Their faces were like newborn babies and their teeth, sharp. The pits were built because Morbids were horrid jumpers and weren't intelligent enough to realize it. An Alrenian could lure the creatures to the pit, jump the wide expanse, and the Morbids would follow, falling to their deaths. She shuddered slightly and pushed on.

Her leg muscles were already complaining after two weeks of having done nothing. She had told herself she'd leave her grief at home, but she was finding it hard to do. Her father had been her last link to her mother. Now he was gone, and nothing seemed to matter anymore.

It wasn't like it had been a complete surprise. Her mother had died in a fall. Most transporters died young as their bodies became too tired, too old, for the physical demands of the job. It was either die falling or be banished to the ground. Would the second option have been such a bad fate? The contamination of the Great Destruction would last for centuries. Uluns had adapted to the toxic properties of the ground, but those born in the trees were more susceptible to the poisonous earth and its contaminated water. Living on the ground meant the possibility of dying of ground sickness.

But at least we would have had a chance for a life together as a family.

She pushed the thoughts away and silently scolded Jack for planting seeds of discontentment. She didn't have the luxury of *what ifs*. It was her duty as an Alrenian to do her part.

Being a transporter wasn't such a bad job. She'd carried everything imaginable—food, clothing, medicine, bird carcasses, wood. Heavy things required the elaborate pulley system of ropes, but most other common items were still carried to their destination by transporters. She found that moving through the trees, and leaping the occasional expanse without a bridge, made her adrenaline surge. Thinking of it now sent her heart racing.

She began running, her feet springing off the slats. She inhaled deeply, and the heavy scent of leaf and soil brought her a soothing sort of happiness.

I've missed this.

She arrived breathless. As she crossed the small entrance bridge to the landing platform outside post 21, she stuffed some loose strands of hair back up into her cap and lowered the brim a bit more to cover her eyes.

Here goes nothing. Act like a boy.

Two soldiers stood guard by the door, while a short, stocky man in a fine silk shirt and cap studied a sheet of paper attached to a thin slab of wood. He was muttering to himself.

As she drew nearer, the regal-looking man glanced up at her. His bulbous nose was full of craters reminiscent of damage from a hailstorm. This was no doubt the queen's chamberlain—the overseer of the queen's household and affairs. *Or* was he simply dressed to mimic the real chamberlain? She was sure she'd be with a decoy queen.

"Name?" he asked, sounding bored.

Wynter swallowed. Would she'd be able to say such a ridiculous name without choking on it and giving herself away? She attempted to lower her voice. "Beamus." She stopped there, unable to finish.

Jack is going to pay for this.

The man checked his paper, then glared at her.

"Last name?" he said impatiently.

She cleared her throat and spat out, "Trout." It came out more like a cough and less like an actual word.

The man's brow creased. He checked his paper again, eyed her warily, then waved her through.

She pushed open the swinging door and let her eyes adjust to the small, dank room. It smelled of green hickory nuts and sweat. *There's no way they're bringing the real queen here.* It was a very un-queenlike place.

A half dozen soldiers were scattered around the room, checking equipment. Some were sharpening the array of knives they kept on their hip belts—others checking the strings on their bows. They barely looked up from their tasks to register her presence. She was grateful for that at least. Hopefully no one would look at her too closely. She didn't want to think of what would happen if she got caught impersonating a male. Not to mention the illegal use of the ridiculous alias Jack had stuck her with.

Lady M, as they called the postmaster there, was standing behind the receiving counter. There was an array of packs stacked and ready for transport in the holding room behind her. The older woman eyed Wynter suspiciously. She was a hard one to slip anything past. She was gritty and rough like oak bark, and she would just as soon string you up by your ankles as look at you.

Wynter crossed her arms and melted into the dark recess of a corner. The last thing she needed was for Lady M to recognize her.

The air in the room felt stagnant and too thick to breathe. She closed her eyes and pulled out the wolf medallion from underneath her tunic and kissed its cool surface. Perhaps it was foolish to bring it out in the open, but it reminded her of her father, and it soothed her to hold it in her hand.

Father would want you to carry on. You need this job.

She took a deep breath, tucked the medallion safely away, and opened her eyes.

The door to the post shot open. Everyone in the room came to attention. Two stiff-looking soldiers surveyed the room. One went back to the holding area behind Lady M and then called out, "All clear."

The door swung open again and the man with the hammered nose announced, "Her Majesty of Ferran."

Everyone in the room immediately made a show of bowing, including the bristly Lady M.

The chamberlain glanced at Wynter. She immediately lowered her eyes, thankfully remembered to bow at the waist instead of dropping into a curtsy. However, her eyes rolled back up when she heard the rustling of feet and smelled the scent of gardenia flowers wafting through the sour air.

A young woman graced the doorway like a fresh spring appearing suddenly in a dry desert. Her long black hair was plaited in an elaborate design. The resulting braid hung over her shoulder and down the front of the long, red-silk gown she wore. A dazzling array of embroidered flowers flowed cross-body from the shoulder to the hem. Her face was pale with a hint of red in her cheeks, and her almond-shaped eyes were like blue fire.

There was a gold ring on the woman's right hand. A ring embossed with an eagle.

Wynter let out an involuntary gasp.

Daughters of Alrenia. She's the real queen.

She'd seen the queen, *once*, when she was very small. This was not the same queen, but she was equally as young and beautiful. Wynter wondered if this queen was a Healer like the queen who had healed her grandmother so long ago. Some queens were Healers, others weren't. But all agreed that the gift was endowed from above, and that fact alone was enough to solidify in their minds that the true heir to the throne of Ferran came from the royal line of the late King Rodolf's daughter, Alrenia.

The chamberlain barked orders to the soldiers who would now take the queen on the next leg of the journey. No one knew the route or plan, and only now would the queen's new escorts be told where they were going. At least, that was the story told among her fellow transporters about how the queen managed to travel in such guarded secrecy.

A young boy was called in. He carried a cross-body sling on his back. He was directed toward Wynter. He shrugged off his pack and handed it to her. She reached out her hand, willing it not to shake. He might as well have been handing her a pack of rattlesnakes.

I'm actually going to carry the queen's bag. How can they trust someone named Beamus to carry her bag?

Calm down!

She took the bag and wiped away the sweat on her forehead with the back of her hand.

Once the chamberlain finished instructing the soldiers, he approached Wynter with determined, squatty steps, made more pronounced by his short stature.

"Mr. Trout."

She winced ever so slightly at the name.

"That sling will remain on your back at all times. You will follow after the first solider and will remain in his shadow until the next post. Do you understand these orders?"

"Yes." Her voiced cracked. She cleared her throat and tried to lower her voice an octave. "Yes, sir."

His eyes didn't portray any sense of confidence in her answer, but he continued.

"If, God forbid, the party should be attacked, your job is not to protect the queen. You're a transporter, not a solider. Do you understand this distinction?"

She nodded this time, not trusting her voice to remain steady.

He frowned. "Very well."

The soldiers lined up in their assigned places. Swordsman at the front. Archers in the rear. Wynter moved quickly to the front and fell in line behind the commander, his rank made clear by his shaved head. He towered over her and was at least a foot taller than the rest of the men. This was likely by design. He would be able to see beyond the men following him.

The blade sheathed at his hip was larger than any she'd ever seen, and it seemed to radiate a heat of its own, making it difficult for her to breathe.

The queen waited like an obedient child until preparations were complete. To Wynter's horror, Lady M came out from around the counter and approached the queen. M bowed awkwardly as if it was the first time she'd ever done it.

"We thank you for your visit to post 21, Your Majesty." M then bowed her head and held out her hand, offering the queen a fresh white orchid. The queen looked taken aback by the gesture. The men nervously shuffled their feet. The room seemed to be holding its breath.

The queen reached out a delicate hand and plucked the flower from M's hand, then slid the flower into her braid by her ear.

Immediately, the chamberlain barked orders to depart, and the whole party moved as one as they disappeared into the treetops.

5

GIDEON

ideon made his rounds among the people—a remnant
of what was once a great kingdom. The faces of the
cooks, weavers, food gatherers, and builders all held
the same questioning gaze.

Will you be able to lead us?

Many of them nodded at him respectfully. Others looked
away. The state of their encampment was grim at best. His father
lay dying, the food supply was dwindling, and those who had
defected were more numerous than he cared to admit. Staying
loyal to the royal line of Ulu had little benefit these days. Part of
him didn't blame the deserters. Resources were becoming scarcer
with each passing year. The Great Destruction had shattered
their world, and ever since the sky rained down fire like snow,
the world of Ferran had struggled to regain its once bountiful
lands. Years of civil war and fighting for survival, and the Uluns
were no closer to regaining the throne of Ferran or its land.

Gideon stopped and talked to a clothier. The man was
dipping wool in blue dye made from the woad plant. His hands
were permanently stained, and he was missing several teeth.

"This will make a fine blue coat for you, my lord. Once I line
it in squirrel, it will be perfect for winter."

Gideon smiled. "I have no doubt." The man's friendly words lifted his spirits, if only for a moment.

At least one person believes we'll make it to winter.

The clothier returned to his work with increased vigor, spurred on by Gideon's approval.

Gideon moved on to his reeve who was talking and gesturing wildly to a group of women field workers. Tomas had originally been a carpenter, but his quick wit and meticulous attention to detail had caught the eye of the king. He'd been Gideon's father's reeve, overseeing the needs of their people for many years now. His age showed in the white of his beard, but his abilities were as sharp as ever. There'd never been a time when Tomas hadn't known exactly how much the workers needed to produce, whether it was weapons, candles, shoes, or turnips. Tomas anticipated the needs of the people like a master sculptor envisions the finished piece long before he lifts a hand to the stone.

As Gideon approached, Tomas waved off the women and greeted him with an exaggerated bow. "Your Majesty."

"I'm not king yet, Tomas."

Tomas straightened, his expression turning serious. "No. But you soon will be. The physician says your father continues to decline."

"Yes. I'm afraid he's not much longer of this world."

Tomas nodded. "I'm sorry. Your father is a good man."

Gideon wasted no time moving on to more important matters. "How's the food supply?"

Tomas frowned. "Not good, I'm afraid. The land needs a rest. The crops grow weaker and smaller every year. We need to move north and look for more fertile ground and new game."

Gideon rubbed his brow.

"We've no choice," Tomas explained. "The land simply cannot sustain us much longer. Perhaps if we were to make peace with Valen and his followers?"

Gideon's hand automatically went to his blade. "I won't ally with traitors to Ulu. They left us. There's no coming back from that."

Tomas sighed. He bent over and fished a small cabbage out of a barrel and placed it in Gideon's hand. "We have two months of food left. We either move north, or we starve. Even then, we may still starve."

Tomas disappeared into the camp. Gideon tossed the cabbage into the barrel. Everything depended upon Lark and his men now. If they captured the Alrenian queen, that would change everything. They could use her to ensure their passage north through Alrenian territory, to the White Mountains where there lay the hope of a new land—a place untouched by the Great Destruction—Isidor. Many had heeded the great King Rodolf's oracle and had tried to find the Iron Gate to Isidor, and all had failed. But with his father's ring and the Alrenian queen's ring, he believed they'd finally be able to unlock the Iron Gate. The words of the oracle were clear.

...the two rings of Ferran are the key to your salvation.

Nothing about his plan was certain, but Gideon believed that if the Alrenian queen fell into their hands, they'd have a real chance at fulfilling the oracle.

6

———

WYNTER

Wynter relaxed as she fell into the familiar rhythm of slats and ropes. Traveling through the trees was like a dance—an intricate choreography of movement and balance. It was as natural as breathing to her. The muscles in her legs and arms felt liberated from her self-imposed confinement. It was time for her to move forward—past her father's death.

She matched the steps of the commander in front of her and tried not to think about the fact that the queen of Ferran was a few men behind her. What were the odds that Wynter would be assigned to the real queen?

Things were going smoothly until they reached an area she hadn't immediately recognized—a southern point known to be an area of concern, yet the only clear path to their southern colony. Her heart leapt when she realized where she was. This was the exact crossing where she'd fallen from the trees twenty years ago. The wolf medallion that the boy had hung around her neck that day now lay against her skin under her tunic—the metal hot against her skin as if the memory burned there.

The commander stopped at the rope bridge and held up a hand. The bridge hung fifty feet above the forest floor. Its knotted workings were like the web of a giant spider. He would test the crossing first to look for signs of attackers.

The day she had fallen from the trees came flooding back with a vengeance.

MOTHER WOKE me with sleepy eyes, fed me, and put me in a sling on my father's back. Only my father was strong enough to transport with the extra weight of a child.

We showed up at a depot and they handed my father a pack. When the man told him the destination, the muscles in his back tensed. I squirmed and pushed against my father's hardened muscles. His trepidation only lasted a few seconds, but it was enough that, even as a toddler, I knew that today was going to be different.

He stuck a hand behind his back and shifted me to his left, then slung the pack onto his right shoulder.

The constant jostling from my father running across bridges made my eyes flutter with sleep and I dozed off. Minutes, hours, meant nothing to me, but when his pace slowed and he stopped, I opened my eyes to see what had interrupted my slumber. The woods were quiet, no birds sang their songs. There was an eerie calm in the air. His breath was quick and laborious, and a moist heat rose from his back. But this was always how he was during a brisk run.

He looked across the long expanse of a single rope bridge. He hesitated, searching the ground below. The sun disappeared as though a light had been extinguished. He stepped out onto the thick rope and balanced his soft shoe on its shaky surface. I wobbled left and right as he put one foot in front of the other. My head hung precariously far over the sling as I stared down at the thick foliage of the forest floor. Some of the large leaves below began to move in rhythm with my father steps. When he stopped, the leaves stopped. It was like magic—when my father moved, the ground moved. How my father was able to do something so wonderful? I tried to speak and pointed my chubby finger. He quickly shushed me and tried to shift me to the middle of his back, but I wanted to see the moving plants beneath us, and I threw my weight back to the left. Quite suddenly, my father's body grew rigid and he took off in a run. The plants below us moved just as quickly as my father's steps. The ground was chasing us.

We were only halfway across when a black-hooded figure rose from the thick cover, and an arm pulled back a string connected to a long stick. Something struck my father in the shoulder above me and the strap of my sling split in two. I tumbled out of the sling and fell between the guide ropes. I did not cry out, my father did.

"Wynter! Wynter!"

He lay on his stomach on the rope and reached out his hand, grasping for me. He looked afraid, and I tried to summon a cry. Then small hands caught me, and I was no longer falling. I looked up at the black hood above me, but there was only a dark hole and I couldn't see a face. The hood looked me up and down. Its hands tightened around my small body and then it ran through the waist high foliage. I don't know how, but I knew I shouldn't be there on the ground. My home was in the trees. Something was wrong.

The hands held me tentatively, awkwardly. If the black hood dropped me would I fall again to a new place? Finally, the hood stopped and placed me quickly on the ground and backed away, as if it were afraid of me. I looked up at the trees, amazed at how big they looked from there. I pedaled my feet and arms in excitement. The black hood squatted down next to me. I couldn't see eyes or a nose, only a hint of a mouth. Its hand pulled the hood back, and a young boy with shoulder-length, curly black hair stared at me. Never had I seen such dark eyes. I puckered my lips and held my breath. My face flushed with the heat that always proceeded my loud cry. But sensing my anxiety, the boy lifted me up his arms and held me out in front of him like I might be poisonous. I pushed my lower lip out further, and then he spoke.

"Don't cry." He seemed unsure what to do next. I didn't like unsure, and I let out a whimper. He sat down and placed me on his lap. "Here. This will make you feel better. It will protect you." He put his hands behind his neck and removed a necklace that looked like a coin with a wolf on it. I liked shiny. He tied it around my neck, then took me back through the green underbrush and tied me to a rope that my father *had thrown down. My father's pack fell beside the boy's feet, then suddenly I was being pulled into the air, and before I knew it, I was back in my father's arms. We watched as the boy ran away with the pack.*

WYNTER'S BREATH quickened with the memory. The woods were quiet, just like that day with her father.

I'm not a baby in a sling. I'm the queen's transporter.

The barrel-chested commander removed his bow and snatched an arrow from his back. He threaded the arrow in the bow and stepped out onto the bridge.

Wynter stood at the precipice of a memory, and she couldn't stop it from replaying in her head. The boy could have, *should have*, killed her, but he had not done what was expected of him. The fact that she remembered the day so clearly was a phenomenon she'd never understand.

The commander made quick steps, looking left and right, his bow aimed at the green undergrowth below. He stopped midway and motioned the group forward. She swallowed and placed one soft shoe on the rope and one shaky hand on the guide rope. Normally she was as quick as a squirrel, balancing on the single center rope with no hands. But she was nervous, so today she would hold on.

She worked her way toward the center, feeling the rope behind her move with the weight of the rest of the accompaniment. She dared a small look below though the commander was keeping careful watch. The large-leafed plants of the forest floor were still and silent. Yet she imagined them moving and thrashing about like dozens of sharks in a deep ocean that she'd often heard stories about.

"Speed it up, transporter," the commander barked.

She released the guide rope and let her feet carry her instead of her fear. She focused on the commander's strong and reassuring presence. Her anxiety was nothing more than a memory.

When Wynter reached the commander, he lowered his bow and turned to lead the party the rest of the way across. That's when an arrow landed in his left temple and he fell against the guide rope, his bow and arrow tumbling to the ground. His body bounced off the rope, then he fell sideways through the side webbing and landed on the forest floor with a loud thump.

She gasped, her heart pounding so fiercely she could barely breathe. Arrows arched up all around her. The men behind her were shouting. She instantly ducked down into a crouch, scanning the woods for Uluns. But the forest was veiled in a shroud of green and it gave up nothing of the foe hidden below. The enemy were ghosts.

The men on the bridge yelled for her to move as they shot their arrows aimlessly into the underbrush.

No. No. This can't be happening. Not again.

She willed her feet to move, and the rope bounced beneath her with the frantic activity of the men trying to protect the queen. She dared a glance behind her. A soldier pushed the queen toward Wynter, and she stumbled on her spotless gown, reaching out with a desperate hand. Wynter grabbed the queen's hand and pulled her toward the anchor tree at the end of the bridge while the soldiers behind them fought the invisible force below. Two more thuds sounded beneath her. The words of the queen's chamberlain echoed in her head. *Your job is not to protect the queen.* Yet here she was holding her delicate hand—leading her to safety.

The men urged her forward. More shouts and bodies falling trailed behind her. Wynter and the queen reached the platform at the end of the rope bridge and they hid behind the trunk of the giant tree. The queen was gasping for air and struggled to speak. Wynter didn't understand what was happening. Then the queen collapsed. That's when Wynter saw the arrow sticking out of her back. The queen toppled sideways and tumbled off of the platform and fell like a red angel into the thick ground cover below.

The shout of an Alrenian soldier rang out. "Fall back!"

Arrows were flying everywhere. Ropes with grappling hooks were launched across the bridge. The Alrenian soldiers shot down at the Ulun men climbing up toward them, but they were quickly outnumbered. The queen's small force was over-whelmed, and soon the Uluns were on the rope bridge chasing the men back into the trees from where they'd come.

She'd been left behind—not important enough to save and not important enough to kill.

"No!" Wynter screamed.

One of the soldiers looked back at her before disappearing into the trees on the other side. There was nothing he could do for her nor the queen.

She gripped the straps of her pack and pressed her back against the tree and closed her eyes. What was she to do now? A faint cry came from below.

"Help me."

The queen! She's still alive.

"Please," the small voice cried out.

Wynter couldn't just leave her. She shrugged off her pack and looked for footing to climb down. Without thinking, and with no regard to the idiocy of what she was about to do, she made her way down to the ground limb by limb. She forgot about the danger below and focused on the soft whimpers of the queen until her feet dropped to the ground.

She pushed through the dense brush, following the queen's cry.

Her foot hit something solid and she dropped to the ground and pushed aside the leaves until she found the queen's face. The queen stared up at the broken sky between the treetops. Her body was twisted unnaturally, one leg at an angle that shouldn't be possible. A lump formed in Wynter's throat. She placed a reassuring hand on the queen's face. "My name is Wynter, Your Majesty. I'm here for you."

The queen's eyes moved to hers. There was nothing in her gaze to show that she was surprised by Wynter's attempt to disguise herself as a boy. "I must give you my gift of healing before I pass. I'm too broken inside to fix, and it could be years before another Healer is born."

Sisters of Alrenia. She's a Healer!

Wynter shook her head. "No, Your Majesty, someone from the line of Alrenia must be born with the gift."

Surely the queen can't give away her gift, can she?

The queen coughed. Death was wrapping itself around the queen, pulling the breath from her very lungs. The queen lifted her hand with the gold eagle-crested ring.

"Take it now. Hurry," she whispered.

By law, Wynter had to obey her command. She removed the ring from the queen's hand.

"Put it on."

Wynter complied, slipping the ring on her right hand. It fit perfectly.

The queen closed her eyes and winced in pain.

Distraught, Wynter bent over her and drew her up into her arms. She wouldn't let her die alone on a cold ground. The queen opened her eyes. The light was fading. The queen lifted her hand to Wynter's cheek. Her fingers were cold.

"Now, receive the gift," the queen said.

Wynter's cheek tingled, then burned. Her head swam. Suddenly, she was blind and all she could see were flashes of dark and light.

What's happening?

"You have been chosen to receive the gift. Accept it, and it shall be yours. Reject it, and it will die here."

Wynter said the words without thinking. "I accept." She wanted the queen to die in peace, and if that meant playing along with her last wishes, then she would abide.

The queen's hand fell from Wynter's face and her body went limp. Wynter released her to the ground.

What do I do now? I can't just leave her here. Not like this.

But she didn't have a choice. The Ulun soilders would be

back any minute. The medallion around Wynter's neck turned cool, giving her an idea. She removed the gold medallion and slipped it around the queen's neck. Maybe it would fool the Uluns into thinking they hadn't killed the real queen. No queen would ever wear the symbol of her enemy.

"May you find peace, Your Majesty, and your soul be forever free."

With that, she rose and made her way back to the tree to find her way home. *Home?* What kind of home would she have now that the Uluns had killed their queen?

She looked down at the ring on her hand. A shadow befell her, and before she could turn around, her world went dark.

7

LARK

Lark looked down at the girl. She was wearing boy's clothes, but he could tell by the facial features this was no boy. The rest of his men had not yet returned from chasing after the Alrenians.

"He's a spry one," Lark's cousin, Finn, said cheerfully.

Lark couldn't help but wonder if Finn's constant good humor was a mask or if he was just annoyingly chipper.

"That's no he," Lark replied.

Lark bent over and removed the cap of the unconscious *lad*. Long brown hair spilled out like a snake uncoiling itself.

"Well, I wasn't expecting *that*," Finn said.

Lark turned her over. Immediately, the ring on her right hand caught his eye. *The ring of the Alrenian queen!*

"And I certainly was expecting *that*," Finn added. "That's quite a disguise for some fancy queen."

"Yes, it is," Lark agreed.

Just as the Ulun king's ring never left his hand, neither did the ring leave the Alrenain queen's hand.

"Lark!" A deep voice cried out. "You better come see this."

"Keep an eye on her," he instructed Finn.

He pushed through the thick foliage to where Brendle, his

lieutenant, was standing. Brendle swatted at mosquitoes with his large brown hands. At his feet lay a young woman in a red gown.

"No ring. She wears the Ulun wolf medallion," Brendle said in his matter-of-fact thick, Jutta accent.

It was only through warring in other countries that Brendle had come to be with them now. But it didn't take long for the king to recognize his value and make him Lark's right-hand man.

Lark bent down and straightened the young woman's twisted leg. She was immaculate, even in death. Her face was flawless, her lips stained red with berries. He lifted one of her hands, turning it over. No calluses. Soft.

These hands have never seen a day of work

He reached for the medallion around her neck and held the cold metal in his hand. It was his people's crest—the wolf—representing the royal lineage of Ulu, son of King Rodolf. The Alrenians had backed Ulu's sister, Alrenia, as heir to the Ferran throne. Why was a woman of the eagle wearing a wolf crest?

"What do you make of it?" Brendle asked.

"I don't know," he answered honestly. "The girl over there wears the queen's ring."

"She stole the ring," Brendle suggested, furrowing his brow.

"Maybe."

Their mission was to bring Gideon the queen. Unharmed. If this vision in red was the real queen, they were in deep trouble.

"The attack was rather chaotic. Perhaps someone hit the wrong target," Brendle said as he glanced over at Finn with accusing eyes.

The Jutta were known for their honesty and bluntness. Under normal circumstances, Lark admired this quality. But not today. He gritted his teeth. "Bring the dead woman. Make a travois to carry her on."

He returned to the girl in the common clothes. She was still out cold. "Secure the prisoner to return to camp," he ordered Finn.

"Yes, cousin. With pleasure."

Two women. One in regal wear, the other in commoners' clothes. Identities uncertain. He just prayed that they hadn't killed the real queen.

8

WYNTER

Wynter woke to her head pounding and her hands bound behind her. Her eyes locked onto the green canopy moving above her.

Where am I?

She jostled unforgivingly against the hard wood beneath her.

I'm being pulled?

The distinctive footfall of horses filled in the missing pieces. She was on a travois, which was basically two long poles with netting between them. The terrain they were passing through was so rough that every bump and bobble vibrated in her teeth.

A troop of men marched behind her.

I'm on the ground!

Her heart raced. She looked to her left and screamed. The queen was right next to her, one eye open, her skin as pale as a gray laden sky. Wynter fought her restraints.

Someone ahead, out of her line of vision, called out. "My lord, Her Majesty is awake."

It didn't take her long to realize what had happened.

I've been captured by Uluns, and I'm lying next to my dead queen.

Just that morning she had been sleeping and lamenting the loss of her father. How had she come so far from that?

The horse pulling her and the queen stopped. Footsteps approached on her left—three men. The one apparently in charge stepped up to her. He stared down at her with the darkest eyes she'd ever seen. His beard was neatly trimmed, and his wavy black hair fell just above his shoulders. His clothes were fine but not fancy. He wore simple brown pants and a leather vest with a woolen shirt underneath. He propped a booted foot on the travois and held onto the jeweled hilt of the large knife that graced his hip. Just behind him stood a tall black man with a scowl on his face. His head was shaven in the style common of a Jutta—foreigners to Ferran. The third man, much smaller than the other two, had a messy head of brown hair, an ill-shaven face, and iridescent green eyes. He watched her with a wily smirk on his face.

"Get her up," the man in charge said gruffly.

Wynter was glad to be away from the dead queen, but afraid to face the brooding eyes of her incarcerators. The two men came forward and sat her up, untying her hands and ankles. The soldiers bringing up the rear gathered together, whispering and casting glances her way.

She was pulled to her feet and pushed in front of her dark-haired captor. She had never been this close to an Ulun. This one didn't appear much older than herself.

"What's your given?" he asked.

She looked down at her shoes.

"Let's try this again. My given is Lark."

"Wynter," she mumbled.

"You're the queen of the Alrenians?" he asked.

She quickly lifted her eyes to his "No."

He glanced at her hand and raised an eyebrow.

She raised her right hand and looked at it. The ring—the queen's signet ring, gold and gleaming even in the low light of the forest. The embossed eagle practically soared off the glittering surface. "I—" How could she explain? She turned and looked at the queen's lifeless body. This was all a big mistake.

"I told you she stole it," the dark man said.

"I didn't steal it!" She wasn't a thief. The queen had given it to her, hadn't she? Wynter touched her lips remembering the words she'd spoken only minutes ago—*I accept.*

"So you're the queen?" Lark asked, eyeing her attire.

"Perhaps the queen here is in disguise," the other young man said. "A trick—to fool us."

"You could be right, Finn," Lark said, considering.

The queen would never wear the clothes of a transporter. But they didn't know that. "The queen gave me the ring," she announced.

Lark and the one he called Finn started laughing.

"The girl lies," the dark man said between gritted teeth.

"Gideon will be the one to decide what's true and what's not," Lark said, putting an end to it.

"Gideon?" she asked.

"He's the heir apparent to the *real* king of Ferran," Finn said in a condescending tone.

Heat rose to her face, but she held her tongue. Finn's remark was a dig at the Alrenians claim that Rodolf's daughter, Alrenia, had been the rightful heir to the kingdom of Ferran, not her brother Ulu. When their father, the great King Rodolf died, the twins Ulu and Alrenia, had fought for control of the throne, dividing the people of Ferran. But when the Great Destruction rained fire down on their country, the war had stopped. The land had been poisoned by ash and many had died. Now, thirty years later, they were still divided, and both factions were struggling to survive. But Wynter knew, as all Alrenians did, that the eagle soared above the wolf and that the rightful heir would always be from the line of Alrenia.

Finn held out his arms as if inviting her retort.

"What? Nothing to say, Your Majesty." He chuckled.

Her hands balled into fists.

"That's enough, Finn," Lark said.

Lark drew uncomfortably close to her, and she recoiled.

"I suggest you get your story straight before we get to camp. Gideon is not so easily fooled."

She swallowed the bile rising into her throat. He was right. Her explanation sounded like a lie. She was wearing the signet ring of the queen of the Alrenians. No doubt the Ulun people knew that the queen never removed her ring. She was either going to lose her life, or save it. And it all depended on what she said next.

9
____

WYNTER

ynter walked the rest of the way behind the Ulun horses, next to her dead queen. The sun was already below the trees. Any thought of running had evaporated. Where would she go? She had no idea where she was. Even worse, she knew nothing of the world below the trees. The Ulun world was a mystery to her. She'd probably die of ground sickness within days.

Her head ached and she was afraid, but she needed to push her fears aside. She had to choose what story she would tell this Gideon. She wore the queen's ring. Her thoughts scattered as the one called Lark shouted greetings to the awaiting camp.

Her eyes widened as she stepped into the Ulun world. There were tents as far as the eye could see. People were bustling about —carrying baskets, pushing carts. Steam rose from cooking pots hanging over open fires, releasing the scent of leeks and wild game into the air. A man wearing a bloodied apron wielded a large cleaver, making quick work of the trussed chickens and ducks that floundered at his feet. He plucked them from the ground one by one and finished them with a single whack. She trembled. What would become of her? An Alrenian in the enemy camp?

All activity stopped as they noticed the strange brown-haired girl arriving. Lark led her and his men through a growing crowd of people, though they were strangely silent. She kept her eyes on the ground, afraid to see what hatred lurked behind Ulun eyes. Lark called to the crowd to move aside, but they pushed in just the same. The heat of their day's work radiated off their chests. The breath of their morning meal followed her. Someone spat at her feet as she passed by. She moved closer to the dead queen.

They halted and, mercifully, Lark came and took her by the arm and led her into a tent. The air was musty and held the faint scent of chestnuts and cheese. Crates were stacked three high on a floor of straw. She moved aside as men brought in the dead queen and laid her on top of a section of crates.

Lark surveyed the room. "One inside, four out." The men dispersed. Lark left, leaving the Jutta, the man named Brendle, with her. Brendle lit an oil lamp to brighten the darkened tent. It cast a warm glow across the queen's body. Wynter fought the urge to cry. She inched toward the queen and touched the necklace she had placed around her neck. Even now she missed the weight of it around her own. She traced the familiar mark of the wolf with her finger.

The tent flap was suddenly thrown back and the towering presence of a man entered. She clasped her hands to her racing heart. He walked slowly toward her, Lark on his heels. His cloak touched the ankles of his boots and his white shirt hung partially open, revealing his broad chest. His hair was black as a raven's, matching the intensity of his dark eyes. There was a willfulness about him that commanded those around him without a word. His gaze had an energy that instilled fear in those who didn't know him, and respect to those who did.

Gideon.

He snatched up her hand and examined the ring. Brendle left soundlessly.

"Well, what do you think?" Lark asked.

Gideon dropped her hand. His dark eyes traced over the dead queen, then he locked eyes with Wynter.

She shivered. Never had she seen eyes the color of a moonless night. He seemed to be unaware of the intensity his gaze held.

"Are you the queen of the Alrenians?" he asked.

She opened her mouth, but no words came out. She swallowed and tried again. "No," she croaked.

He frowned at her. "Yet you wear the ring. Is it not true that the ring never leaves the queen's hand?"

"She ordered me to take it. She was dying," she said defensively.

Gideon frowned. She lowered her eyes and fixed them on his boots.

"Just as I told you," Lark said.

"Doesn't the queen usually have healing powers?" Gideon asked.

She raised her eyes to his. Her heart raced. "Sometimes. Yes, but—"

"Then all we have to do is see if you can heal someone," he said folding his arms in front of him.

"I can't," she stammered. Or could she? The queen said she was giving her the gift, but hadn't that just been a dying queen's ramblings? She didn't feel any different than before she'd *accepted* the queen's gift.

Gideon crouched down so his face was level with hers.

"You can't, or you won't?" he asked with a venomous tongue.

"I can't," she said softly.

"This is pointless," Lark said. "Let me fetch our informer."

"Informer?" she asked.

Gideon studied her face. His eyes were endless, unnerving. She held his gaze this time, suddenly angry at the thought of a traitor among her people.

He smirked. "Are you surprised, Your Majesty?"

"Don't call me that," she said feeling heat rise to her face. She stood in the shadow of a man twice her size, yet she found herself growing bolder.

Gideon turned to Lark. "Fetch the informer."

Lark took his leave. Wynter sighed. This was not going the way she had hoped.

"What shall I call you?" Gideon asked, amusement in his tone.

"My given is Wynter."

He nodded. "Okay. Wyn-ter."

The way he said it sounded like he doubted that was her real name. He skirted around her and stood next to the real queen. He studied the medallion Wynter had placed around the queen's neck, then he jerked it from her body. He gazed at the necklace in his hands as though he recognized it. Wynter's hand instinctively went to the empty place at her throat where the necklace had lain. He looked over at her and she quickly dropped her hand to her side. He shoved the necklace in his coat pocket and left the tent without another word.

Night came and Brendle brought her figs and boiled beef, then left. After Wynter ate the strange meal, the wick of the oil lamp sputtered and went out. She fell into a light sleep on the straw floor only to be woken by invading footsteps and the light of a lantern. She quickly rose to her feet and waited for her eyes to adjust. Two shadowy figures pushed someone forward who had been hidden behind them. She stifled a gasp.

Jack? Cousin. Traitor?

Her face reddened. Jack avoided eye contact.

"Well?" Lark asked her cousin.

Gideon stood behind the duo, blending into the dark recesses like a predator. Wynter stared at Jack, afraid to say anything. Despite her boiling rage at his betrayal, she still held a small glimmer of hope that he would help her. It was true that he'd often voiced his dissatisfaction with the lack of action by the Alrenian queen, but Wynter was his family. He wouldn't abandon her, would he?

Jack glanced nervously at the ring on her finger.

She gave him a pleading look. But Jack would do what was best for Jack.

Then he said, "That's her. She's the queen. She wore transporter's clothing to hide her true identity in case of an attack."

Wynter's heart surged. Pure unfettered anger flared inside her. She forgot where she was, and within a matter of seconds she had stepped forward and slapped Jack across the face. Lark grabbed her by the shoulders and pulled her away.

"We can't have you beating our informant, Your Majesty." His voice sounded amused.

She tugged against his hold.

"What about the woman in the red dress?" Gideon asked, finally stepping into the light. "She doesn't look like a transporter."

Jack asked for the lantern and then held it above the queen's face.

"This is the queen's lady. She sees to the queen's needs. A clever deception don't you think?" He handed the lantern to Brendle. "May I leave now?"

"You'll tell your people we have captured your queen and if they try to rescue her, we'll kill her," Gideon said.

Jack nodded and handed Lark the lantern. He turned to leave.

"Wait," Gideon said.

Jack turned.

"Can she heal?" Gideon asked, looking at her.

Wynter tugged against Lark's arms and looked desperately at Jack. The queen had said she'd given her the gift, but she didn't know if she could heal or not. She wasn't from the line of Alrenia.

Please, Jack.

"Not all Alrenian queens are Healers," he said flatly. He slipped out of the tent without even a look back.

She was relieved he had at least spared her from the awkward predicament of having to explain why she couldn't heal, but it had done nothing to temper her anger. Jack had still betrayed her to protect his alliance with the Uluns. A dead queen would be worthless to them.

"Traitor!" she shouted, trying to break free of Lark's hold.

He wrapped an arm around her, pulling her against him. "Welcome to the wolf's den, Your Majesty."

10

WYNTER

Wynter's body relaxed as the cool night air set in. She'd been sequestered in her own tent and now she lay awake thinking of Jack, wondering how long he'd been working with the Uluns. How could he sleep at night knowing he had fed information to the enemy? She thought she had seen regret in his eyes when he'd first laid eyes on her, but his actions had proved that wrong.

Her eyes were fluttering with the heaviness of exhaustion when a shadow passed over her. She opened her eyes to someone crouched beside her. She cried out, then sprang up and pushed herself backward, crashing into the tent wall. Moonlight seeped through the tent flaps, landing on Lark's dark features.

"What are you doing here?" she asked, her voice shaking.

Lark grinned, his teeth glowing white against his onyx beard. "I couldn't sleep and thought now would be a great time for your first hunting lesson."

Wynter clutched her thin blanket to her breast. *Is he joking?*

"Get dressed," he said, standing.

Her hands trembled. His sudden presence inside the tent and in such a small space sent her mind racing. Who would help her if she cried out?

"I hardly think now is—"

He cut off her protest. "You don't get to think—just do. Now get dressed. I'll wait outside."

He ducked out, letting in a gust of fresh air.

She tossed her blanket to the side.

Arrogant. Rude.

What if he was taking her into the woods to slit her throat or something worse? Who would know? He could say a Morbid took her in the middle of the night. It had been clear from their first encounter that he didn't like her. But the fact that she was still alive meant Gideon had some kind of plan in mind for her. She considered screaming, then changed her mind.

He's trying to scare me.

She grabbed clothes from a pile that had been left for her. She stuffed her legs into ill-fitting Ulun pants and slipped into a white shirt, two sizes too big. The sleeves hung to her knuckles. She jerked her long brown hair into a leather tie and shoved her bare feet into her soft suede boots.

At least they let me keep these.

She rushed out of her tent, angry at the lunacy of the intrusion. Lark stood like a black ghost against the moonlit sky, checking the sharpness of his side dagger. She crossed her arms and cleared her throat. He glanced at her obstinate posturing, then chuckled and sheathed his knife.

"This way, Your Highness," he said, lumbering toward the woods.

She stumbled after him, unaccustomed to traipsing over forbidden ground in dark places.

"I doubt Gideon would approve of this," she said, watching her steps as she tried to keep up.

Lark glanced back at her. "How do you know he didn't order it?"

Her face flushed.

Smug. Irritating.

He was playing with her like an animal with fresh prey.

After a long walk that left her breathless and exhausted, Lark stopped.

"Tonight, you'll learn how to catch a snipe." He removed the cloth sack he had tucked into his belt and handed it to her.

She snatched it from his hand.

"First, snipes aren't very bright creatures," he said.

"What's a snipe?" she asked with trepidation.

He ignored the question. "But they can be very aggressive if they sense fear or danger."

She held the sack under her chin like a small child trying to find comfort in its blanket.

"But," he continued, "luckily for you, I'm an expert snipe hunter, and if you do what you're told—" he looked at her and frowned. "I'm sure you'll be fine. Their bite is not so bad. Small flesh wounds. They heal quickly."

One of her knees buckled and she wobbled.

His bright smile lit up the forest. "Okay then." He rubbed his hands together. "Here's how this goes. You stand there with the sack ready to go and I'll rouse them. I'll chase them in your direction and you just hold the sack open on the ground and they'll run right inside."

Wynter sighed. "Do you think I'm an idiot? There's no such thing as a snipe."

He smirked and unsheathed his knife. "Believe what you want, but if you don't want them climbing your legs like a tree trunk, you better have that sack at the ready." He disappeared into the trees.

She opened her mouth to call after him, but it was too late. She was alone, cold, and creeped out.

I'm alone. In the woods. On the ground. I should be dead. Or at least ill with ground sickness by now.

Strange whistles pierced the darkness. "Lark?" she whispered, turning in a circle. The underbrush moved to her left. She quickly knelt down and opened the sack. Her heart pumped like a hammer. She squinted, trying to see through the darkness.

"Here they come!" Lark yelled in the distance.

She gripped the sack tightly. The forest in front of her sprang to life. Sounds sped toward her like a herd of animals—limbs cracked, leaves rustled. Were those claws scraping across the cold ground?

Her eyes grew wider as the sounds grew closer and closer. How big was a snipe anyway?

Lark burst out of the trees so quickly she fell on her backside and dropped the sack. Lark laughed rather heartily.

She looked up at him, embarrassed and angry.

"You should see your face right now," he said.

She jumped to her feet and lunged for his throat. He held her off with one hand while smiling. She clawed at him. "You're a pathetic, rude—"

"Whatever you say, Your Highness."

She shrugged him off then turned away, seething.

He made a fool out of me. I'm never going to survive if I let him have the upper hand.

Suddenly, Lark grabbed her and pushed her against a tree, pressing his body up against hers. She opened her mouth to scream, but he clamped a hand over it and put a finger to his lips.

Voices. Faint but approaching.

"Not a word," Lark whispered.

She nodded, and he slowly released his hand from her mouth.

The voices drew closer.

She tried to push Lark away. The closeness of his face to hers was disconcerting. She had never been this close to a man—ever. He seemed unaffected. His face was stern with concentration— his ear turned toward the voices.

"Word is you have the Alrenian queen." It was a man's voice, deep and strong.

"It's dangerous to be meeting like this, Valen," came a

muffled reply. It was as if the speaker's face was covered, perhaps muted by a hood.

"This changes everything," Valen said. "What's Gideon's plan?"

"I suspect that he plans to use her to get passage through the northern forest and on to the White Mountains to find Isidor."

"A fool's errand! No such place exists," Valen snapped.

"Once his father dies, there's nothing to stop him from abandoning Ferran to the Alrenians."

"We can't let that happen," Valen growled. "We *won't* let that happen. Ferran belongs to us, and a dead queen will make it much easier to defeat the Alrenians."

"The queen should be easy enough to take care of. Accidents happen all the time."

"Whatever you do, make it stick, or I'll have no choice but to do it myself."

"Have a little faith. I have everything in hand."

"When the queen's Alrenian blood flows on Ulun ground, only then my friend, will I have faith."

And with that the voices stopped, and their footsteps drifted away.

LARK WAS quiet on the way back to the camp. He stormed through the woods, batting stray branches, mumbling under his breath. He was like a pot of simmering water that was close to boiling over. She feared speaking to him lest he take his anger out on her.

When they were about to breach the camp, she grabbed him by the arm. He spun around in a fury, clenching his fists. She quickly released her grip and backed away, fearful of what he might do. "They were talking about killing me, weren't they?"

He closed the distance between them and put a finger next to her nose. "It's none of your concern."

He was treating her like a child—someone to be talked down

to. She slapped his hand away. "My life is very much my concern."

He gritted his teeth. "I'll protect you. You've got nothing to worry about."

She felt herself getting angry all over again. She'd been kidnapped, mistaken for the queen, humiliated, and now some ground-dweller was planning God knows what. Any fear she had previously felt evaporated.

She pushed her face close to Lark's and lifted her gaze to his defiant chin. "Excuse me if I don't quite believe you. You've treated me with nothing but disdain ever since you dragged me, literally dragged me, back to your foul camp. So sorry if I'm not rushing to line up for team Lark quite yet."

"I'm not going to let anything happen to you!" he barked. His eyes were as black as Gideon's.

"Of course, you would say that," she retorted.

He grabbed her roughly by the arm. "Let's get one thing straight. I know you're not the real queen. So, don't expect any special treatment from me. You'll play the part until we get what we need—"

"Lark?" A voice came in the dark. A shadow approached.

"Gideon," Lark said, unhanding Wynter.

She rubbed her arm. *If he knows I'm not the queen. Why is he pretending that I am?*

"What's this?" Gideon asked, holding up his lantern.

Lark rubbed a hand through his thick locks. "Nothing. Just thought I'd give her a quick hunting lesson, set a few traps."

Gideon looked Wynter up and down, a puzzled look spread across his face. She suddenly become aware of her ill-fitting clothes and wrapped her arms around herself.

"And what were we hunting?" Gideon asked.

"Squirrel," Lark said quietly.

"Snipe," Wynter snapped. Two could play the game of fools. *You want me to play the part of queen? Fine. I'll play.*

Gideon grinned. "Snipes?"

Lark sighed and turned his head toward Wynter and gave her a "thanks a lot" look.

She smiled smugly.

Gideon frowned. "It hardly seems an appropriate activity for a queen."

This was Wynter's chance to bury Lark. She could tell Gideon how he had treated her, how he knew she wasn't the queen, about the other men in the woods and their unsavory plans. But there was something soft about the way Lark held himself in front of Gideon—respectful, humble. She'd hold her tongue for now.

She stepped forward, deciding to help Lark save face. "It was just what I needed. A distraction."

Gideon studied her face. She held her head high, though she avoided looking into his dark eyes. *The eyes that go on forever.* She coughed into her hand.

"Very well," Gideon said. "Sleep now. We have a long day tomorrow."

She nodded and stepped around Gideon to return to her tent. She took two steps, then hesitated. She turned, marched up to Lark, and kneed him in the groin. He doubled over.

"That's for the snipes."

She spun around and walked defiantly toward her tent. Gideon's soft chuckle faded behind her.

11

GIDEON

Gideon laughed softly as he and Lark headed for his tent. Lark walked gingerly next to him.

"It's not that funny," Lark said.

"It's pretty funny," Gideon said. "You deserved that from her. Besides, it was foolish to take her out into the woods this time of night. Brendle will watch her for now. At least I know he'll simply *guard* her tent."

"Don't be so quick to judge, brother. It was a good thing I did take our queen out into those woods because I overheard something I wasn't meant to hear."

Someone stepped out of the shadows. Lark rushed in front of Gideon and drew his knife.

Gideon held up his lantern. "Uncle."

Lark sighed and sheathed his knife. "Mangus. I could have killed you."

Mangus flashed a sardonic smile. "Fortunately for us both, you did not. The whole mess would have been rather difficult to explain, don't you think?"

Gideon's uncle Mangus was his father's brother and a trusted advisor. Gideon needed Mangus' support, but his ways were as antiquated as his father's, so he had to tread carefully. He didn't want his uncle frustrating his efforts.

"So what's this *thing* you weren't supposed to have overheard?" Mangus asked.

Gideon frowned and gestured with his lamp. "Inside."

The three of them ducked inside Gideon's tent. Mangus made himself comfortable, taking a seat. Gideon plopped the lantern on the table.

"What are you doing up at this hour, Uncle?" Gideon asked.

Mangus smiled. "I could ask you the same thing."

Gideon removed his cloak and flung it onto the only other chair.

"Is it true?" Mangus asked. "Have you got the Alrenian queen?"

Lark shot Gideon a look. Gideon hesitated, something told him Mangus already knew the answer to his question. Parading Wynter through the camp had made quite the stir.

"Yes. Our Ulun informer confirmed it only a few hours ago."

Mangus took a deep breath and rubbed a hand across his bristly white hair. "I wish your father was awake for this. All our lives we've waited for this moment. The moment when we finally kill the Alrenian queen."

Gideon poured himself a cup of water. He needed to think quickly. His uncle wouldn't be so easily convinced that they needed to keep the queen alive so they could gain passage through the northern Alrenian forest, much less search for Isidor.

He downed the liquid in one gulp and set the cup down on the table, twisting it in circles. "We're not going to kill the queen. Not yet."

Mangus' eyes widened. His face reddened.

"We're going to look for Isidor," Lark blurted out.

Gideon sighed.

Mangus sprang to his feet. "Have you lost your mind? Isidor is a myth! A fantasy concocted by a mad king on his death bed.

Our people have searched the White Mountains. There's nothing there!"

Gideon cast Lark a look of displeasure. This wasn't the way he wanted this to go, but Lark was headstrong, and he had made it clear to Gideon on numerous occasions that their father and Mangus were their past and that their own generation was the future.

"It really doesn't matter what you think, Uncle," Lark retorted.

Mangus made a move toward Lark which spurred Lark forward. Gideon pressed a hand into Lark's chest. "This isn't helping."

Lark hesitantly backed away. Gideon turned to his uncle. "You may not agree with what we plan to do, but I would like to have your support. When I'm king, I'll depend on your good advice, just as my father has."

The words didn't seem to soothe him. "Yet, you've already decided to search for Isidor without consulting me?" Mangus retorted.

"I was planning on talking to you about it, then I received word that we might have a chance to capture the Alrenian queen. Things have moved more swiftly than I had planned."

Mangus folded his arms.

"We're going with or without you," Lark said.

Gideon clenched his teeth and looked at Lark. He loved his brother, but his mouth was like the rapids of Glasser River.

Mangus closed his eyes and cracked his neck from side to side. He took a deep breath and opened his eyes. "Does Niko know?"

"No." It was doubtful his father would ever wake up, and even if he did, Gideon would not share his plan with him. It was better if his father died in peace.

"That's some small consolation." Mangus took pause. "I suppose I have no choice. The decision has already been made."

He gave Lark a spiteful glance then looked back to Gideon. "You have my support, on one condition."

"You're in no position to make demands," Lark said.

"Lark!" Gideon's patience was running thin.

"Don't keep me in the dark about your plans. I want to know what you know."

"You have my word," Gideon said.

Lark let out a small sigh.

"Where is the queen's ring?" Mangus asked. "I suppose you also believe the two rings of Ferran are needed to open the Iron Gate to Isidor?"

Lark put a hand to the blade at his side and stepped toward Mangus. "The details are not your concern."

Mangus showed no signs of being intimidated by Lark's posturing. If nothing else, he seemed to be feeding off of Lark's contempt. He furrowed his brow and continued, ignoring the slight.

"Surely you're not letting her continue to wear it! What if she tosses it away?"

Gideon took a calming breath. "She won't. A queen or king never removes their ring. You know this."

Mangus stiffened slightly.

"Besides, we might need her *and* the ring to open the Iron Gate. If both the queen and the ring are the other key, it's best to keep the two together. Less chance of one or the other disappearing."

To Gideon's surprise, Mangus seemed to accept the explanation, though the slight crinkle of his lips clearly showed his difference of opinion.

"Now young Lark, what is this thing you overheard in the woods?" Mangus asked.

Lark had a white-knuckled grip on the hilt of his knife. Mangus and Lark had never had a very hospitable relationship. Lark had always been a hothead, and Mangus treated him as an undisciplined youth instead of a nephew.

"Valen was in the woods tonight," Lark finally said.

The mention of his name made Gideon's skin crawl. Valen had worked against the king, convincing others that Niko had given up the fight for Ferran. By living in relative peace with the Alrenians, the king was all but conceding the throne. Usurper was a kind word for a man like Valen.

Mangus took a step closer. "Are you certain?"

Lark nodded. "He was talking to someone, but I couldn't make out the voice."

"The traitorous bastard," Mangus said. "What is Valen doing here? I thought he and his dogs had gone north."

"I believe someone in our camp is feeding him information," Lark said.

"Who?" Mangus pressed.

"Like I said, I couldn't make out the voice. But I heard enough to know that Valen wants the queen dead, and whoever he was talking to was ready to deliver."

Gideon's stomach soured. Another traitor in their midst was the last thing he needed.

Mangus straightened his aging shoulders. "It appears we have a problem."

Gideon's jaw clenched. *Mangus expects me to ask for his help.*

He didn't want to be beholden to his father's brother, but he needed him. At least for now. Too many of the people still looked up to him and respected him. He couldn't afford another uprising so soon after Valen's exodus. He considered for a moment.

"Of course, I need you to look into this," he said to Mangus. "The people will likely be more willing to confide in you. Perhaps you can find something out about this *informer*."

Mangus pursed his lips. "But of course. A level head is what is needed in these kinds of situations."

This was a dig at Lark, but Gideon let it go. "Thank you, Uncle."

Mangus cleared his throat and looked at Lark.

Gideon narrowed his eyes at his brother in warning.

"Yes. Thank you, Uncle Mangus," Lark said with a tinge of sarcasm.

Satisfied, Mangus excused himself and Gideon breathed a sigh of relief. With Mangus in their corner, things would go much smoother. He rubbed his tired eyes.

"Why do you bend to him?" Lark asked gruffly.

Gideon was not in the mood to debate politics with his brother. Luckily, they were interrupted by Brendle who barged into the tent unannounced. Gideon could tell by Brendle's stiff posture that something was wrong.

"What is it?" Gideon asked.

"The girl has fallen ill."

The color drained from Lark's face. "She was fine…"

"She has the fever," Brendle said stoically.

"Sons of Ulu," Gideon growled.

Ground sickness was unpredictable. Some lived. Some died. But almost always, if the fever came, they died. Over the generations, the Uluns had built up an immunity to it, but some, mostly children, would still become stricken with it. The Alrenian tree dwellers were even more susceptible.

"If she were the real queen, she would not have contracted ground sickness," Brendle said.

Gideon held up the hand of caution. "We were told she's not a Healer, Brendle. Besides, she is still human, even if she was a Healer."

Brendle grunted his dissatisfaction. "I should get back," he said. "She'll need tending to, medicines." He turned to leave.

"Wait," Gideon said. He looked at Lark. "Lark will see to her needs."

Brendle glanced at Lark uncertainly.

"You'll stay by her side until she recovers," Gideon said, addressing his brother. "Brendle, you're dismissed for the night."

Brendle wasted no time in leaving. That's one thing he liked about Brendle. He may have been a man of few words, but he always followed orders without question.

Lark stood speechless. Gideon would use this as a lesson to his brother. No more games with the queen. Besides, his behavior with their uncle had been out of line. His brother needed to be reminded who would be king. Gideon didn't cow to Mangus, and he certainly didn't cow to his little brother.

Lark's face burned with indignation, but he said nothing and left abruptly.

Gideon rubbed his stiff neck. A sick queen, an Ulun traitor in their midst, an unflappable uncle, and a dying king father. And all the Uluns of Ferran awaited his next move.

He collapsed onto his sheepskin pallet without undressing and fell into a fitful sleep. Some time in the night he woke in a dripping sweat, awakened by the same drowning, faceless Alrenian queen.

12

WYNTER

Wynter held a high fever for three days. The ground sickness had come without prejudice—even for a queen. It had all started when she'd returned from the woods with Lark. Her stomach had churned and soured and suddenly she was losing what little food she had eaten next to her pallet. After that, she'd barely registered anything that went on around her. She remembered crying out for her mother sometime during the light hours, only to have a young girl with golden braided hair hold a cup of warm liquid to her lips. Sometimes she'd open her eyes and a dark shadow would be lurking above her. She knew it was Lark. One night she'd woken to find him sleeping near her. She had been too weak to care.

Finally, on the fourth day, she woke up with a clear head. The fever was gone, and the small pangs of hunger had replaced her nausea. She sat up, and the same young girl who had tended to her, hurried to her side and offered her a cup.

"What is it?" Wynter asked.

"Dandelion and black walnut. It helps clean toxins from the body."

She was young, with a kind face and a sweet voice. In fact,

she was the youngest person Wynter had seen since she'd arrived.

"Thank you," Wynter said. She sipped its warm contents. It was earthy and sweet.

The young girl sat back on her heels and smiled. "I'm Kidron."

"What happened?" Wynter asked, though she was sure she already knew.

"You had ground sickness. We have a lot more toxins on the ground than you do in the trees because of the Great Destruction."

Wynter took stock of her rumpled attire and felt her matted hair.

"You'll be fine now," Kidron added cheerfully. "It's a miracle really. Once people have the fever, they usually die."

Had her *healing* powers saved her after all? She took a whiff of the shift she wore and winced. "I need to bathe."

"Okay. I can take you to the river."

Kidron grabbed some clean clothes then helped her stand. She was a small little thing, but she was strong. She wrapped an arm around Wynter's waist and led her outside. Wynter blinked against the sunlight and marveled at how something as small as fresh air suddenly felt like a luxury.

Kidron guided her through the woods. "How old are you?" Wynter asked.

"Twelve."

"Why haven't I seen any other children?"

"The women have stopped having children."

Wynter tried to hide her shock. The implications were staggering. The Uluns would surely die out. This should have been good news for an Alrenian, but she was surprised to find that it made her feel sad. She let the subject drop, afraid further questions would appear disingenuous.

They made their way through the woods and then down an embankment. Kidron helped her undress and guided her into the frigid waters. Living in the trees, Alrenians only ever took showers with rainwater. The sensation of complete immersion in dark waters was frightening. Forget the fact that she couldn't swim. She didn't realize she was holding her breath until Kidron had to remind her to breathe.

She lathered and rinsed herself off the best she could with the soap bar Kidron had provided. It came off black on her skin, which seemed counterproductive to getting clean, but Kidron assured her it worked as good as any Alrenian soap.

Kidron provided her with a form-fitting gown made of gray wool with long, tight sleeves that touched her knuckles. The hem sat right at her ankles. She'd never worn a dress in her life. It would have been very impractical for a transporter.

Kidron braided Wynter's hair in a single braid down her back. Now that she was clean and dressed, reality began to seep back in.

I'm a prisoner. Lark knows I'm not the queen. There are Uluns who want to kill me.

"Well, well, well," Lark said, coming out of the woods.

Wynter crossed her arms. "Is this dress your idea?" she snapped. It suddenly occurred to her that the dress might be another one of his games, serving to further humiliate her.

He held up his hands in surrender. "Nope. All Kidron."

Wynter looked over at Kidron and raised a questioning eyebrow.

Kidron shrugged. "You're a queen. You should dress like one."

Lark grinned, and she couldn't help but notice that he was rather handsome. She frowned at how annoying the thought was.

"Well, it's ridiculous," she said, peering down at the gown. "I can't do anything in *this*."

Lark came closer. Too close. She closed her eyes as he leaned in next to her ear. "All you need to do is look pretty."

Her face reddened. The nerve. Women were obviously undervalued in Ulun society.

He took a step back looking smug and self-satisfied.

They were right back where they'd left off the night of the fake snipe hunt. Apparently her sickness had done nothing to temper his attitude toward her. She straightened her shoulders and lifted her chin. "What about the secret plan to kill me?"

That got his attention. His jaw tightened and his eyes narrowed.

"What?" Kidron asked, looking horrified.

Lark shot Kidron a dark look. "Wait back," he said sternly.

Kidron sighed but complied and navigated to the edge of the woods, keeping just in sight. She removed a knife, hidden at her ankle, and swirled it in her fingers.

Wynter turned her attention back to Lark's frown.

"You're not in any danger," he said unconvincingly.

"Not from what I heard a few nights ago."

He pulled back his cloak to reveal a large blade at his hip.

She smirked. "Is that supposed to impress me?"

"Nobody gets to you without going through me. You've nothing to worry about."

"So you say."

He let his cloak fall back over his knife. "My job is to protect you at all costs." His tone seemed sincere.

"Why? As you've said, I'm not the real queen."

"Until I say otherwise, you're the queen. So if you want my protection, you'll play the part, and keep this between us."

Wynter didn't know why Lark was deceiving Gideon about who she really was, and she didn't care, but she wasn't convinced Lark was the great defender he claimed to be. She glanced in Kidron's direction. "I'd feel better if I had a weapon."

He chuckled. "That's not going to happen."

She held her shoulders back and stood taller. "And why not?" She had no idea how to use a knife to defend herself. Her knife skills were limited to cutting rope and peeling back tree bark for some quick sustenance. But she'd like to have some-thing to depend on besides Lark.

"Oh, I don't know," he said waving a dismissive hand, "maybe because I don't want to be murdered in my sleep."

His words reminded her that during her feverish nights, she had woken several times to find him next to her. Suddenly, the argument felt petty. He seemed to notice her change in demeanor and now eyed her suspiciously.

"Thank you," she said softly.

His eyes registered a curious surprise.

"For taking care of me—during my illness," she explained.

His face paled slightly as if he had been caught in the act of thieving. He shifted uncomfortably. "Kidron took care of you," he said.

"Of course. That's what I meant to say. Thank you for Kidron."

He nodded and looked behind him at Kidron. "She's under my feet constantly. You've been a good distraction for her."

"Under your feet?"

Lark smiled at her.

So he can be charming when he wants to be.

"She's our half-sister—a daughter of the king. Her mother died during childbirth. Unfortunately, that gives her a certain amount of free rein which usually includes her incessant nagging for me to teach her knife fighting."

Wynter glanced at Kidron who was watching them with a careful eye.

This could work in my favor. Kidron could be a wealth of information.

"I'd like Kidron to be my companion." She tried to sound queen-like, but her face flushed despite her efforts.

Lark raised an eyebrow and scratched his forehead as if perplexed by the request.

"Are you sure?"

"Yes," she said, trying to speak as one with authority.

He smirked and made a show of bowing low. She knew he did it in jest, so she let it go.

He motioned back toward the woods. "Shall we?"

She grabbed up the folds of her skirt and strode toward Kidron. Lark announced to Kidron that she would now be the queen's maid, then he disappeared into the woods.

Kidron smiled brightly. She seemed pleased with the news. Her smile warmed Wynter.

"Is this okay with you, Kidron?"

"It would be my honor, Your Majesty." She made an awkward attempt to curtsy.

"Kidron, let's not be so formal," Wynter suggested.

Kidron smiled shyly. "Like friends then?"

Wynter smiled. "Yes. Like friends."

They walked through the woods. Lark's cloak flowed between the trees in front of them.

"Kidron," Wynter said, "do you know how to use that knife of yours?"

Kidron bent over and produced the blade from her ankle.

"How well?" Wynter asked.

Kidron stopped, planted her feet, and threw the knife straight into the woods ahead of them. It landed in a tree trunk right beside Lark's head. He turned and frowned.

Wynter couldn't resist a tiny smile. "Could you teach me?"

"Absolutely," Kidron said. She ran ahead to fetch her knife.

13

GIDEON

Gideon studied the maps at hand while he rubbed the wolf medallion hanging around his neck. If they cut through the Alrenian northern forest, they'd reach the White Mountains in six to seven days. He clenched his fists. Trying to find Isidor was a huge gamble, especially now that their food supply was dwindling. He would be risking the lives of all the people who had been loyal to the line of Ulu. But fleeing to surrounding countries wasn't an option either. Those countries were caught up in wars, many of which Ulun mercenaries had fought in. His people didn't need more war. They needed a new start. He had the two rings, but what if this new world didn't exist?

His father had been adamantly against looking for Isidor. King Niko wanted one thing—Ulun control of Ferran. But Gideon was a realist. His people would slowly perish if they didn't find Isidor. Ferran was still recovering from the Great Destruction, the Ulun women had lost too many children to war, and there hadn't been a baby born in twelve years—not since Kidron. The seer, at least, believed in the last oracle of King Rodolf. And though Gideon was not one to rely on oracles or prophecies, he felt he had no choice but to try and find the mystical land of Isidor. And since the part of the oracle about Ferran splintering into two factions had already come true, he'd just have to hope that the rest would follow.

A guard stuck his head in the tent. "Someone to see you, my lord."

Gideon nodded.

The seer strode in.

Gideon leaned back in his chair. "What is it, Gotz? I'm busy."

Gotz eyed the stack of maps on the table. "I can see that." He took a seat across from Gideon, wincing slightly. "The bones aren't what they used to be."

"What do you want?" Gideon asked.

Gotz fingered the edges of the maps, clearly feigning interest. "Have you thought any more upon your dream? The one about the girl—the queen?"

"No."

Gotz pursed his lips. "You've captured the Alrenian queen. I assumed—"

"You assumed wrong."

"I see," Gotz said, tapping his fingers on the table. "I heard the dead girl, the queen's maid, you brought in with the queen was wearing a wolf medallion." Gotz eyed Gideon's neck. "So I see it has found its home again."

Gideon knew what Gotz was getting at. In the dream that haunted him, the faceless woman wore the medallion and the queen's ring. Now that he had both, Gotz would use it as evidence of the accuracy of his vison. But nothing in the oracle had said anything about marrying.

"I will never unite with the queen."

"Even if it saves your people?" Gotz asked.

Gideon rubbed his temples with one hand. "I don't have time for this, seer."

Gotz waved a hand across the table. "Yet you spend hours making plans that you are not sure will work."

Gideon stood and paced. "How do you know what I have planned?"

Gotz raised an eyebrow. "I'm a seer. I see things you know nothing about."

Gideon stopped pacing and crossed his arms. "I'm not my father. I won't build our kingdom on your dreams and visions."

Gotz looked up at the ceiling of the tent as if all the answers lay there.

"Where has my father's rule left us, hmmm? Starving. Childless. Deserters. I have to find a better way—a better future," Gideon said.

Gotz glared at him. "You have the answer; you refuse to accept it."

Gideon laughed. "Unite with the Alrenian queen? Marry her? She's barely more than a child."

"Yet, that is what you must do."

Gideon slammed his hands on the table in front of Gotz. "How could that possibly save our people? Will our women suddenly conceive? Will it put food on our tables?" he barked.

"Your stubbornness certainly won't save us."

Gideon straightened. "Neither will an old man's ramblings."

Gotz stood and calmly hobbled toward the way out.

Gideon felt a stab of regret watching the old man. "Will you back my decision to head north?" Gideon asked. "The people will look to you."

Gotz stopped without turning around. "Isidor?" he asked softly.

Gideon's muscles tensed. He had told no one of his plan, except for Lark and Mangus. Yet the seer seemed to know. He *always* knew.

"Yes. I will back your plan. On one condition."

Here it was. The catch.

He turned and looked at Gideon now. "You'll at least consider the union with the queen."

Gideon worked the muscle in his jaw back and forth. "I won't change my mind."

He could've sworn he saw a twinkle in Gotz's eyes. "As you say," Gotz replied.

Gideon was left wondering if he was playing the seer or if the seer was playing him. He shook the thought away and changed into his more regal wear—a clean muslin shirt and a black over-coat. It was time to tell his people of the plan to search for new land—for Isidor.

14

FINN

"Gideon is calling the people together," Finn said to Mangus.

"I'm aware, son."

Finn stifled a yawn as his father strode around his tent in a robe searching for his dress clothes.

"Why did you summon me?" Finn asked.

He hated when his father sent someone for him. One would have thought Mangus was king the way he put on airs.

Mangus held up a gray woolen tunic. He stuck his finger through a hole near the collar.

"Blasted moths." He tossed it aside.

He stopped his momentary search for a proper shirt and looked at Finn. "I summoned you because I want to know what you've found out about Valen's informant who's hiding among us. It's been three days since I asked you to look into it." His tone was one of a master to his servant.

Finn bit his tongue and stuck his thumbs into his belt. "Nothing so far. Whomever it is, he is very clever."

Mangus frowned. "I want him found."

"I'm aware. I'm doing my best."

"Well your best isn't good enough." Mangus sneered.

Finn smiled. "Of course."

Mangus fumbled around inside a trunk and pulled out a burgundy tunic. "Ah, much better." He threw off his robe. Finn looked away. The sight of his naked father was not something he wanted imprinted upon his mind.

"I'm assuming there's more to why you called me here," Finn said.

Mangus jerked his pants off a chair and slipped them on. "There's the other matter of the queen."

"She's recovered from ground sickness," Finn said.

"Yes, yes. I know," Mangus said with a wave of this hand. "I'd rather hoped she wouldn't."

His father looked at him pointedly.

Finn smirked. *The devil shows his true colors.*

"I'm not sure I get your meaning, Father." Finn displayed his best puzzled face. Playing dumb would irritate Mangus.

Mangus scowled. "Sometimes I think you have rocks in that head of yours."

Finn continued to stare quizzically at his father.

"We can't allow her to live. Gideon has some grand idea of finding Isidor. He needs her to gain passage through the northern Alrenian forest."

Finn tapped a finger on his cheek. "Uh huh."

"Blasted, Finn. Stop toying with me!"

"Why not just let Valen's inside man handle the job," Finn suggested.

Mangus' face turned bright red. "Because he is a traitor to our king and the Ulun people," he spat. "If I can't have Valen's head, I'll have the head of whomever he's got working inside of our camp."

Finn was beginning to enjoy stringing his father along. "What are you asking me to do?" He knew, of course, but he wanted to make his father work for it. Was Mangus' face turning purple?

"I want you to arrange an accident for our Alrenian queen!"

"What's in it for me?"

Mangus stepped in front of him. Was that sweat on his fore-head? Finn tried not to grin. "Get it done," Mangus said between gritted teeth.

Finn took a step back and made a low bow. "As you wish, Father."

He left and walked through the camp feeling quite satisfied with himself. He had his father right where he wanted him, in the palm of his hand. Oh, he'd take care of the queen, all right, but not because Mangus wanted it done. Finn had to pacify Valen and make him believe that he was doing *his* bidding. But nothing could be more contrary to the truth. Finn was playing the game he needed to play, and when the time was right, he would take the throne for himself.

He started whistling.

15

WYNTER

"There is really no need to learn to throw a knife," Kidron said. "The idea is to keep the knife in hand. Once you throw it, you no longer have a weapon."

Wynter one-eyed the tree in front of her, clutching the knife in her hand. "Then why did you learn to do it?"

"Because it's cool, and I like messing with Lark. Catching him off guard keeps him on his toes."

"Okay. Well, those reasons sound good to me."

Kidron shrugged. "If you say so."

Wynter pulled her right arm back and threw the knife. It hit the tree, bounced off, and landed on the ground. She frowned and looked at Kidron.

"It's not as easy as it looks," Kidron said. She ran and fetched the knife. "First of all, you're holding it wrong. Don't clutch it in your fist."

Wynter shook out her hands. Kidron took Wynter's right hand and placed her thumb dead center on top of the grip.

"Now, three fingers on the back. Pinky finger hangs off."

Kidron let go of her hand, and Wynter let the blade settle. She eyed the tree.

"Now," Kidron said, "you want your left shoulder facing your target, so your body is at a slight angle."

Wynter adjusted her stance.

"Try to throw straight, blade flat."

Wynter pulled back and threw her whole weight into the release. The knife hit the tree and fell to the ground.

She sighed. "What am I doing wrong?"

Kidron retrieved the knife again and placed it in Wynter's hand. "Part of it is knowing how many rotations it takes for the point of the blade to arrive first. The distance will dictate how hard you need to throw it."

Wynter was frustrated, but not deterred. Again and again, she threw the knife. Kidron gave her pointers each time, tightening her form, until finally, the blade buried itself into the trunk of the tree. Wynter's heart beat furiously. She grinned at Kidron.

"One out of fifty. It's a start," Kidron said.

Wynter didn't care. She'd practice until she mastered it. She didn't know what awaited her. If someone was going to try to kill her, she wasn't going to go down without a fight.

Lark stepped out of the woods in his dark cloak, taking them by surprise.

"What's this?" he asked, frowning.

Kidron ran to the tree and pulled out the knife. "I was just practicing. Wynter wanted to watch."

Wynter nodded and said, "Fascinating."

Lark raised a suspicious eyebrow but said nothing further about it.

"Get back to camp, we're packing up."

Wynter's heart fluttered. "What do you mean, packing up?" she asked.

"We're leaving, Your Highness. Pick up your skirt and get back to camp." With that, he turned and strode back into the woods.

Wynter turned to Kidron, her heart racing. "Where are we going?"

"I don't know. But I have a pretty good idea."

"Where?"

"Isidor."

WYNTER MADE work of packing her meager belongings. She didn't understand why the Uluns were leaving. They were known to be nomads and travel the lands of Ferran for resources, but from what she could tell from their camp, they hadn't been north of the Alrenian middle forest in a long time. But if what Kidron said was true, that they were leaving to search for Isidor, then perhaps Gideon was not of his right mind. Isidor was a myth—part of the ramblings of a past king—King Rodolf. It was supposedly a place hidden beyond the White Mountains, where the land had not been destroyed by the Great Destruction. It was protected by a secret entrance that could only be opened by some magical key. She had heard the tales—they had been passed down through the generations, but she'd never known anyone who actually believed Isidor was real. She grew angry at the absurdity of her predicament. Leaving middle forest would dash all hope of her ever returning home, however slim that hope was.

Lark poked his head into her tent as she was folding up the ill-fitting pants and shirt she had been given a few nights ago.

"Come in," she said flatly.

Lark stood awkwardly as she packed her clothes into a leather satchel.

"Are you going to try and find Isidor?" She stopped folding and looked at him.

"Yes."

Heat rose to her face. "It's a foolish thing to do," she snapped.

Lark closed the distance between them and talked down to her. "The only fools here are the Alrenians. Let's see how your people fare when they no longer have our wool or leather."

Her face burned with indignation. "We don't trade with Uluns. You're a liar!"

She tried to turn away from him, but he jerked her back around. "Where do you think the leather on those shoes of yours came from? Trees? We've been trading for years."

"You're hurting me," she said, pulling against his grip.

He released her. "The land has given up everything it has left. If we don't find Isidor, we'll all perish, including the Alrenians."

She rubbed her arm. "If what you say is true, I should warn my people. Let me go. What use could I possibly be to you?"

Lark grinned. "You're our ticket, Your Highness. You're not going anywhere."

"What do you mean ticket?"

"We have to pass through the northern forest—Alrenian territory. You think they're just going to let us walk right through?"

"But I'm not the queen!"

He smirked. "That is true. But they don't know that. You wear the ring. That is all that will matter."

"What they say about Uluns is true," she spat. "You're just a bunch of Grunts."

Lark chuckled. The fact that he'd found the slur funny made her even angrier, and she balled her hands into fists. The knife Kidron had given her burned at her ankle, but she had promised only to use it if her life was threatened. Before she could think on the blade any further, Lark retorted with a counter slur, "At least I'm not a high and mighty Stump."

He made a low bow and left.

She screamed at her tent walls in frustration.

16

———

GIDEON

Gideon pulled his black stallion to a halt next to Lark's brown and white speckled mare. They surveyed the camp's packing progress from atop a hill.

"I heard there was a small disturbance this morning," Gideon said.

Lark's horse whinnied. "If you mean a spoiled queen having a fit, then yes, there was a small disturbance. It was nothing I couldn't handle."

"I don't want her handled," Gideon said.

Lark looked over at him. "Since when?"

Gideon kept his eyes on the camp. The reeve, Tomas, was barking orders as supplies were loaded into wagons.

"The seer says I need to unite with the queen." He glanced over at Lark. Lark's jaw hardened and his grip on his horse's reins tightened.

"Since when did you confer with our father's seer?"

"I keep having a dream about a faceless woman. She's drowning in the river and I try to save her. I bring her back to the shore but it's too late. She's dead. She's wearing the ring of the Alrenian queen and a wolf medallion."

Lark didn't speak right away. The horses snorted.

"Gotz gave you a vision?"

"Yes. The same faceless woman says to me, *Until the wolf unites with the eagle, there will be no peace, and we shall all perish. Come, let us begin.*"

"What are you saying?" Lark asked, his voicing raising an octave. "Uniting with the Alrenian queen betrays everything our ancestors fought for. What our brother died for."

"I know."

"And what of Hilran? She's still unmarried, no doubt still holding out hope that you'll take her as your bride."

Gideon sighed. "I have no intention of marrying Hilran."

Lark turned his horse around toward camp. "The Alrenians spit at us, Gideon. They call us Grunts."

"I know this too."

"I love you, brother. But you better think long and hard before you try to erase the past."

Gideon listened as Lark galloped away. He didn't want to believe that he needed to unite with the Alrenian queen. Yet the dream had woken him again last night. Only this time he had felt a gut-wrenching loss for the queen that had followed him into the waking hours. But he would not be the king who bowed down to the eagle. That would not be his legacy. He would lead his people to Isidor and start anew.

He turned and rode back to camp.

17

LARK

Lark stood at a distance and watched Wynter and Kidron as they loaded their belongings into a wagon. He sharpened his blade on a smooth stone, trying to work off the pent-up energy that was driving him to madness. Gideon's talk of a dream about uniting with the queen was disconcerting, but he didn't have time to worry about visions. There was a traitor in their midst, and he had no idea who it was.

Valen had definitely been there that night in the woods. That much he was certain of. He was a stain on the Ulun people—a deserter and a usurper. He had recruited half of their men and women to break free from the king's rule, claiming Niko had all but handed the Alrenians the throne by not doing more to claim it. Valen had convinced them that it was time to fight their own wars at home and reclaim their kingdom. He said the Uluns had lost too many fighting other men's wars as mercenaries. That part was true, but only because they needed the spoils of war to keep their people alive. Valen saw this dependency on others as weakness, but Lark saw it as strength. Without the spoils of other men's wars, their people would have starved by now. But the losses of war had been great, and the Ulun people were tired.

So now they stood divided, Valen on one side and Gideon on the other. Valen wouldn't be satisfied until the queen was dead and the Uluns had reclaimed the throne of Ferran. Only Wynter wasn't the real queen.

He knew he should tell Gideon that she wasn't the real queen, but he couldn't bring himself to spoil their plans. He had told the Alrenian informant, Jack, to say that Wynter was the true queen and not the beautiful dead woman that lay on lowly crates. If Gideon knew the truth, Lark feared the plan to find Isidor would end right then and there. What if Gideon thought using a fake queen to gain passage through the northern forest was too risky? All their plans to find Isidor would fall at the wayside. He couldn't let that happen. Their people needed hope. That meant Lark needed Gideon to believe Wynter was the queen. The whole future of the Ulun people depended on her.

He told himself he would tell Gideon as soon as they were through Alrenian territory – especially before Gideon could do anything so foolish as to marry Wynter. The seer's interpretation of Gideon's dream was hardly reliable. Gotz had served his time, and to what end? The Ulun people continued to fight for survival. The seer's words were meaningless. Lark would have to work harder to keep him from poisoning Gideon's mind. He and Gideon needed to stay focused until they passed through the Alrenian's northern forest. If they found Isidor, they'd find fertile land—a land of plenty where they could prosper once more. And if they had to use a fake queen to do it, so be it. Lark would make sure that Gideon saw the plan through. He didn't need to be honorable. That was Gideon's job.

I'm doing the right thing.

Now he just had to ensure that Wynter stayed alive.

He'd been lost in the soothing sound of blade against stone when shouts erupted, and a commotion ensued near Wynter and Kidron's wagon. He sheathed his knife and ran toward the crowd gathering around their wagon. He pushed people aside, searching for Wynter. His eyes widened when he found her propped against a wheel with an arrow sticking out of her left shoulder. He fell to his knees beside her. Kidron was gaping at Wynter's wound in horror.

"What happened?" he asked Kidron.

She shook her head. "I don't know. I'm sorry. I should have—"

Lark ripped the dress from around the arrow to assess the wound. Wynter cried out in pain. The wound was gushing blood.

"Whoever did this is not going to get away with it," Kidron barked. She disappeared into the crowd. He started to call after her, but Kidron had a mind of her own—a very stubborn one.

Wynter moaned and her eyes fluttered. He was losing her. He shouted orders to some of his soldiers who were already pushing back the crowd. "Search the surrounding woods!" He gingerly lifted Wynter into his arms.

The arrow was Alrenian. The shaft was birch with goose feather fletching. Ulun arrows were made from ash and turkey feathers. But why would the Alrenians risk coming so far from their territory to kill their own queen? Something told him this attack came from much closer to home. Someone wanted to make this look like an Alrenian attack.

Whoever did this is diverting the blame to protect themselves. It has to be Valen's inside man.

The color had drained from Wynter's face. Blood poured from the wound and soaked into her dress. He cursed under his breath and ran toward the tent of the doctor. His soldiers pushed people aside, making a clear path as he passed shocked faces, murmurs, and looks of reproach. Wynter's head fell back. She became limp in his arms like a small child who had fallen asleep.

No. She can't die.

Relief flooded over him when he spotted the doc's tent still standing. Moving camp always resulted in its share of injuries, so the doc's tent stayed at the ready until the last wagon pulled out of camp.

Lark rushed into the tent. The doctor was wrapping a splint around a woman's middle finger.

"What's this?" Barrow asked, looking annoyed at the intrusion.

"Get out!" Lark shouted at the woman.

The woman looked nervously at Barrow and he sighed. "Have your husband finish the wrapping." The woman nodded and fled the tent.

Barrow stood and motioned for Lark to put the girl on his worktable. He wiped his hands on a rag. "I never thought I'd see the day where I'd have to treat an Alrenian Stump."

"Keep your tongue in check, Barrow," Lark warned.

He gingerly laid Wynter on her side on the table. Some color had returned her face, and the bleeding had slowed.

Barrow huffed, then wet a sponge in a basin of water. Lark ripped the back of Wynter's dress so that the wound could be accessed from the front and the back.

"You're going to have to back up if you want me to treat your *queen*," Barrow said from behind him.

Lark stepped aside.

"You should wait outside," Barrow said, cleaning the blood away from the exit point of the arrow.

"I'll stay."

Barrow shot him a look of disdain. "Hmmm. You don't trust me?"

"Just do your job."

Barrow examined the wound. His eyes widened.

"What? Is it bad?" Lark asked nervously.

"What is this?" Barrow said, looking at Lark.

"What's what? She has an arrow in her shoulder!"

Barrow frowned, stepped back, and motioned him forward. "See for yourself."

Annoyed and growing more impatient by the minute, Lark pushed past the doctor. Wynter's skin had healed around the arrow. The skin was pale and pink as if it was the most natural thing in the world for the arrow to be there. "Sons of Ulu," Lark whispered.

"She's a witch," Barrow said.

Lark spun around. "No. By all the saints…she's a Healer."

Wynter's story about the queen giving her the ring may have been true, but she failed to mention that the ring hadn't been the only thing the queen had given her.

This changed everything.

18

____

LARK

"**I** won't treat her," the doctor said sternly.

There was fear in the man's eyes despite his harsh tone.

"Get out!" Lark spat.

"May the spirit of Ulu forgive this treachery," Barrow retorted.

"Leave now, or I'll cut you from stem to stern," Lark warned.

Barrow grabbed a box of supplies and bumbled his way out of the tent. Lark would deal with him later. Right now he had to get that arrow out of Wynter's shoulder. Just as he drew his knife, the tent flaps flew open and Kidron walked in.

"Why is Doc—"

"Not now," he said bitterly.

Kidron approached cautiously. "Is she…"

"She's not dead. Just the opposite."

Kidron narrowed her eyes and moved in closer. "Sons of Ulu. The wound is healing around the arrow. What are you going to do?"

"Well we can't leave an arrow in her shoulder, now can we?"

"But—"

"Get on the other side. When I tell you, pull the arrow out."

Kidron nodded and rounded the table. She gripped the arrow in her hands and nodded at Lark.

He took a deep breath, broke off the end of the arrow, then took his blade and cut into Wynter's shoulder right at the entry point. Wynter jerked to life and screamed. She flailed her arms, trying to guard herself against Lark.

"Be still. I'm not trying to kill you."

Wynter tried to sit up. "Help me! Help!"

He grabbed her arms. Kidron rushed around to his side, trying to calm Wynter.

"It's okay, Your Majesty," she said, taking her hands into her own. It was hardly the time to be gentle, and Kidron's child-like admiration for Wynter was grating on his nerves. But at this point, he'd kiss Wynter's ring if it meant she'd be still.

"What's going on here?" Gideon's voice broke through Wynter's screams.

Great. Could this get any worse?

"The queen has healed around the arrow in her shoulder. I have to cut it out," he explained.

"Gideon. Help me!" Wynter cried out, turning toward his voice.

To Lark's surprise, Gideon threw off his cloak and came to their assistance. He stood at the top of the table by Wynter's head and held her still. She screamed in protest. Gideon nodded imperceptibly at Lark.

Kidron resumed her position at Wynter's back, gripping the shaft of the arrow.

"Here goes nothing," Lark shouted over Wynter's piercing scream.

GIDEON STARED AT WYNTER. She was in a state of semi-conscious-ness, but she was calm. The arrow had been removed. Kidron was fussing over her, cleaning the wound with fresh water. The skin had only taken a few minutes to heal over.

She lied. She said she couldn't heal. No Alrenian was going to make a fool out of him.

"Leave," Gideon barked at Kidron.

She cowered under his strong words. He felt a stab of regret at the harshness of his tone. Over the years, he'd not been the brother he should have been to her. It was clear by her reaction that she feared him, but it seemed too late to remedy the mistakes he had made with her.

Lark put a hand on Gideon's shoulder, trying to calm him. But he was angry, and he wasn't going to let go of it anytime soon.

"Both of you. Out," Gideon said evenly.

Lark hesitated.

"Please," Gideon said quietly.

Lark and Kidron exchanged furtive looks, but they complied and left him alone with the queen.

Wynter mumbled and fretted as if she were having a bad dream. He poured a vessel of water, then went and stood at her side. A pale pink color had returned to her cheeks. Her brown hair fanned across the table. Her dark eyelashes fluttered, though her eyes remained closed. Her face held a youthful innocence that almost made her beautiful. He had to admit, her eyes were a kind of blue that made him look twice. But any kind of union with this queen was out of the question—vision or not.

He threw the water in her face. She gasped and sprang up, sputtering, eyes wide. She wiped a hand across her face and stared at him in astonishment.

"How dare—"

"Get up," he said, cutting her off.

She looked around as if trying to piece together what had happened. She looked down at her torn, bloodied dress and lightly fingered the scar below her shoulder. "I was hit," she said.

"I said get up," he said, more harshly this time.

"Where's Lark?" she asked, furrowing her brow.

What little patience he had left retreated. He took her by the arm and pulled her off the table. She fought against his grip.

"Unhand me!" she cried.

He ignored her plea and drug her with him out of the tent. Lark and Kidron were waiting outside and exchanged surprised looks upon seeing Wynter in tow.

"Gideon," Lark said, coming after him.

"Don't follow," Gideon barked, shooting him a look of warning.

Wynter pulled against him, stumbling, prying at his grip with her fingers. The people in his path stopped what they were doing to stare.

Let them stare. Let them see that I'm in charge and that the Alrenian queen will bow to the wolf.

Gotz stepped out of the dying king's tent as they approached, as if he'd known they were coming. Gideon avoided his gaze and pushed Wynter to the ground at Gotz's feet.

"Take her to father."

Wynter wept, but not even tears were going to stop his resolve in this matter.

Gotz glanced at Wynter's crumpled figure and wet hair, then looked up at Gideon. "Was this really necessary?" he said quietly.

Perhaps the dramatic tear through the camp had been undue, but he wouldn't be admonished by his father's seer.

"She's a Healer. See if she can heal him."

Gotz took a deep breath. "Very well. If that's what you wish." He held out a hand to Wynter. "Come, my dear."

She raised her gaze to the old man, relief in her eyes. Perhaps she thought the old man kindly. She placed her shaking hand into his withered palm and rose to her feet, drawing close to him as a child would to its mother.

"You should attend," Gotz said to Gideon.

Gideon glanced at the girl's downcast eyes.

Gotz continued, "I don't want to be accused of anything nefarious."

Reluctantly, Gideon gave a small nod. Gotz led the girl into the tent and Gideon followed. It had been a while since he had attended his dying father. He excused his neglect by telling himself he had important duties to perform—but it was more than that.

What son waits anxiously for his father to die?

Bringing the girl to his dying father's side was nothing more than an attempt to relieve some of his guilt.

The tent where his father lay was dark except for the lard candles that burned all around him. The solemn sight gave the illusion of his father resting in a bed of flames. Hilran stood next to his father, waving a smoking bundle of sage over him. Even in a simple gown, she was beautiful. Her long black hair glistened in the candlelight. She glanced over at Gideon, and they shared a moment like they used to when they were kids. At one time, he thought they might wed, but that time had passed.

The bittersweet smell of the sage filled the room, and Gideon wondered if this was what death smelled like—burning candles, mixed with the scent of smoldering herbs.

The bed that served as his father's sick bed had been made special for him. The mattress had been stuffed with duck feathers and the pillow with crushed nut shells. It was a bed fit for a king and not a luxury afforded to the rest of them.

His father's face was stricken with the gray pallor of sickness. *This* was the great King Niko, short for Nicholas, named after the mythical Greek god of victory. An honorable name for a great warrior. But Niko had driven the Ulun people to near extinction. His ways of old were no longer working. Fighting as mercenaries in other countries may have provided them much needed supplies, but the losses had mounted, and their numbers were dwindling. His father's plan to kill the queen had amounted to nothing, and as he'd gotten older, he'd grown complacent even in that. It was up to Gideon now to save the people of the wolf. It was a job that should have been his older brother's, but he had died fighting their father's mercenary wars.

"Thank you, Hilran. You may leave us," Gotz said.

She curtsied and left the tent.

Gotz led Wynter slowly to the king's side. Gideon stayed by the doorway wondering if this had been a mistake.

But what kind of man would I be if I didn't try to heal my father?

Gotz glanced back at Gideon as though waiting for him to realize his foolishness in bringing the Alrenian queen to his father. It was too late to turn back now.

19

WYNTER

Wynter stared down at the sullen, wrinkled face—a face subdued by whatever illness lay beneath its façade.

"What's wrong with him? she asked quietly.

This is the great Ulun king, Niko? A weak, old man lying at the edges of death?

"We don't know," Gotz said. "He complained of pain in his lower abdomen. The doctor treated him with every known remedy, even some Alrenian medicine. Now he has a fever. We fear it won't be much longer."

Wynter fidgeted. She had healed from an arrow wound in minutes. It was obvious to everyone now that she was, in fact, a Healer. The queen had not been delirious; she'd been serious about giving Wynter the gift. But she had no idea how it worked, or if she could heal anyone else besides herself. She could feel Gideon's dark eyes on her and it pierced her to the soul, so strong was his presence.

She'd only witnessed a healing once, when she was very small, so small, she remembered holding on to her mother's pant leg. It was unusual for the queen to heal anyone who wasn't of royal lineage, but Wynter's grandmother, Eliza, had been the queen's favorite seamstress, and she had insisted on attending her. Wynter hadn't fully understood the significance of such an event at the time. Only later did she learn that the queen did not heal everyone. The memory came flooding back.

THE QUEEN CAME ONE MORNING, *early, while clouds of mist still hung in the trees. It made her appearance all the more startling, as if she had stepped out of a dream where gossamer nymphs and winged horses lived. Her gown was white silk. Red embroidered flowers snaked up the thigh of her right leg, intermingling with green vines. She wore a dark cape tied at the neck, and when she removed her hood, Wynter pointed a chubby finger in case her mother had failed to notice the pale skin and rose-colored cheeks of a beauty never before seen in the middle forest. Her mother pushed down Wynter's arm. Wynter understood this to mean that she must remain silent. She stuck her thumb in her mouth.*

The queen removed her cloak and handed it to a man who Wynter had just now noticed. He took it, bowing reverently. Wynter bent at the waist in mock adoration. The queen knelt down next to Eliza. Eliza's eyes were closed. For two days, Wynter's mother had dropped to her knees and prayed to God for a miracle. Wynter wasn't sure what a miracle was, but what she was feeling in the room right now felt like what a big word like that might mean.

The queen gazed at Eliza lovingly, then placed her hands on Eliza's shrunken shoulders. The room seemed to hold its breath. She ran her hands down Eliza's arms and across her chest and abdomen as if smoothing out the wrinkles of a morning bed. Then she stopped suddenly and stiffened. Wynter drew closer to her mother and wrapped her arms around her mother's leg, clinging tightly. Her mother placed a hand on top of Wynter's head to soothe her, but Wynter did not feel soothed, she was afraid.

The queen's back arched, and her breathing deepened. So strong and deep were her breaths that Wynter whimpered quietly. Her mother picked her up, shushing her softly. The queen fell backward, and the guards rushed forward to catch her. Her face was ashen. Was she dead like the birds they ate for dinner? Wynter cried aloud, piercing the quiet room. Her mother bounced her up and down, whispering, "It's okay. It's okay." Wynter reached out a hand toward the queen as a soldier carried her away in his arms. Her small hand grazed the white silk, and she stopped crying, for it felt like she had touched that special place her mother called heaven.

A little while later, Eliza opened her eyes and sat up. There was much laughter and smiling after that. The neighbors came and brought gifts—coming to witness the miracle. Five years later, Eliza got sick again. The new queen did not come. She had not known her grandmother in the same way. So Eliza died, and the joy of the day of the miracle evaporated as if it'd never happened. Six years later, Wynter's mother died in a fall. And then there were two—her and father.

WYNTER GLANCED BACK AT GIDEON, but his eyes were cast in shadow. She shivered and drew her arms around herself and once again studied the man in the bed. She had to at least try. There was going to be no talking her way out of this. She had the gift of healing. For all intents and purposes, she was the Alrenian queen.

She straightened and pushed her shoulders back, the memories of her childhood the only thing to assist her. She placed her hands on the king's arm. His body radiated with heat.

He definitely has a fever.

She moved her hands up and down his arms waiting for something to happen. Tears built behind her eyes. Gotz stepped forward and took her right hand and placed it on the king's abdomen.

"Close your eyes," he instructed.

As she closed her eyes, cool tears fell down her cheeks.

"You must empty your mind," Gotz said.

Wynter let his voice guide her.

"You must have a heart that desires to heal."

She nodded. She was surprised to find that she wanted to

help the king. It was not even a thought, it was an innate desire that she could no more control than hearing or seeing. Her body relaxed. Then something radiated up her arm. Something dark and unsavory moved beneath her fingers. It traveled to her mind, seizing her with pain so severe, her breath caught in her throat. Her body became rigid, frozen in its grasp. The disease had no shape or form, but it was ugly and numerous—spreading through her so quickly, she became consumed by a suffocating madness. She pushed back, surprised to find that she was able to move through the all-encompassing mass.

If I can move through it, I can capture it.

The thought was hers, yet she had no idea where it had come from. She pulled the black sickness into herself as if taking a piece of string and twisting it into a ball. She pulled and wound the endless treachery. It was strong, but she was stronger, yet her will was fading as the pain continued to seize her body. She could barely breathe. She held on. The darkness consumed her until she was no longer conscious of reality, just cruel, unending darkness. Her body shook; there was but a breath left in her.

The end is close, I can feel it. If I just hold on a little longer, I will have it.

The sickness would be hers and she would suffocate it. She spiraled down a long, dark hole.

I can't breathe. I've lost.

WYNTER WOKE up feeling groggy and worn. She was moving. Wheels beneath her bounced over rock and earth. She opened her eyes and found that she was in an enclosed wooden wagon that was akin to a moving coffin. The only light seeped through the small slat windows near the ceiling. Before she could sit up, Kidron was at her side.

"Thank the sons of Ulu you're alive," Kidron said.

"What happened?" Wynter asked, pushing her hair out of her face.

"You don't remember?" Kidron asked, sounding surprised.

Wynter waited for her head to clear.

The king.

She grabbed Kidron by the arm. "The king?" She held her breath.

"He's still alive," Kidron said sweetly.

"But is he…healed?"

"No. But his fever came down."

Wynter deflated. *I failed.*

"Apparently, it was too much for you."

"Too much?"

Kidron took her hand. "His illness was too far gone for you to heal. That's what Gotz said."

"Who's Gotz?"

"The king's seer. He was the one there with you."

So the man who helped her through the healing was a seer—a Prophet. It was known that Uluns were sometimes given the gift of prophecy, much like the Alrenians were given the gift of healing. But what did Gotz know of a Healer? He had helped her with the healing as if he had known what to do.

Kidron rubbed Wynter's back. "You did the best you could. I bet you were amazing."

Wynter smiled wearily. "I suppose." The truth was, she remembered very little of what had happened. Only that there had been excruciating pain, and now she felt weak.

The wagon came to a halt. Kidron popped up and peeked out a slatted window. "We're stopping to make camp." She returned to Wynter's side and helped her to stand. "Gotz said it may take a few days for you to get your strength back."

Wynter accepted her help. She could barely hold herself upright. Kidron threw open the door and took Wynter's hand. Someone shoved a step under the door and Kidron assisted her down. The bloodied, torn dress from earlier was gone, and she was now wearing a dark blue, woolen dress. She took a deep breath, which mostly smelled of horse sweat and earth. The sun had dropped below the tree line, casting late afternoon shadows into a large meadow. She squinted against the setting sun. "Where are we?" she asked.

"One day from the Yellow Fields," Kidron said.

Lark rode up on his brown and white mare and dismounted. He handed the reins to a boy who led the horse away. He studied Wynter while he took off his leather gloves.

"How are you feeling?" he asked, his voice steady and deep.

She held his eyes for a moment.

He carried me to the doctor. He cut open my shoulder to remove the arrow. He took care of me.

His look of concern faded at the realization that she was staring at him. He turned to Kidron. "Give us a moment."

Kidron sighed and stomped off.

"I suppose I owe you a thank-you," Wynter said, wrapping her arms around herself.

The place where the arrow had pierced her shoulder mildly ached—like a distant memory.

"I was just doing my job," he said flatly.

She thought she read something else in his eyes.

"Is that all I am? A job?"

He frowned and squeezed his gloves in his hand. "That's all you can be," he said quietly.

"I see," she said, looking away.

"We should get you something to eat."

"Of course." Why did she feel disappointed? Did she really think that the son of the Ulun king could actually care for her? She had seen something in him that was unexpected—kindness. Maybe it was the healing, but something in her made her feel more connected to Lark's feelings. She saw things more clearly than she had before.

"I'd like to see Gotz, if you don't mind," she said.

He looked at her intently as if he might say more. Finally, he motioned to Kidron who appeared to be helping a family unload for the night, but Wynter had a sense that she'd been mostly pretending in order to stay nearby. She came running.

"Take her to see Gotz," Lark said flatly, and then walked away.

For some reason, watching him leave made her feel sad—abandoned. She dismissed her feelings and refocused.

Kidron led her to the far edge of the meadow where Gotz had started a small fire. Two tree stumps had been set upright for seating. Something pungent simmered in a small black pot.

"I'll be back later," Kidron said and disappeared back across the meadow.

"Please sit," Gotz said, gesturing to a vacant stump.

She straightened her dress beneath her and sat as demurely as one could on a stump. She considered the irony.

A Stump on a stump.

Only *that* life was lost to her now. She didn't know what or who she was anymore.

Gotz took a cup, ladled some of the hot liquid into it, and handed it to her. "This should help with the fatigue."

Hesitant, she took the cup and let it warm her hands while she stared into the white flames of the fire. She had so many questions, she didn't know where to begin. So instead, she stayed silent and sipped the bitter tea.

Gotz stood and rumaged around some crates and came back with two slices of cheese. Her stomach growled at the sight of it. She accepted the white piece graciously. The cheese melted pleasantly in her mouth.

After her less than stellar healing performance, she started at the only place that made sense. "I assume you know I'm not the real queen?"

Gotz nodded.

"Does Gideon know?" she asked.

Gotz warmed his hands on his cup. "He probably does. But it is better for him to believe that you are."

"How does it work?" she asked. "The healing?"

Gotz stared into the flames and nodded as though he had expected the question. "I don't know *how* it works, only what frame of mind you must be in."

She took a sip of tea. She might have been imagining it, but she could already feel her strength returning to her.

"There are many tales of Healers," Gotz continued. "It's hard to say what is true and what isn't. I have made notes throughout my many years, garnering what I can from history, and from those claiming to have witnessed healings. As you know, this is more often an Alrenian trait."

She lowered her cup and held it in her lap. "Why couldn't I heal the king?"

"A Healer cannot heal a mortal wound. It was simply too late. He's been sick for some time."

"I'm sorry," she said softly.

Gotz rose again and reached out a gnarled hand for her cup. She placed it in his palm, and he refilled it. The sadness in his face showed that he cared for the king.

"Why did you tell Gideon that it was a bad idea for me to try to heal the king?"

Gotz studied her face, considering. "He wasn't doing it because he wanted his father healed."

"I don't understand."

"He brought you to his father because he was angry," Gotz explained.

She gazed into her tea. "Yes. He was angry at me for lying about being a Healer."

Gotz laughed softly. "No, my child. At himself. At his father. But not you."

She looked up, confused. "But he dragged me to his father's tent like a common criminal."

Gotz furrowed his brow. "Yes, and I'm none too pleased with him on that account."

He took their still-full cups and set them aside. Then he

looked at her with those wise blue eyes, wrinkled yet kind. "It would ruin Gideon's plans if his father recovered." He paused to throw another log on the fire. A cloud of sparks rose into the darkening sky. "You see," he said, "he was angry after you healed from the arrow, because everyone would *know* that you're a Healer. What would people say if he didn't take you to heal his own father—the king of the Ulun people? He had no choice. And if his father would have recovered, all his plans..."

Wynter was starting to put the pieces together. "He wants his father to die?"

Gotz shook his head. "Not in the way you think. He certainly loves his father, but his father is from a different time, and Gideon's generation thinks the Ulun people have suffered unduly under his rule."

"Why are you telling me all this?" she asked.

Gotz poked at the fire with a stick. "You'll need to understand Gideon."

The sun had almost disappeared, and the air was growing cooler. She held her hands above the flickering flames. "I understand that he hates me," she said more curtly than she meant to. She looked over at Gotz. "He treats me with contempt. Like a... a...Stump."

Gotz grinned and tapped his stick on the ground. "You are very important to him. He just hasn't realized yet."

"Important? I'm nothing more than a pawn!"

Gotz came to her and took her hand as a father would a daughter's. "Be patient with him, dear. Your lives are bound together now. Deep down, he's a good man."

What did these strange words mean? They were *bound* together now? Fear filled her heart.

"What are you saying?" she asked. "I don't understand. How are we bound together?"

Gotz dropped her hand and gazed off into the horizon. Dusk was upon them. His eyes lit up with the reflection of the fire. "Until the wolf unites with the eagle—"

"Gotz!" came a voice out of nowhere.

Wynter jumped and Gotz snapped out of his reflection.

Gideon glared down at them from atop his black stallion. The horse let out a series of snorts. Gideon pulled up on its reins. "The queen needs her rest," he said, looking none too happy.

Wynter tried to hide her disappointment at having her conversation with Gotz cut off. Gideon had interrupted something. Something it seemed he didn't want her to hear. Gotz bowed slightly at the waist. "Of course, my lord."

Gideon turned the horse and held out a hand to Wynter. Her stomach churned. After their last encounter, she didn't relish the idea of being near him. But Gotz's words had given her some hope—*deep down he's a good man.* Perhaps Gideon's gruff side was not all there was to him.

She thanked Gotz for the cheese and tea, then placed her fingers into Gideon's large hand. He lifted her up onto his horse, placing her sideways in front of him. Before she could consider their awkward proximity to each other, he kicked the horse and they bolted across the meadow, past the camp, and up the hill that rose above them. She held on to the horse's bridle and closed her eyes. She had never been on a horse. It was frightening, yet exhilarating, to feel the wind in her face and through her hair. Goosebumps formed on her arms. The cool air enveloped her. She had no idea where they were going. Perhaps he would kill her. But something whispered in her ear.

Until the wolf unites with the eagle... What did it mean?

The horse slowed and Gideon dismounted. She opened her eyes and he held his arms out to her and she slid into them. He lowered her safely to the ground the way one would unload a parcel.

He looked out upon the camp as if examining troops. The tents were lighting up like thousands of paper lanterns, one by one. It was quite beautiful. She wrapped her arms around herself and rubbed them for warmth. Gideon immediately removed his cloak and laid it across her shoulders.

"Thank you," she said softly. It was the first kindness he had ever shown her.

They stood together in the fading light—silent and unmoving. She didn't dare speak. It seemed words meant very little to this man. He had shamed her by dragging her across camp in a bloodied, torn dress. A night standing on a hill seemed a respite. Finally, he spoke.

"I owe you an apology," he said, his voice authoritative but sincere.

She wondered how much of his pride he had sacrificed to offer words he likely did not mean.

"I treated you poorly. I have no excuse."

She glanced over at him, but he continued to stare into the camp.

He's a good man, deep down.

She had yet to see any goodness, so great were the walls Gideon had built up around himself. Yet she admired his strength and couldn't help but view him with a sense of kingly awe at the challenges he faced leading the Ulun people.

She pulled his cloak more tightly around her. The scent of him filled the air—a combination of animal musk and fire.

"I'm sorry I couldn't heal your father," she offered.

Perhaps a truce was in order now that he had taken the first step. The horse nuzzled Gideon in the ear. He rubbed the horse's nose.

"Tomorrow's a big day," he said.

"The Yellow Fields," she replied.

He looked at her now, though his eyes were hidden in the darkness. "We'll go out together to meet the Alrenian representative at the edge of the northern forest."

"I understand." She was the Uluns' ticket through Alrenian territory—a hostage.

"What will become of me after?" she asked.

Gideon gathered the horse's reins and mounted. "We should return to camp." He held out his hand.

So that's it.

She was going to be killed once he got what he wanted. Gotz's words were nothing more than false hope. She took his hand, and in a flash, they were riding at a full gallop back toward camp.

20

GIDEON

Gideon returned to his tent to find Lark waiting inside for him.

"Make yourself at home," Gideon said, throwing off his cloak.

"Where have you been?" Lark asked.

"Out." Gideon sat in the chair across from Lark and removed his boots.

"Out, like riding off into the sunset with the queen?"

Gideon tossed his boots to the side, then stood and pulled his white shirt off over his head. "Are you spying on me, brother?"

Lark chuckled. "Hardly. Besides, it's my job to protect the queen. Remember?"

Gideon ignored him and poured himself a drink.

"Care to share?" Lark asked.

"No."

"Fine. We'll move on. I have concerns about tomorrow."

Gideon frowned. "What kind of concerns?"

"Safety concerns."

"Who's? Mine or the queen's?"

"Both, actually. I'm certain that the arrow meant for Wynter was not from an Alrenian bow."

Gideon tapped the tip of his cup with his finger. "The arrow was Alrenian?"

"Yes. But one readily available anywhere in camp from souvenir mongers."

"You think it's Valen's mole trying to kill the queen?"

"I'm sure of it."

"We knew searching for Isidor might be an uphill battle, brother," Gideon said.

"Yes, I know. But without the queen, we don't stand a chance of making it through Alrenian territory."

"I assume you have a plan?" Gideon asked.

"Of course. Don't I always?"

Gideon sat, removed his socks, and propped his sore feet on the edge of the table.

Lark wrinkled up his nose. "Really, must you?"

"My tent."

"There are others besides me keeping one eye on the queen," Lark said.

"Who?"

"Finn, for one."

"Mangus has likely asked for his assistance in rooting out our mole." Gideon cast Lark a humorous look. Their cousin Finn was no soldier, much less a killer.

Lark raised an eyebrow. "Finn might not have the physical qualities of a soldier, but he's an excellent bowman and much slyer than he looks."

"Uncle Mangus appears to be loyal, and Finn usually tows his father's line."

"May I remind you that uncle was initially against the search for Isidor. He bowed to your wishes rather easily, don't you think?"

Gideon rubbed his chin in contemplation. "You think he could be our mole—playing both sides?"

"I wouldn't discount either one of them. I've noticed Mangus has yet to produce the traitor."

Gideon's night guard stuck his head in the tent. "I'm sorry, my lord. Lord Finn is here to see you."

"Speak of the devil," Lark said quietly.

Gideon lowered his feet to the ground. "Send him in."

Finn ducked inside and bristled slightly upon seeing Lark. "Sorry for the lateness, but I saw your tent still aglow."

"It's fine, Finn. How can I help you?" Gideon asked.

"My father and I wanted to offer our services tomorrow at the Yellow Fields. We can easily scout with the others. This would be a perfect opportunity for the mole in our midst to make another attempt on the queen's life. I have no doubt he or she will up their game now that we're so close to Alrenian territory."

Gideon studied Finn's face. His words were sincere, but his forehead was moist with nervous sweat. Gideon looked to Lark. "Lark?"

Lark tapped his fingers on the table. "I have my most trusted men in place, Finn. Why should I be concerned with traitors in their midst?"

Finn forced a smile. "Not every man is loyal to the line of Ulu, though he may appear to be so." Then as an afterthought added, "My lord." He bowed slightly.

Gideon stood and clasped Finn on the shoulder. "Thank you, Finn. We appreciate your loyalty as well as uncle's."

"We are glad to offer it."

Gideon dropped his hand. "We could always use extra men on the perimeter."

Looking satisfied, Finn bowed and departed.

Gideon rubbed the back of his head and looked at Lark.

"What?" Lark asked, shrugging.

"*Why should I be concerned with traitors in their midst?* Your question sounded more like an accusation. We can't afford animosity between us and our uncle. People still look to Mangus as a trusted advisor of our father."

"I suppose I can pretend to trust them, but I have to consider

that this visit was likely an attempt to mask their true loyalty."
Lark stood. "I better go check on our queen before I turn in."

Gideon nodded. Lark gave him a pat on the back, then withdrew.

Gideon blew out his candles and fell onto his pallet. So much could go wrong tomorrow. But what choice did he have but to look for Isidor? His father's mercenary wars had decimated their numbers. Many had defected with Valen. The women in the camp were barren. If only he could just close his eyes and actually rest. Lately there had been no peace in dreams. Always the dream came of her—the faceless woman—the Alrenian queen.

Until the wolf unites with the eagle, there will be no peace.

He drifted off to sleep. Sometime during the night, the dream woke him. Only this time, he saw part of her face. Her eyes—blue as a cloudless sky.

21

FINN

Morning came and brought all the possibilities of Finn's future with it. Finn listened to Mangus squirming in his saddle next to him. They waited close to the Yellow Fields until Brendle gave the signal to move forward and fan out.

Finn kept a casual eye on the queen. It looked like Kidron was trying to explain to her how to ride a horse. Gideon and Wynter were to ride across the Yellow Fields to the edge of the forest to meet an Alrenian representative. Gideon had sent word by pigeon at the break of dawn. *Let the Uluns pass through the northern forest and the queen's life would be spared.* They would show the Alrenians their queen and agree to terms for passing through the northern forest.

"I don't know why you volunteered me for this," Mangus grumbled.

Finn looked over at his father. "You want the queen dead, don't you?"

Mangus scowled. "Keep your voice down," he spat.

Finn grinned. "We're quite alone father."

"Erring on the side of caution was never your strong suit."

Finn shrugged off his father's insult and twisted in his saddle in order to look at his father more directly. "We're both strong bowmen. Wouldn't it look more suspicious if we didn't offer our services? We must appear supportive."

Mangus frowned. "Just make it stick this time. You made a sloppy mess of the last attempt, hitting her in the shoulder. Bah."

The flames of anger simmered inside Finn, but he held his tongue. He was used to being treated with contempt by his father, but it was becoming more difficult to ignore.

He offered his father a smile. "Don't worry. After today, you'll never have to see her face again.

"Hmph. We'll see."

22

WYNTER

Kidron gave Wynter a boost onto Lark's mare. Wynter's hands trembled. She'd never ridden a horse by herself, and Kidron's attempt at instructing her did nothing to allay her fears. It didn't help that the ridiculous dress she was being forced to wear was too bulky, making it virtually impossible to sit comfortably. She clung tightly to the reins and the horse jerked its head in protest.

"Just relax," Kidron said, rubbing the horse's nose.

Wynter nodded and took a deep breath, then let it out slowly. The morning was cool, but she had broken out into a sweat beneath the heavy cloak that Lark had insisted she wear.

Kidron silently led the horse to the edge of the Yellow Fields. There was no sign of Lark, and she found it frustrating that he had been making himself more and more scarce. To her horror, she had developed certain feelings for him, and she thought he might feel the same. But now she was starting to wonder if she had imagined something that wasn't there.

It's his job to take care of me. I've been seeing what I wanted to see.

She gazed across the place known as the Yellow Fields. This was no ordinary field. The grass, if one could even call it that, was as tall as a man, and it swayed back and forth with the wind while the sunlight reflected off its slender, yellow tips. Beyond the great blades was the northern forest, wide and deep and dark. She temporarily forgot about her fear until someone said, "It's time."

She looked over. Gideon sat on his dark horse, his face hidden by the hood of his cloak. His horse pawed at the ground and whinnied.

What if the Alrenians of the northern forest saw through her little act of pretending to be the queen? The gold ring on her finger proved her claim to be queen, but what if Jack had gone back to her people and told them that the real queen was dead? Word would have made it to the northern colony by now.

Brendle shouted a command. A small troop of soldiers she recognized as Lark's band of men, including Finn, were spread out to her right and left. They moved forward, blending into the long blades.

Why isn't Lark here?

She turned to ask Kidron, but the horse lurched forward at Kidron's soft slap to its rear, and Wynter moved into the Yellow Fields, alongside Gideon.

The long blades of grass bent beneath the horses' hooves, breaking as easily as the weavings of a delicate spider web. It was clear that no one ever trekked through the field. The surrounding blades were pristine. She wanted to dismount and set her ear to the ground and listen to the voice of the strange grass. Would its roots speak with loud pops like a beech tree, or would there be a gentle sizzle like a fire, crackling a delicate song. She longed to be home in the safety of the trees, but she feared she may never return.

Gideon did not speak nor did she wish him to. She lifted her eyes to the forest and traced the treetops, looking for movement, people. What would Gideon do with her once they were through the woods—when she was no longer needed? She turned her head to ask him when a loud *swoosh* went by her ear and Gideon lurched backward on his saddle and fell to the ground. Free from its rider, the stallion galloped away, mowing down the grass in its path.

Wynter's horse rose up on its hind legs. She settled the horse and stared down at the arrow that had pierced Gideon's cloak. He wasn't moving. She didn't know if her people were trying to save her or if the Ulun traitor had been trying to take her life. She glanced up at the trees, realizing she was yards away from safety.

This is my chance to run.

She dug her heels into the horse and clicked her tongue like Kidron had taught her. The horse bolted toward the trees. She was soaring through the grass, the horse carrying her to freedom. And for the first time in days, the unsinkable feeling of hope rose deep within her.

She bent low over the horse and kicked harder into its sides. Once she was in the safety of the trees, there would be zero chance of Lark's men apprehending her. The perimeter defenses of the Alrenians were no match for a small group of Ulun bowmen.

A grin spread across her face. She almost wished she could see the expression on Lark's face when he realized she was lost to him.

The woods came at her so fast, she thought she had run into a tree when she found herself lying flat on her back in the grass. The world spun around her. She blinked against the sun and a shadow passed over her. She shielded her eyes and tried to focus. Gideon's face glared down at her from atop a brown horse. His dark eyes were flaming with anger—his rage apparent in his furrowed brow. Was she hallucinating? There was no arrow in his chest. He wasn't even on his black horse.

Feeling the impact of the fall, she rose shakily to her feet and stripped off her cloak, letting it fall to the ground. With the chance of freedom removed, her mind immediately returned to her captor.

"I don't understand," she said breathlessly. "You were—" She looked back from whence she had come.

Gideon dismounted. "Get back on your horse," he said gruffly.

Wynter looked to the trees. She could make a run for it.

"Get back on the horse," he repeated, closing the distance between them. He reached out and took her by the arm. She struggled, wanting to be free from his touch.

"If you're here, then who took the arrow back there?" she snapped.

He released her, and she stumbled backward. The seriousness of Gideon's expression said it all.

She shook her head. "No. No!" She turned and ran back through the flattened grass. *Not Lark.*

"Wynter!" Gideon called after her.

23

MANGUS

Mangus waited nervously, hidden in the grass. He held the reins of Finn's horse waiting for him to return. Shouts had erupted five minutes ago. Finn had no doubt hit his target, but he was taking too long getting back. Mangus gritted his teeth. If Finn didn't return soon, they'd both be caught in a very sticky predicament. He could concoct a cover story, but the truth was always better than a lie. Lies had a way of exposing themselves regardless of the cleverness of the teller.

Finn came running toward him. Mangus breathed a sigh of relief. Soldiers approached from their right.

"You lingered too long," Mangus spat, tossing Finn his horse's reins.

Finn seemed calm. Too calm for someone who had just killed the Alrenian queen. Mangus opened his mouth to speak when a trio of Lark's men rode up.

"Lark has been hit. Did you see anything?" one of them asked.

Finn grabbed Mangus by the arm.

"I'm afraid I did," Finn said.

Mangus looked at Finn and pulled against his grip. "What are you doing?"

Finn tightened his grip and reached behind Mangus' back and produced an arrow from his quiver.

"I think you'll find that this arrow matches the arrow used against the attempt on the Alrenian queen's life, and Lark's."

The men looked at each other, confused.

"This is outrageous. That's not my arrow. Finn planted it there!"

Finn shook his head. "This pains me greatly, Father. But even I can't undo your traitorous actions."

Finn nodded toward the men. They dismounted and took Mangus forcefully by the arms.

"You're making a big mistake. I'm the king's brother," he yelled. He fought against his restrainers.

"You won't get away with this Finn!" he screamed as they led him away.

24

WYNTER

Of course it was Lark. It was his job to keep her safe—to keep *Gideon* safe.

She stumbled into what had already become a clearing of flattened grass. Several men on horses stamped about, some shouting. Brendle was bent over Lark. Lark's hood had been pulled back. The arrow in his chest looked like a stake pinning him to the ground. Brendle locked eyes with Wynter and shook his head. She shot forward and fell to her knees, pushing Brendle out of the way. Lark was still alive. He smiled at her, though it was more like a grimace.

"You fool," she whispered harshly. She ripped his shirt open. Blood spilled from his wound like a rushing river. The arrow was planted right next to his heart. Her head swooned.

I can save him. I'm a Healer.

"You can't save him," a voice said.

She looked behind her. Gideon stood next to his horse, looking defeated. It infuriated her. She turned back to Lark and lowered her face to his and cradled his cheeks in her hands. "I'm going to save you," she whispered.

"It's too late," he said, his eyes distant.

"Don't say that. You care for me. I know you do."

He looked at her now. "It doesn't matter. You're meant for him." He looked toward Gideon.

"No," she said firmly.

He reached up and cupped his hand over hers. "He's not so bad. I promise."

Tears slid down her cheeks. She shook her head. He coughed and a small bit of blood seeped from his mouth. She pulled her hand from his face and rolled him to his side. She broke the tip of the arrow off. Lark cried out in pain.

"Wynter!" Gideon shouted. She rolled Lark onto his back and pulled the arrow from his chest. Lark screamed, and a gush of blood sprayed from the wound. She placed her hands on the opening and pressed down hard. She closed her eyes and let herself go. Immediately, her mind became dark and chaotic. So many obstacles came at her. She plunged forward, searching, feeling her way to the source of Lark's lifeblood. So much blood. So much pain. It was in her hands, her arms, her body. It was like being burned alive.

I can do this.

She wrapped herself around every bleeding wound—tending it, giving it life—her life. The faster she worked, the angrier the blood fought her.

I won't give up.

She poured herself into Lark. The blood slowed, but still it came.

Hands pulled her away from Lark. Her eyes flew open. Lark turned his head toward her. "I'm sorry," he mouthed, and his eyes went vacant, staring into nothingness.

"No! No!" she cried, tearing at the arms that held her. "Let me go. I can save him."

Gideon spoke roughly in her ear. "He's gone."

A sob escaped her, and she went limp. Gideon let her collapse to the ground. She stayed on her knees staring at Lark's lifeless body, trying to make sense of what had just happened.

"Find out who did this," Gideon barked. And suddenly, the horses shifted, and the men were tearing through the grass.

She sat back on her heels. Hot tears fell down her face and under her chin. Lark's blood was already drying on her hands. She'd never felt so alone.

Gideon took a knee by Lark and shut his brother's eyes. He looked over at Wynter.

"Why didn't you let me save him? He's your brother!" she cried.

Gideon stared at his lifeless brother. "The wound was mortal. You can't heal a mortal wound," he said flatly.

"But it was working! The bleeding was slowing." Once again, she couldn't heal. She didn't deserve to hold the gift of healing. She wasn't the queen. She never would be. She stood, defeated.

Gideon said nothing.

Lark *had* cared for her, but some of his final words were troubling.

"What did he mean, *I was meant for you*?" she asked.

Gideon rose to his feet. "Nothing. He was delirious."

She wiped her tears away. Several men came running through the grass, Kidron among them. When Kidron saw Lark, she immediately ran to Wynter and wrapped her arms around her, burying her face into Wynter's side. Wynter held Kidron and glared at Gideon, accusing him with her eyes. Several shouts came from nearby, and Brendle rode up on his horse.

"We think we have our man," Brendle said.

"Who?" Gideon asked between gritted teeth.

Finn came down the path into the clearing, an arrow in his hand—an Alrenian arrow. The same kind of arrow that had been pulled from Wynter's shoulder. The same kind of arrow she'd just pulled out of Lark.

Gideon put a hand to his sword and took a step toward Finn.

Finn held up his hands. "It wasn't me." He stepped aside, and two of Lark's men dragged Mangus into their midst. Mangus shouted his innocence, cursing at Finn and the men who held him. Gideon's face turned red. It all happened so fast after that. In one swift movement, Gideon slid his sword from its sheath and turned in a circle of fury. The men holding Mangus jumped aside, and Gideon's blade sliced through Mangus' neck, sending a spray of blood across the men nearby. Mangus' head thudded to the ground.

Kidron screamed in horror. Wynter pressed Kidron's face into her shoulder, in an attempt to shield her from the madness.

Finn dropped to his knees and cried out, "Father!"

A man galloped up on a horse, breathless. He momentarily paused as he took in the chaotic scene. Then he looked at Gideon and said, "I bring urgent news. The king is dead."

25

WYNTER

They wrapped up the bodies of Lark and the king like tightly bound packages and put them in back of a wagon. Wynter didn't know what had happened to Mangus' body. It had disappeared like he'd never existed. No one even murmured his name. Not even Finn.

Her attempted healing of Lark had left her feeling drained, just like it had after she'd tried to heal the king, only this time, she had not taken the healing so far as to lose consciousness.

It only took a few hours for the Ulun camp to regroup, and to her displeasure, Brendle had her up on a horse and riding back out to the Yellow Fields even while she could still smell the remnants of Lark's blood on her hands.

This time, there was a whole company of men on horses that expanded the width of the field. It had the look of war, but weapons were not drawn. The delicate blades of grass no longer swayed in the wind—its harmonious song had been destroyed by the stampede of horses from earlier.

Gideon did not look at her, nor she at him. This was business. Developing feelings for Lark had been foolish. From here on out, she would play her part, nothing more. The Ulun people were her enemies, not her friends. She decided right then and there that she'd never let Gideon see her cry again.

Brendle flanked her left side and Gideon her right. Gideon no longer had the sword he'd used to kill Mangus at his side. It had been replaced with a large knife.

They rode through the fields—a solemn march accompanied by birds singing in the distant trees and in the dying grass beneath them. She fought back tears and tried not to think of Lark's last words. *I'm sorry.*

As they approached the woods, she became restless. There was no movement in the trees. The wind from earlier that morning had died down. The trees should've been teeming with soldiers. Maybe they didn't want to appear defensive. This was a transaction after all. Gideon had sent word by pigeon that morning.

She side-glanced at Gideon. His face held a scowl. *What has he done with the sorrow of losing his brother and father in the same day?*

The line of Ulun horses plowed through the field, destroying what was left of its pristine existence. Gideon held up a fist, and the men slowed as they approached. There was still no sign of an Alrenian representative. They were ten feet from the tree line.

The company of men halted. Gideon dismounted, approached her horse, and held up a hand. She simply gave him her hand like a prisoner to its ward, and he helped her to the ground.

Maybe the Alrenians will try to save me. I am their queen, after all.

Brendle shifted to dismount when Gideon stayed him with his hand. "Follow on horse," Gideon instructed.

Wynter glanced up at Brendle. His large brown eyes seemed to be trying to reassure her. He was not Ulun, he was Jutta. Perhaps he understood a little of how she felt. Or, like Lark, he was only doing his job. She had already surmised that Brendle would be her new caretaker.

She followed Gideon to the trees, her eyes frantically scanning for any sign of friend or foe.

"Something's wrong," she said.

"Maybe they're setting a trap," he suggested.

"No. This is something else. I need to climb up and see what's wrong."

"Yeah, that's not going to happen," he said.

Her face flushed with anger. Her hands clenched into fists. "I'm not trying to escape if that's what you think. Someone should have been here to greet us, and you know it."

He wouldn't make eye contact with her, but motioned Brendle forward.

"Take a small group through the woods around our perimeter and see if they're setting a trap," Gideon said.

Brendle nodded and gathered five others. They split up and rode to the forest edges and disappeared.

Being left alone with Gideon was almost more than she could bear. He paced and ran his hands through his hair. He was king now. She was the Alrenian queen. It had been seventy-five years since the twins Ulu and Alrenia had been born joint heirs to the throne of Ferran. Alrenia was the firstborn. She had been gifted a Healer, a natural leader. Ulu came second. He had been gifted with prophecy and had become a great warrior who led many men as mercenaries to fight the wars of other countries surrounding Ferran. But when the king died, the twins had fought for the throne. The people of Ferran divided, and each group pledged their allegiance to a different heir. Then the Great Destruction had come down from the heavens, destroying much of the land and leaving Ferran not only divided, but devasted as well. Now here she was with Gideon—king and queen together, yet their worlds couldn't have been further apart, and she wondered if such a thing as hope existed at all.

Finally, after several painstaking minutes, Brendle and his men rode out of the woods right in front of where she and Gideon were standing.

"Well?" Gideon asked.

"The place is abandoned," Brendle said.

Wynter's stomach dropped. *No.* Brendle must be mistaken. Maybe her people were in hiding. Her heart raced. She didn't think after that. She took off running toward the woods.

"Wynter!" Gideon barked.

She kept running. She pushed through the underbrush, scanning for a tree she could climb. She passed below bridges and tree homes, but there wasn't an Alrenian in sight. Gideon's angry footfalls pursued her, and she caught glimpses of Brendle and his men riding their horses through the less dense areas of the forest next to her. But their pursuit did not deter her.

Soon she found an old bent oak. She gathered up her dress in a bunch near her waist and bounded up its gnarled branches, scaling up the tree, grabbing, pulling, swinging, and jumping to the next tree until she pulled herself up to a slat bridge. There were several tree homes clustered nearby. She ran to each one, pushing open doors to ransacked, barren rooms, upturned mattresses, empty trunks, the smell of decaying apples, beeswax, and empty nut shells. She climbed down a ladder to gain access to a lower rope bridge. She dropped the last few feet to a landing platform. When she turned around, she cried out. Gideon was standing there against the tree. He was breathing heavily, sweat running down his temples.

"Don't ever do that again," he said, his eyes aflame.

Wynter swooned. *Where was everyone? The whole colony gone?*

Gideon wiped the sweat from his forehead onto his sleeve. He peered over the edge of the small platform they were standing on and quickly turned and placed a steadying hand on the tree.

He's afraid of heights. The thought gave her some small sense of pleasure.

"We should go," he said.

"My people are gone," she said. "Did you do this?"

His eyes narrowed. "No."

"Then who?" she snapped.

Gideon remained silent, but there was a definite displeasure in his face. He knew something, and he didn't appear to be happy about it. The night she'd been in the woods with Lark, she'd heard two men plotting to kill her. Were they responsible for this?

"Was it Valen?" she asked.

Gideon's face flamed red. He grabbed her arm. "Where did you hear that name?"

She pulled against his grip, angry at his harshness. She said nothing.

"I'll say it again, where did you hear that name?" he asked between gritted teeth. He got right in her face. She tried to remain calm, but he towered over her and his closeness was all consuming. She swallowed and set her feet.

"That first night, when Lark took me into the woods to hunt, we overheard two men talking about trying to kill me. One of them was named Valen."

Gideon stepped back, gripping the hilt of his knife so tightly that his knuckles turned white. He cursed under his breath.

"Who is he?" she asked.

Just when she thought he wouldn't answer, he spoke. "He's a traitor to the Ulun king. He managed to convince a large number of our own to rally against the king and they left camp. They want to destroy the Alrenians and claim Ferran as their own."

"Valen did this?" she asked, suddenly feeling the weight of the situation.

Gideon faced her again. "I don't know. Maybe."

Heat rose to her face. "Isn't that what you want too? To destroy us and claim Ferran for the Ulun people?" In her mind, Gideon was no better than Valen.

His jaw tensed. "No. That's not what I want."

His answer surprised her. He no longer needed her as his ticket to get through the northern forest. This was the Uluns chance to finally kill the Alrenian queen. Why wouldn't he seize the opportunity while it was right within his grasp?

"Will you kill me?" she asked.

His expression softened. "No."

"What is it that you want?" she asked, fearing the answer. If he didn't plan on killing her and claiming Ferran, then what was he planning?

"Not this," he said, looking around. "We should go," he added.

She didn't understand why he would let her live, but she wasn't going to tempt luck by giving him time to reconsider. "We can continue north until we find a safe way down," she suggested.

He nodded.

They crossed the rope bridge, her balancing on the rope with hands free, him holding on to the side ropes, trying not to look down. Several bridges later, Gideon asked to stop. They stood in the middle of a fairly high slat bridge. A low hum permeated the air. Wynter tried to place the insect-like noise. Gideon was catching his breath when a glob of clear liquid fell on him from the crown of the trees above. He frowned and wiped the strange substance from his face and examined it. She took his hand and sniffed the tacky goo. He looked up.

"Wynter," he said quietly. She followed his gaze to the tree-tops. The blood drained from her face. Something in the trees pulsed like a slow heartbeat. The canopy was so dense, the sunlight had been completely blocked out. But there was a mass there—a large, undulating mass of inhuman flesh—a Morbid hive.

Wynter grabbed Gideon's face and forced him to look at her. "We're going to quietly move off this bridge. You understand?" she whispered.

He nodded.

There wasn't just one or two Morbids, there were more than she could count. The monkey-like creatures were sleeping in a huge group in the treetops, latched on to one another so that they appeared as a whole. It was a defense mechanism to look larger and deter predators. Size mattered in the animal kingdom, though whether the Morbids were human or animal, she did not know. Legend was that they were demons that had fallen to earth during the Great Destruction. She had no idea if they were truly demons, only that they were violent creatures with an appetite for the queen. And here she was—a delicacy, only feet away.

Gideon quietly unsheathed the knife at his hip, and they moved slowly, carefully calculating each step. The humming of the Morbids rose and fell like the gentle purring of a cat. Her heart pounded so hard, she feared the Morbids would hear it.

Is this what happened to my people? Morbids?

She feared the same fate for her and Gideon if they couldn't slip away unnoticed.

They had just made it to the end of the bridge when Gideon's foot slipped through a gap between the slats with a loud crack. Wynter looked up at the mass in expectation, while Gideon tried to remove his foot from the splintered hole. The humming continued, and the cluster continued to move like a gentle breath. She tugged at Gideon's leg, trying to help him, while keeping her eye on the creatures above them. Gideon quickly freed his boot, but it was too late. A single Morbid fell to the bridge, shook itself off, and caught sight of them.

No. Oh no.

The Morbid screeched, sharp teeth bared—calling to the others.

"Run!" Wynter grabbed Gideon by the sleeve and grabbed up the folds of her dress. They ran to the end of the bridge, skirting around the large tree that anchored the bridge via a circular platform. A mixture of slat and rope bridges continued as far as the eye could see, but if she stopped, they were dead, so she kept running. Panic set in as she began calculating the odds of outrunning the little demons.

Bang!

The bridge shook as Morbids dropped from the trees and landed on the wooden slats behind them. The screeching grew louder as more and more woke and joined in the pursuit. Gideon stayed right on her heels, but speed belonged to the Morbid. If she didn't find a Morbid pit fast, she and Gideon would be overcome in a matter of minutes.

A Morbid scuttled past them, crying out to its friends. More followed.

They're trying to surround us, cut us off.

Gideon struck out at them with his knife. Wynter's blade rested at her ankle, but there was no time to stop and unsheathe it. She needed to focus on finding a Morbid pit in a place that wasn't her home. Their odds of survival were growing grimmer by the minute.

"I hope you have a plan," Gideon grunted as he slayed a Morbid, which screeched loudly before he tossed it aside.

"I'm working on it."

They scrambled across a rope bridge. Some of the Morbids were following in the trees above them. Others crawled beneath the bridge, lashing at their ankles. They were slowly becoming trapped.

A Morbid dropped from the tree crown and landed in front of Wynter, gnashing its teeth. Wynter stopped. Gideon was fighting off the attack from behind them. She crouched, drawing up her hem higher and reached for her knife. But before she could draw the blade, an arrow pierced the Morbid's side and its eyes rolled back. It tumbled between the ropes and plummeted to the ground. Wynter looked below. Gideon's men were sending up arrows as fast as they could. They shouted instructions to each other, focusing on the easiest targets. She silently thanked God, pushing ahead, calling to Gideon to keep up. That's when she saw it, twenty feet out—a big, beautiful M painted on a square piece of board. *A Morbid pit!*

"I can't keep them at bay much longer. There are too many," Gideon shouted above the screeches.

"Twenty feet!" she shouted.

"Twenty feet, what? Until we die?"

Daughters of Alrenia! How can I explain a Morbid pit in thirty seconds?

A Morbid leapt in front of her. She kicked it, and it sailed into the air.

"Brendle! A little help here," Gideon shouted.

More shouts from Gideon's men erupted from below. Wynter jumped down to a slat bridge five feet below them and landed in a crouch. Gideon sheathed his knife and followed. The Morbids rained down like large hailstones.

"Now would be an excellent time to let me in on the plan," Gideon said between gritted teeth.

A Morbid jumped on his back. He reached behind him and grabbed it, broke its neck, and tossed it to the ground. At the end of the bridge was a Morbid pit—a large gap between the trees that no Morbid could cross.

"You're going to have to trust me. We're going to run to the end of this bridge and jump."

Gideon continued snatching up Morbids and tossing them aside. His face was full of bleeding claw marks. He had protected her from the brunt of the attack. "Are you out of your mind? We're sixty feet in the air."

"We jump across," she said. "The Morbids can't make it."

He looked past her to the end of the bridge while punching a Morbid in the face and asked, "How far is the jump?"

"Eight feet."

His eyes widened.

"It's the only way."

She'd never actually seen the theory put to the test, but she trusted it would work. *If* they made it across.

"For the love of Ulu," he said. He took two Morbids and smashed their heads together and released them to the ground below.

"Are you ready?" she asked, not quite sure whether she was.

He nodded. Arrows flew over their heads, and Morbids continued to drop down around them. And still, more came.

She focused on the platform on the other side of the wide expanse.

My father died leaping seven feet.

She shook the thought away, quickly ripping the skirt off her dress. Then she sprinted with every ounce of strength she could muster. With every step, her leg muscles burned, but she dug deeper and pushed harder until she was off the bridge and in the air, her arms swinging. And like a miracle, her feet hit the platform on the other side, and she set down a hand to steady her landing.

She stood and turned around. Gideon was standing at the edge of the slat bridge looking at the large expanse between them.

"You can make it, I promise," she shouted.

He seemed hesitant, unsure. A Morbid jumped on his back. Others tried to follow Wynter and fell to their deaths. It sounded like giant pinecones falling from the trees.

The Morbid on Gideon's back dug his tiny, clawed hands into Gideon's eyes and wrapped its legs around his neck. Gideon pulled at the creature, but to no avail. He fumbled for his knife, but as soon as he got it out of its sheath, he dropped it, and it tumbled to the ground. Gideon twisted and pulled at the creature.

"Turn around!" she shouted, her heart racing. She pulled the knife from the strap at her ankle.

Please don't let me kill him.

Kidron had taught her how to throw a knife, but she never thought she'd ever have a reason to actually do it. But if there was ever a time, this was it.

Gideon seemed momentarily disoriented.

"Turn your back to me," she shouted, using her voice as an anchor.

He turned, his hands still pulling at the creature. She aimed, pulled back her arm, and released the knife. There was a loud *thunk*. She placed a hand on the tree trunk behind her, steadying herself. Gideon turned to face her—his eyes wide. Had she missed? Her stomach twisted into knots. To her relief, Gideon pulled the limp creature off of him, stared at Wynter's knife sticking out of its back, then dropped it off the precipice. He wasted no time. He ran back down the bridge then bolted toward her, Morbids running by his ankles. He leapt into the air. Time stopped.

She closed her eyes. There was a giant boom. She opened her eyes to find Gideon, scratched face, breathing heavily. She slumped to the platform. The Morbids fell one by one to their deaths, until there were no more.

26

GIDEON

Gideon rested his elbows on his knees and bowed his head. The claw marks on his face burned with a bitter vengeance. What had happened to the Alrenian colony? If it had been an attack by Morbids, there would have been bodies. No, the Morbids must have moved in after the Alrenians were gone. The lost colony had the mark of Valen all over it. Why did he care? His people had made it through the northern forest. But the cost had been greater than he'd expected. His brother had lost his life because of his uncle's betrayal. Lark had tried to warn him about Mangus, but Gideon hadn't wanted to believe his uncle would work with a man like Valen.

He raked his hands through his hair and stared at his boots. He was alone now, and the loss of Lark and his father fell on him like a crushing weight. The only real family he had left was Kidron, but she was like a complete stranger to him. Lark had been his anchor to the world. He'd kept Gideon in check, and the people responded to his good-natured humor. Gideon was under no illusion that he had the same charisma or rapport with his people. He was moody and ill-natured. A trait he no doubt had inherited from his father. He was black or white. He needed gray in his life—he needed Lark.

How could he lead the Ulun people alone? And the queen—Wynter. He had not forgotten Gotz's words. In order for the people to survive, he needed to marry the queen. Nothing made sense. Besides, she hated him. He might be hard-hearted, but he would marry for love, not duty.

Finn ducked inside the tent. "You wanted to see me?"

Gideon gestured toward the empty chair across from him. This wasn't a conversation he was prepared to have, but have it he must.

Finn sat down but avoided eye contact, staring at the crack between the tent flaps instead.

Gideon took a deep breath. "I believe your father is the mole who plotted with Valen to kill the queen."

Finn grimaced. "I suppose he was."

Gideon rubbed his hands together. "I was hasty with his sentence, but it would have been the same regardless."

"I understand."

Finn looked at Gideon now. "I didn't know, I swear on my mother's grave. Mangus always acted like he loathed Valen."

Gideon nodded. "We both have fathers whose legacies will follow us."

Finn stood, preparing to leave. "I won't hold it against you—killing my father."

"I didn't expect that you would."

Finn gave a quick nod and left swiftly.

Gideon leaned back in his chair and stared at the single flame of the candle. Tonight, the people celebrated the shallow victory of making it through the northern forest. Tomorrow, he would bury his brother and father and they would crown Gideon king. Did it made him a monster that he hadn't afforded Mangus the same honorable burial as he would his brother and father? Finn hadn't protested when they'd left Mangus' body behind. How could he? Mangus had dishonored the family.

He rose and removed a razor from a small wooden box. Then he sat at his table and shaved his head. His dark locks floated to the ground. Tonight he began mourning the loss of yet another brother and his king father.

27

WYNTER

Wynter stood at the edge of the camp. The Ulun men and women laughed and shouted by their campfires. Sparks rose into the sky as more logs were added to the flames. It would have almost been beautiful if she had not lost so much—Lark—her people.

A small group of soldiers was gathered around a cage that sat on the crest of a hill. They had captured a Morbid and were now tormenting it by dragging a stick across the bars of its prison. The creature screeched and hissed. The men laughed.

Not too far from there, Gideon's tent stood aglow with candlelight. She wrapped her arms around herself, shuddering against the cool night air. Kidron had cried herself to sleep. Her only real family was gone, and she was left with a brother who barely gave her the time of day. It had been all Wynter could do to muster the strength to console the girl. Her own future was empty and more uncertain than ever. Gideon had not killed her. Yet. That didn't mean he wouldn't.

She jumped when someone stepped up next to her. It was Brendle.

"Sorry to have startled you," he said.

"It's okay," she said quietly.

"It's hardly a time for celebration," he said.

"A whole Alrenian colony is gone. This is a great triumph for them."

"There are no winners here."

She turned and looked at Brendle. His dark skin glistened in the firelight. His eyes held something wise and profound. He didn't seem to belong here.

"Why are you here, Brendle? These aren't your people. You're Jutta."

He shifted and rested his hand on the hilt of the blade at his hip.

"Why don't you return to your own?" she asked.

"Lark and Gideon saved me as mercenaries in a war where they had no compulsion to care what happened to a man not of their own kind. Yet, save me they did."

"So you're an Ulun now?"

"This is where God put me, so I must see what he will have me do."

"You think he wanted you to be dragged from one war into another for some greater purpose?"

He looked at her now, the whites of his eyes were large and intimidating. "War is the evil work of man, not God."

Her frustration grew. Why wasn't Brendle angry? This wasn't his home, his people. Yet he seemed so sure that this was where he was meant to be. Was this also her destiny? Did she even believe in such a thing? She was taken by force, virtually a prisoner. Yet, were her and Brendle's circumstances so different?

She closed her eyes and asked the question she wasn't sure she wanted to hear the answer to. "How can you know the difference between the plans of man and the plans of God?"

When he didn't answer, she opened her eyes. He was looking past the fires, into the night as if the answer lay somewhere hidden in its deep recesses. Then he turned and walked away.

"Brendle?" she called after him. She was afraid to be alone.

"I'll be close by." Then he disappeared into the darkness.

There was shouting from the hill above her. The men tormenting the Morbid had grown tired of their game and were leaving, but not before hurling a slew of insults. Without thinking, she wandered into the camp and found a barrel of drinking water and ladled out a cup. She was ignored by the Ulun people as if she didn't exist. She was Alrenian—an unwanted presence. She would never be accepted here.

She climbed the hill, though her aching muscles protested. The encounter with the Morbids had drained her, and though she feared it, she felt a sense of kinship with the frail creature at the top of the hill. It too was taken from its family, imprisoned and mocked.

At first, she stood at a safe distance studying the small creature. It was lying on its side, breathing heavily, eyes closed. Its bald head and tiny limbs made it look like a starving child. It didn't react to her presence, so she approached the wooden cage and knelt down by the small latched door. The cup wouldn't fit through the slats. She'd have to raise the door a few inches and push the cup inside. The Morbid continued to pant, but it remained very still. She slid out the stick that secured the door latch, watching for any sudden movement from the Morbid. Her heart pumped fiercely. After all, this was one of the creatures that had tried to kill her and Gideon. She lifted the door a few inches, then carefully, using one finger, slid the cup into the cage. The Morbid opened its large eyes. She froze. As if understanding her kind gesture, it remained still. Its dark eyes were haunting. Was this really a demon that had come down with the fires of the Great Destruction? It seemed so frail and innocent.

She let her guard down a moment too long. Suddenly, the Morbid lurched. She didn't realize what was happening until it had a hold of her arm. Then everything went black.

SHE AWOKE *in the woods and immediately inhaled a cloud of smoke.*

The woods were on fire. The treetops burned like giant torches and flakes of leaves fell in golden wisps all around her. She turned frantically, looking for a way out. She covered her nose and mouth with the sleeve of her gown. A baby's cry pierced the crackling of the trees. She stumbled toward the sounds of the infant, using its loud wail as a beacon. She didn't understand what was happening. She was sure that just a few minutes ago she had been about to give the Morbid a drink of water. Was the sky raining down fire again like the day of the Great Destruction?

The baby's cry grew louder. Was she getting closer? The smoke was slowly suffocating her and her eyes stung with its bitter turmoil, yet she pushed forward toward the piercing cries. The baby needs me. I need to save it. *She didn't understand where these thoughts were coming from. She ran until she burst out of the woods and found herself at the edge of a river. The air was clean, smokeless. Lark was standing there holding the child. The baby had stopped crying. She glanced behind her—the world was in flames, but this place, this world, was serene and untouched.*

I'm dreaming.

Lark smiled at her and then looked down at the child in his arms. She moved slowly toward them. She was afraid, but not of Lark—of the child. She stood in front of Lark, happy to see him alive. He shifted the baby in his arms so she could see its tiny face. The baby was sleeping now.

"I have to admit, he's one beautiful baby. Just like his mother," Lark said.

"Who's his mother?" she asked, mesmerized by the child's angelic face. She had never seen a face so beautiful. The child's lips moved as if he was dreaming of suckling at his mother's breast.

"I have a suggestion for a name," Lark said.

She lifted her gaze to meet his.

He smiled at her. "Lark is a good strong name." He handed her the baby. Panic rose in her chest. Why was he giving her the baby? The world was falling apart all around them; what was she going to do with a baby? Yet when she gazed at the boy's face, she forgot all about the destruction behind her.

She looked up. Lark was leaving, his cloak floating behind him.

"Lark!"

He turned around. There was sadness in his face.

"Where are you going? Whose baby is this?" she asked desperately.

He opened his mouth to speak. A blinding flash pulled her back to reality.

28

GIDEON

"You must come speak to the girl," Brendle said.

Gideon was sitting in a chair rubbing his newly shaven head. He wasn't in any kind of mood to converse with the queen. He sighed. "I'm in mourning."

"There is no time for such things as this when you are king," Brendle reminded him.

"I've lost my father, brother, and uncle in the same day." Gideon dropped his hand to the table and studied Brendle's face. His skin was as dark as a raven's feathers, his eyes large and accusing. The knife at his waist looked like a child's toy, so large was his frame.

"What's wrong with the queen?" Gideon asked.

"You've made it through the northern forest. She thinks you no longer need her. She's anxious."

Gideon picked at the edges of the rough wood table. "We both know she's got nothing to worry about. We need the two rings of Ferran to open the gate to Isidor. And since I don't know if she has to be actually wearing the ring for us to open the gate, she is most certainly safe."

Brendle's right eye twitched—almost imperceptibly. Gideon

had learned this tell of his a long time ago. *He thinks I should come clean with the queen. Tell her about Isidor.*

"You should tell her," Brendle said matter-of-factly. He made no move to leave.

Brendle was not going to take no for an answer, and though Gideon was in no mood to address the queen, he respected Brendle. This was a man he would need at his side now more than ever. He would do this for him if for no other reason than to ensure his loyalty.

"Did she say she was concerned for her life?" Gideon asked.

"She didn't have to."

Gideon stood, swiped his cloak off the back of the other chair, and they headed out. Shouts of laughter rose into the night sky, and the smell of burning wood and fresh meat turning on spits made him long for the time when he had gathered with his own family to celebrate victories after their mercenary soldiers had returned from war with their spoils.

Brendle led the way using only the light from the fires to guide them. They were walking across the grassy hill next to his tent when Gideon spotted Wynter crouched by the cage where the captured Morbid was being kept. He and Brendle took off running. She was on her knees in the clutches of the creature, her body stiff and shaking with convulsions.

"Bow!" Gideon barked, holding a hand out to Brendle. The creature's eyes were closed, but its face was bright red and its small teeth were bared, so tight was its grip on Wynter's wrist.

Within seconds, Brendle had a bow and arrow in Gideon's hand, and Gideon released a shot directly into the cage, right into the Morbid's chest. The creature's eyes shot wide open. It shrieked, then collapsed.

29

WYNTER

Wynter blinked her eyes a few times. It took a minute for her to realize where she was. A hooded figure and Brendle stood above her. She sat up and everything came rushing back.

The Morbid was giving me a vision. Lark was about to tell me about the baby.

She scrambled to her hands and knees and crawled to the cage, only to find that the Morbid was dead. An arrow stuck out of its chest. She whipped around. The cloaked figure pulled back its hood. It was Gideon. His head was shaved. A bow dangled from his hand.

"Why did you kill it?" she screamed.

Gideon pulled his hood back over his head, then turned to leave. She jumped to her feet and barreled after him, only to have Brendle block her path.

"The creature was hurting you," Brendle said gently.

"It was giving me a vision!"

Brendle's eyes widened. He turned and looked at the retreating Gideon and then back to Wynter. "No such thing as this can happen."

"Well it did," she snapped.

Brendle reluctantly moved aside so she could pass. She dashed after Gideon, angry and hurt. Tears flowed down her face. Why did she feel like she had abandoned the baby? The vision wasn't real, but it had felt real, and her feelings of loss for the baby and for Lark were as real as the tears falling down her cheeks.

She followed Gideon straight into his tent. When he turned and swept back his hood, he seemed surprised to see her.

She was slightly taken aback by his shaved head, but she was too angry to care. "Do you just kill everything that crosses your path?" she said fiercely.

He ignored her, removing his cloak and tossing it across a chair. His eyes, the ones that could send you cowering into a corner, were less threatening without all his dark hair. He seemed more vulnerable somehow.

"Would you have preferred that I let the creature kill you?" he said dryly.

"He wasn't hurting me."

"You should retire. It's late. You can thank me tomorrow."

Gideon sat and removed his boots and socks and tossed them to the side. His feet were wide and strong like she would imagine an ancient gladiator would have.

"Thank you?" she hissed. "There is nothing that you could ever do that would require me to thank you."

He leaned back in his chair and stared at her.

"Lark is dead because of you. You only care about yourself. You killed your uncle without blinking, without even inquiring of his innocence. What kind of person does that?"

His eyes were soulless, like there was nothing left inside him. Instead of pity, hate grew inside her. Her heart pounded so severely that her chest ached. "I've never loathed someone as much as I loathe you," she said. The tears she swore she'd never spill again, fell freely.

He gazed at her without a trace of anger in his face. "Then you are in good company, because I loathe myself."

His response shocked her. His words may have been the most honest thing he'd ever said, but it wasn't enough to erase the past few days. She glared at him through her tears, feeling nothing.

"Then there is justice in the world after all," she said.

With that, she left. Brendle was outside waiting for her, but he let her pass and run into the night. She returned to her tent and lay beside Kidron and held her until the tears stopped flowing. That was when she decided she was going to escape.

30

WYNTER

It was first light, and the mood in the camp was somber—a stark contrast to last night's celebrations. People were already gathering and making preparations to bury King Niko and his son, Lark. Women had gathered flowers and grasses and were weaving them together between two large branches to create pallets on which to carry the dead. Wynter was amazed at the intricacy of the woven patterns. Purple and pale pink wildflowers woven with grasses gave the green deathbeds the feeling of a luxurious tapestry.

Hilran, the woman who had attended the dying king, and another woman, had fetched Kidron to dress her and do her hair. It made her sad to think that Kidron would stand at Gideon's side and watch as the only two people who had ever really cared for her were laid to rest. She felt bad that she was going to be leaving Kidron behind, but she reminded herself that these were not her people. The distraction of the dual funeral was just what she needed in order to slip away.

There had been no sign of Gideon or Brendle that morning, but Brendle's men were always nearby, watching. It would be harder to give Brendle the slip, but it would not deter her from leaving. She needed to return to her people and let them know about the missing colony and the rogue Uluns bent on the destruction of the Alrenians. And there was the matter of the ring. It needed to be returned to the rightful heir, along with the gift of healing. If that was even possible.

She looked at the ring's glimmering gold surface and the beauty of the golden eagle. She'd become accustomed to its presence and rarely gave it a thought anymore. But it was not hers to wear. She wasn't the queen, and she had yet to heal anyone except herself. She was an imposter, and she needed to return to her former life. She was a transporter. That was her destiny.

She ate breakfast at the community table where fruit and bread had been laid out. As usual, she ate alone, but she needed to keep up the appearance of routine until the right moment came for her to slip away. The two women across from her, dressed in simple woolen shifts, watched her warily. They were probably wondering why she was still there—why the king had not disposed of her now that they were through the northern forest.

A horn sounded. The people wrapped up their meal quickly, swallowing last bites and dusting leftovers from their fingertips. They moved in a kind of organized chaos to the top of the hill. She followed, searching the crowd for Brendle. She spotted him just to her right, behind her. *He's watching me.* She'd have to find a way to blend in, disappear.

She advanced her way to the front of the crowd, ignoring the murmurs and whispers that she had no doubt were Alrenian slurs.

Stay focused.

She planted herself right at the front, and the people filled in around her. Finn was standing at the edge of the crowd. He seemed as solemn as the others. There was nothing in his face to betray the fact that he'd just lost his father in such a sudden and brutal way. Perhaps he was still in shock.

Gideon stood next to the two pyres made of juniper branches —the final resting places of his father and brother. Kidron was by his side, putting on a brave face. The women had woven her unruly blond tresses into an intricate braid fit for a king's daughter and had managed to get her to wear a simple burgundy dress. No longer would Lark be there to care for young Kidron, and Wynter's heart broke for her.

Gideon showed no signs of mourning. His face was resolute, emotionless. She felt a stab of guilt remembering the horrible things she had said to him last night after he'd killed the Morbid. For a brief moment, Gideon looked at her, and chills ran down her arms. She couldn't look away, she didn't want to, despite how she loathed him. *What is this madness?* But then the crowd settled, and the music began. The moment was gone.

Someone played a reed flute. It was a somber melody—a pure sound that carried like a breeze. The emotions of the losing her mother and father flooded over her. They had not been given the honor that these two men were to receive.

The people quietly parted behind her. She didn't understand what was happening, until men came through, carrying the woven pallets with the bodies wrapped in shrouds—King Niko and his son, Lark.

The people were silent, and only the footsteps of the pall-bearers could be heard above the light symphony of the flute. She held back the desire to touch Lark as he passed—a final goodbye.

When the crowd began to close in as the procession passed, she slipped through the disorder of the moment and came out at the back of the assembly. No one had seemed to notice.

Racing through the camp, she grabbed a half-eaten apple from the morning table and made her way to the edge of camp where the horses were tied to trees. She spotted Lark's brown and white horse and approached slowly, offering the apple as a bribe. It bit off a large chunk as she slowly unwrapped its reins from around a tree limb. She gently led it away from the other horses, offering the last bit of apple to entice it along. Once up onto the saddle, Wynter glanced nervously toward the crowd at the top of the hill, but all the attention was on the service. Pulling the horse to the left, she took one look back at the camp, and dug in her heels.

She rode as fast as she could though she was fearful of riding back through the northern forest where her people had once thrived. The Morbid attack was still fresh in her mind. Though now that she had received a vision from the captured Morbid, she wondered if the real purpose of the Morbids was to be some kind of messengers rather than destroyers. The vision of Lark and the baby had seemed hopeful, but the burning forest had been an omen of destruction.

If only I knew the meaning of such a vision.

Lark had been about to explain who the baby was when Gideon pierced the creature's heart. Now she'd never know. Holding the baby in her arms had felt so real that her heart now ached for the unknown child.

Why does it feel like I'm leaving him behind?

Nothing made sense.

After several hours of riding, the rushing water of a river caught her ear. Wynter slowed and followed the sound down an embankment, through clusters of tree saplings that had found root at river's edge.

She dismounted and led the horse to the water to drink. She knelt at the edge and splashed her face, lamenting the fact that she'd failed to plan properly by not bringing food and water.

She dried her face with the hem of her skirt, looked across the river, and froze. Staring at her point blank was the blackest of wolves she'd ever seen. Its black coat glimmered with shades of midnight blue and black. It studied her with its icy blue eyes. Thankfully, the horse had not yet seen it.

Wynter rose slowly to a crouch and carefully reached out and took the horse's reins. The wolf watched. She inched closer to the horse, continuing to let it drink water, but preparing to make a quick mount and escape.

Is the wolf alone? I might be able to outrun one, but not a whole pack.

She expected it to make its move, but instead it sat down. Its eyes never left hers, but the look was docile, not threatening. There was a strange understanding that seemed to pass between them.

It's not going to hurt me.

Before she could think on it further, shouts erupted from the other side of the river. The wolf bolted. She mounted the horse, pulled the reins sharply to the right, and dug her heels into its flank, urging it up the steep embankment. The pounding of horses' hooves closed in—voices with it.

It can't be Gideon, the direction is all wrong.

Her heart raced.

Whoever they are, they don't know I'm here. They're probably after the wolf.

She looked back. There were four of them—Ulun by the look of their beards and dark hair. One of them spotted her. She snapped the reins and shouted to the horse. The splash of water behind her told her all she needed to know. They were coming after her, not the wolf.

31

GIDEON

Gotz spoke kind words about King Niko and Lark—words Gideon had heard before when they had buried his older brother, then his mother. Gideon spun his father's ring on his finger—the ring of the king. He hadn't wanted a ceremony. He'd simply put the ring on his finger. It would take time to become used to the cool feel of metal on his hand. It felt more like a chain around his neck.

He glanced over at Kidron. What did he know of a young girl? It seemed his burdens grew like a festering wound. Wynter's unkind words from last night lingered, and he wondered why he would think of it now when sorrow should be the only thing upon his heart.

When Gotz finished speaking, a group of ladies sang a dirge—their voices somber, releasing a deep melody.

Surely he has borne our griefs and carried our sorrows, yet we esteemed him stricken...

The words were haunting, yet he found himself feeling nothing.

Smitten by God and afflicted...

His jaw clenched. A small hand slid into his. He looked

down, surprised at Kidron's simple act of kindness. He fought back the emotions that threaten to overcome him.

Not here. Not now.

He held her tiny hand knowing it was likely all the comfort he'd be able to give her in the moment.

The song concluded. The pyres were set ablaze. It was over. Two lives reduced to one small, final moment—a ceremony marking one's death with nothing but embers left of their existence.

Hilran led Kidron away. For that he was grateful. She would comfort her—give her what he couldn't. He thought of what Lark had said about Hilran holding on to the hope that Gideon would marry her. But he had no heart for a wife. Maybe it was because he'd watched too many women become widows. Being king would only increase that risk for anyone who was unlucky enough to call him husband.

Kidron looked back at him, seemingly hesitant to leave him. But when he didn't show any sign of protest, she turned back and followed Hilran.

Brendle approached him, breathless and sweaty, Finn on his heels. "Wynter is gone."

Gideon frowned. "Gone?"

"She slipped away during the ceremony. I tracked her going southwest," Brendle said.

Gideon's heart leapt. "That's where Valen and his men are."

Brendle nodded.

"They'll kill her without a thought," Finn said.

So she's decided to run.

He couldn't say he blamed her. He had treated her poorly from the beginning, and last night he had done nothing to bridge the gap between them. Why had she been so upset about him killing a Morbid? A vision, she'd said. It had been giving her a vision. The idea was ridiculous. He had half a mind to let her go. But the truth was he needed her—and her ring.

He gritted his teeth. An altercation with Valen was the last thing they needed. But Finn was right. If Valen were to capture the queen, it would be her end.

He rubbed a hand over his mouth. "Round up sixty men."

Brendle and Finn left him, calling the men to arms.

Gideon hurried to his tent, threw off his formal jacket, and grabbed a cloak. Outside, Finn had Gideon's black stallion waiting for him. He stuck a boot into the leather stirrup and the thunder of hooves marked the exit of him and his men from the camp.

32

WYNTER

Wynter did the best she could, but she was no horseman. The men were riding on both sides of her now. She caught glimpses of them as she traversed trees. It wasn't long before they had her hemmed in. Her horse brayed and rose up on two legs. She lost her grip and fell to the ground. She lay there paralyzed, unable to breathe. The men who had been in pursuit dismounted and stood over her. She gasped and air filled her lungs.

"What do we have here?" A large, barrel-chested man with a shaved head and a beard wrested her to her feet. He lifted her hand with the ring and licked his lips. His eyes sparkled like a thief admiring his stolen treasure. He dropped her hand and eyed her slim features.

"You're kinda scrawny for a queen."

The other men chuckled. She crossed her arms and tucked the ring away.

"Do you know who I am?" he asked.

She said nothing, but she had a strong sense that this was the man who she and Lark had overheard in the woods, plotting to kill her.

Valen.

He circled her now, probing her with his eyes. She fumed at her stupidity. She had landed right into the hands of the man who wanted her dead. She had traded relative safety for a sword.

"Where is Gideon heading, and why is he keeping you alive?"

She remained silent.

He stopped in front of her, drawing uncomfortably close. "Nothing to say, Your Majesty?"

His breath reeked of soured goat's milk. She tried to mask her displeasure. He grabbed her forcefully by the arm. She winced. This made him smile. "Let's see if you're more talkative after a night in the cage."

He pushed her toward one of his men who chuckled and caught her in his thick hairy arms. She buried her temper and her will to fight, afraid of what an outburst would trigger.

Her hands were bound in front of her and she was hoisted back up upon Lark's horse. For the second time, she'd been kidnapped by Uluns. But these weren't just any Uluns. These were the deserters Gideon had described—the ones who wanted war with the Alrenians. She'd just handed them the perfect prize —the queen of the Alrenians.

She looked down at her gold ring—the symbol of her people. The engraved eagle seemed to be judging her.

I've done everything wrong. Because of me, my people are in more danger than ever.

It had all started the day she'd climbed down to the ground to help the dying queen. If only she'd fled with the other Alrenian soldiers, she wouldn't be in the predicament she was in now. Her impulsive decision to flee Gideon's camp had only worsened matters. Her good intentions had once again caused more harm than good.

It wasn't long before they arrived at Valen's camp. It was nestled in a valley between two mountains. The man riding next to her held the reins of her horse, and Valen's party of men paraded her through their camp like a prize. Jeers of "hail to the Alrenian queen" were shouted out in mock adoration. Others shook their fists and spat on the ground as she passed. They were loud and boisterous—a sharp contrast to the silence she'd received upon entering Gideon's camp.

The hunting party stopped suddenly, and she was pulled off the horse. She fell to the ground, and the people laughed and crowded in, yelling words she'd never heard before. A tall woman with a head of ragged, short hair, broke through the crowd and pulled Wynter up by her collar. She tugged her along until they reached the far edge of the camp where a line of bamboo cages, no taller than a child, stood. Other prisoners held on to the rough bars and peered out at her. "Queen Mother! Great Healer! Save us!"

They're Alrenians!

The woman shoved her into a vacant cage at the end, sending her sprawling to the dirt floor.

"You won't be saving anyone tonight, Your Majesty." The woman chuckled, secured the cage, and sauntered off.

Wynter crawled into the corner and drew up her knees, covering her ears with her hands, trying to drown out the cries of her people in the cages next to hers. They expected her to do something. There was nothing she could do. She wasn't their queen.

What have I done?

33

GIDEON

Gideon, Brendle, and Finn surveyed the valley below.

"How many fighting men do you think Valen has?" Gideon asked.

"I'd say two hundred at least," Brendle said.

Gideon sighed. They were outnumbered. "Are you sure they have her?"

"Yes. She's being held in those cages on their right flank," Brendle said.

Gideon nodded.

"What do you want to do?" Finn asked.

"We wait until dark. Start preparing fires."

34

WYNTER

"Hey."

A female voice shattered Wynter's fitful slumber. She was surprised to find that she'd fallen asleep and now night was upon them. She pushed herself up, unsure from where the voice had come.

"Over here."

It took a minute for her eyes to adjust. There was a girl in the cage next to her. The whites of her eyes glowed in the darkness.

"What are you doing here, Wynter?" the girl asked.

She knows me?

Wynter crawled over to the bamboo bars that separated them. She couldn't believe her eyes. "Six?"

Six grinned—her smile lighting up like a spark. They grasped hands between the bars.

"What are you doing—" they both said at the same time.

Six was an Alrenian bridge builder. She was Jutta, like Brendle. Dark skinned with beautiful brown eyes. She had been sent to the northern forest months ago to help mend bridges. She was a few years older than Wynter, but they often encountered each other during Wynter's transport runs, and Six would call out to her to avoid certain routes that were being worked on. It had

156

mostly been a working type of relationship, but they had always been on friendly terms. Wynter would sometimes bring Six and her crew surplus fruit.

"You first," Wynter said.

Six eyed the ring on Wynter's hand but continued. "The northern colony is gone."

Wynter nodded. "I know. It was overrun with Morbids when we went through there."

Six lowered her voice. "It wasn't Morbids that destroyed the colony."

"I know. Uluns," Wynter said.

"I don't understand it. The Uluns haven't attacked us directly in years," Six said. "Why now?"

"These aren't ordinary Uluns," Wynter explained. "They're deserters, intent on destroying us and reclaiming Ferran."

"That explains the lack of a king," Six said. "Unless you count that thug Valen. He seems to be the one calling the shots." Six touched Wynter's ring. "Why are you wearing the queen's ring?"

"It's a long story." One she was not so eager to repeat. The dead queen's vacant eyes were still fresh in her mind.

"We received word that the queen had been captured by Uluns while she was in route to the southern colony."

"She was killed," Wynter said softly. "She gave me the ring right before she died."

"Daughters of Alrenia! What are you saying?"

"She also gave me the gift of healing."

Six's eyes widened. "You're...You're the queen?"

"For now," she said. "I escaped my Ulun captors. I was trying to get back to the queen's colony so I could restore the ring and the gift to the rightful heir of Alrenia. Valen intercepted me."

"This is unbelievable. Jack said you were dead. Killed in the attack on the queen."

Jack. Cousin. Traitor.

She had thought little of him since the day he'd told Gideon she was the real queen.

"He's here?" Wynter asked, her eyes narrowing.

"No. But, he brought word to the northern colony of the queen's capture. He was there when we were attacked, but I don't know where he is now."

So he's still keeping up the ruse that the queen's still alive.

She tried to hide her anger. For now, Jack's betrayal would stay a secret. If he was dead, there was no point in resurrecting his sullied past.

"Why weren't there any bodies?" Wynter asked. She wasn't sure she wanted to know the answer.

Six squeezed Wynter's hands. "They didn't want to leave behind any evidence of their heinous crime. The ones who didn't escape were killed and carted off."

"I'm glad you're okay, Six." That was all she could think to say.

Six nodded. "They only kept a few of us. The ones they thought would be useful. Being a bridge builder saved my life. What are we going to do, Wynter?"

"I don't know." A small part of her hoped Gideon cared enough to come for her.

Why would he? The last thing you told him was how loathsome he was.

"We pray for a miracle."

35

GIDEON

"Are all the fires prepared?" Gideon asked.

"Yes, my lord. All one hundred of them," Brendle said.

The risks were high. Valen knew all the Ulun war tactics. It was possible that he wouldn't fall for Gideon's trick.

"My lord. May I speak freely?" Brendle asked.

"Of course."

"Valen knows this tactic. He will know the fires were set to look like we have more men than we do. He will attack, not retreat. We've shown him our hand, as you Uluns like to say."

Gideon couldn't resist a small smile. "That's what I'm counting on."

Brendle bristled slightly.

If I can fool Brendle, there is hope.

"You and I will take our best fighters to the south side of the camp. Have Finn instruct the others to light the fires at sunset. If I'm right, Valen will march toward the fires. Once Valen is close, have the remaining men retreat into the woods. Valen will follow, and then we attack his camp from behind. By the time he figures out what has happened, it will be too late."

Valen was no fool, but Gideon only needed him to be foolish once.

The expression on Brendle's face changed from confusion to understanding. "Yes, my lord. But I believe Finn should remain with us."

Gideon raised an eyebrow. "You have a reason for this, I assume."

Brendle hesitated.

"You may speak freely, Brendle."

"I don't trust him."

Gideon wasn't completely shocked by Brendle's revelation. The pair didn't exactly sing each other's praises.

"He's family."

"So was Mangus."

"Pick another soldier to organize the lighting of the fires. Finn rides with us."

GIDEON SAT atop of his stallion on the south side of the valley above Valen's camp, hidden out of sight with the rest of his men. The Ulun camp below them was lit with night fires and candles aglow within tents. He prayed Wynter was still alive. Brendle had assured him that he had located her in one of the cages at the west end of the camp, along with other cages filled with Alrenians. He knew now that it was Valen who had attacked the northern forest, and that he wouldn't stop until all Alrenians were eradicated. That was why Valen had opposed the king. He and his followers wanted Ferran, though the lands were ravaged and poor. It's what Gideon should have wanted, but something inside him had changed. The fight for Ferran seemed lost a long time ago when the Great Destruction had come. He wanted to start over—bring his people to a new land. Isidor. A land he wasn't even sure existed. He prayed everything he was doing wasn't for nothing.

He and his men waited—Brendle at his side. Finn was only a few horses down as Brendle had requested. The horses snorted in anticipation. This would be his first battle as king. There were men much older than him ready to follow him into battle. They'd put their faith in a twenty-eight-year-old simply because he was the son of King Niko. Was it fate or duty that had set Gideon's path?

He looked over at Brendle. His eyes were closed, and his lips were moving silently. It gave Gideon some comfort to see Brendle praying. Surely, God listened to a man such as Brendle. Why would God listen to a man like Gideon? One with doubts? One with fears?

He rested his hand on his sword's hilt. *If only Lark was by my side.*

The first flames of their fires across the valley sparked to life. Now they waited until the last fire had been lit. Brendle rode off to double-check their perimeter.

36

WYNTER

No one had come by Wynter's cage since her capture. The only reason she was still alive was because Valen wanted to know what Gideon was up to. Valen was no doubt letting her squirm and imagine all the horrible things he would do to her if she didn't talk. As soon as he got what he wanted from her, she was as good as dead.

Her stomach growled. She hadn't eaten anything since morning. She glanced over at Six. Her eyes were closed, but she was humming a song. Wynter let her be.

She gazed out the back of her cage at the open field, fighting the urge to cry. That's when she saw it—the wolf. It hung back, far enough where it couldn't be spotted. Its eyes sparkled, despite the low light. Was it following her? Why?

"Six," she whispered. She wanted to make sure she wasn't imagining it.

Six opened her eyes and Wynter pointed toward the wolf. Six moved closer to the back of her cage and peered out. "Daughters of Alrenia!"

The wolf ran off.

"You saw that right?" Wynter asked.

Six stared at her unblinkingly. "You have a spirit wolf."

"A what?"

Six crawled over to their shared wall. "A spirit guide."

"This is not Alrenian teaching."

"No. It's Jutta. My people believe every person has a spirit guide. If you're ever lucky enough to see it, it means you've been chosen for something great, and you must pay careful attention."

Wynter didn't know what to say. She didn't believe in such things, but it was strange that she'd seen the wolf twice in one day, and that his eyes seemed more human than animal.

"Maybe it's *your* spirit guide," Wynter offered. "You're Jutta. I'm not."

Six laughed. "We worship the same God. Besides, if it were my spirit guide, you wouldn't have seen the wolf earlier."

Wynter's mouth fell open. "How did you—?"

"I didn't. But now I know for sure, it's yours, not mine."

"What does it want?" Wynter asked.

Six smiled. Her smile was a beacon of white. "You ask the wrong question."

Six sounded like Brendle. Jutta words were mysterious, but something in the way they talked was beautiful and full of truth.

"What's the right question?"

"Will you follow?" Six explained.

I'm locked up. How can I follow?

She was lost in thought when Six cried out. "Wynter! Look."

Fires above the valley came alive, one by one until the entire camp of Ulun traitors was bathed in light.

"Gideon." The hope of an escape sent her heart racing.

"Who's Gideon?" Six asked.

"The new king of the Uluns."

"Good grief. We're going to be caught in the middle of a civil war?"

"No, we're going to get out of here."

"What? How?"

Wynter didn't know what Gideon had planned, but the distraction he would cause was all she needed to break free.

"If only we could arm ourselves," she said, tugging on the bars of the cage, looking for a weak spot.

"I was saving this for just the right time," Six said. She dug with her hands in the back corner of her cage and came back with a small knife.

"Six! Why haven't you tried to escape?"

"They told us if we tried, they'd kill everyone who remained."

Wynter stretched her hand through the bars. "Here, give it to me. When the time is right, we'll get ourselves out of here."

Six nodded.

Shouts erupted. Men and women scrambled from their tents and gathered too deep inside the camp for Wynter to see what was going on. A single guard was left at the cages with the prisoners. He glanced at them warily, as if they were somehow responsible for the unwanted company in the hills above them.

Six counted off each fire as it was lit.

"What do the fires mean?" Wynter asked.

"Your Ulun friends are showing their numbers to Valen."

"Why?"

"It's a fear tactic. An invitation to surrender."

Valen's men were organizing. Women were scrambling, squelching the evening fires. The camp grew darker except for the torches being lit by Valen's men. This did not look like a surrender. Suddenly she feared for Gideon.

The organized chaos didn't last long. Valen and his men rode out of camp straight for the hill of fires. They weren't surrendering, they were attacking.

37

GIDEON

ideon and his small army waited in the shadows as Valen rallied his followers and headed up the hill on the opposite side of the camp toward the fires that Gideon's men had set.

He's taking the bait. He has no idea we're about to attack his camp from behind.

Gideon's jaw worked back and forth. His horse fidgeted. His heart pounded. He closed his eyes and breathed slowly in and out, preparing himself for the attack. He had to forget that he'd just lost his father and brother—forget that he was alone in this.

His soldiers' horses stomped their hooves. The wind blew from the north, bringing with it the scent of the fires set by his men. Saddles creaked, horses snorted. A silent trepidation hung in the air.

"We find the girl and retreat," Gideon whispered.

"Yes, my lord," Brendle said. "The men have their orders."

Gideon wondered why Brendle hadn't challenged his plan of attack. Lark would have wanted to destroy Valen and make him pay for his betrayal. And as if Brendle had read his mind, he said, "There's a time for everything. Valen's day of reckoning will come."

Valen's men crested the hill on the other side. Now the men Gideon had left behind would draw him into the woods, feigning retreat.

He tightened his grip on his horse's reins. "On my word," he said. The men shifted in their saddles and called quietly to each other with words of encouragement. Torches were lit.

"Now!" Gideon yelled out.

The horses burst into motion, driving down into the valley as a united wall of blades and bone. The ground itself seemed to be driving them forward. The horses pumped in rhythm, like rolling thunder. Once they were within range of the camp, Gideon's bowmen sent a hailstorm of flaming arrows into the traitors' camp. Screams and shouts began as the arrows hit, and tents erupted into flames. Gideon unsheathed his sword and a chorus of scraping metal followed as the others pulled their own blades.

We'll take as little blood as possible.

He bellowed a war cry to encourage his men forward—one he had heard his father yell many times, only now it was his turn.

The camp was mere feet away. Men and women ran for cover. From the looks of them, they were not fighters. Valen had taken his best men with him.

A surge of strength pulsed through Gideon's body. The second barrage of arrows filled the air around him, and the wave of horses and men tore into the camp. He swept his blade down, dropping three armed men in a row. He avoided their eyes as they collapsed to the ground. As long as he kept his blade in motion, he could stay numb to death.

Brendle pulled away to head for the cages that held the queen. Gideon leapt off his horse as men with short swords and axes ran toward him. He spun, sweeping his blade in a crusade of death. He cut through souls and they dropped to the ground. He shoved an older man out of his way, wrenching his makeshift weapon from his hand and tossing it aside. Gideon paused, watching as his men sliced through those who tried to fight back.

A warrior's yell erupted from behind him. Gripping his blade with both hands, Gideon turned to face a snarling axman swinging his huge weapon. Gideon ducked down fast and thrust his sword upward, slicing into the man's groin and taking him from the fight.

Valen's people screamed and ran for cover. Many abandoned their weapons, while others continued to fight through the smoke and chaos. Gideon made his way toward the cages, his sword held at his side. He punched those who came at him without a weapon and slaughtered those who were armed. The smell of blood and smoke filled the air. The power and glory of battle was not lost on him. It was a thrill that should have repulsed him—yet he found himself hungry for it, and it made him sick at heart. For just a moment, he found himself losing focus, and he just stood there taking in the horrifying scene of limp bodies and broken bones. Heads were splayed open. Gaping wounds spilled blood all around him. Any thrill he was feeling in the moment passed quickly. He forced himself to continue, embracing the surge of adrenaline and letting his reflexes take over once again.

A group of men charged him. He swept his blade with wide, aggressive strokes.

This is necessary for my people. For Wynter.

It was his right to kill the Ulun traitors. He was king. He was meant to lead his men in battle.

Tents fell to the ground a few feet away as his men hacked their ties and tossed flames on top.

Gideon whistled for his horse.

How many lives will be lost here today?

His horse appeared out of the smoky haze. He mounted in one swift movement and charged toward the western end of the camp where Brendle had headed to rescue the queen. His men fought in his wake, closing ranks behind him.

38

WYNTER

Wynter's heart raced. She and Six looked at each other, trying to gather courage.

A shout erupted somewhere in the distance. Suddenly, the thunderous sound of horses' hooves descended upon them. The ground shook, then a volley of flaming arrows fell from the night sky and landed within the camp, setting tents ablaze.

Wynter pulled at the bars of her cage. If one of those arrows landed on their cages, they would go up in flames.

"Let us out!" Wynter shouted at the guard. Soon, all the Alrenian prisoners were shouting and rattling the cages.

The guard, looking nervous, drew his sword and turned his back on the prisoners.

"Are you ready?" Wynter whispered. Six nodded. Together, they kicked at the back of their cages until the poles gave way.

"Hey!" The guard shouted.

Wynter scrambled out into the open. Nothing but field lay beyond them.

"Wynter, help."

Six's shirt was caught on a splintered pole. The guard was

running toward them. The other Alrenian prisoners, seeing their opportunity, began kicking out the back of their cages.

Wynter ripped the cloth and freed Six right as the guard came around the corner. Wynter crouched and held the small knife in front of her. What match would she be for a man with a sword? He grinned knowingly and approached. Suddenly he stopped, his eyes widened, and he fell forward. A spear had been planted in his back. She looked up to see Brendle's wide eyes blazing with the reflection of fire.

"Run!" She grabbed Six's hand and they took off running. Other Uluns, mostly women, and now the prisoners, were running into the fields. Wynter followed and tried to blend in with the fleeing crowd.

The air became unbearably smoky as more arrows landed and set some of the field grass on fire. She glanced back, searching for Brendle's horse, but the only riders she saw were still circling the camp.

She pulled Six out of the fleeing crowd and headed west into the darkest recesses of the valley. They came to a copse of trees and were about to disappear inside when the wolf appeared. His eyes glowed with a steely blue intensity. He growled this time and hunched his back so that his hair stood up. Wynter tightened her grip on the knife and held it out in front of her.

Six batted Wynter's hand down. "No. He won't hurt you. It's a warning. We have to go back."

"What? We can't," Wynter said. "We have to get back to the queen's colony." She moved forward. The wolf bared its teeth and growled louder. She moved left. The wolf moved left. She moved right. The wolf moved right. Each time it bared its teeth in displeasure.

Six grabbed Wynter by the arm. "Please. We have to go back."

Wynter gritted her teeth. She wouldn't go back, spirit animal or not. She'd get around the wolf one way or another.

She turned around to find Gideon glaring down at her from atop his horse. "Going somewhere?"

She glanced back to see if the wolf was still there. It was gone. She sighed and dropped the knife.

39

WYNTER

The trip back with Gideon and his men was long and arduous, with only torches to light the way. It didn't help that their caravan cut back through the northern forest *again* and Wynter had to reface the reality that the northern colony had been lost and that there was little hope of her ever returning to her own colony. At least Six was with her. Wynter had insisted, in a very queen-appropriate fit, that Six be allowed to return with her. The other Alrenians, she assumed, had escaped. In the mayhem and chaos, there was no real way to know.

She and Six rode on a horse together, Six sitting behind her. Ten horses ahead of them were Gideon and Brendle. Finn had situated himself close to her, no doubt on Gideon's orders.

Gideon was none too happy with her. The mood was as solemn as the funeral procession for the king and Lark had been. Men had been lost during her rescue, others injured. It was a marvel more were not killed. From what she could ascertain, Gideon's men on the north side of the valley drew Valen's men into the woods. Before Valen could realize what was happening, Gideon's small army was attacking from the south. His camp had been decimated and burned to the ground, and Gideon's army was long gone. Valen had been left with embers.

"He's one good-looking man," Six said.

Wynter snapped out of her reflection and looked ahead. "Brendle?" He was Jutta like Six.

"What? No. The king," Six said. "My *lord*, Gideon," she added in a silken tone.

Wynter frowned.

"Is he married?" Six asked.

"No," she said a bit too harshly.

"All the better."

For some reason Six's flirtatious ramblings annoyed her. They were prisoners, not potential wives.

"He's cold," Wynter said flippantly.

"Nothing a woman's touch couldn't cure."

Wynter turned in the saddle and gave Six a chastising look.

Six held up a hand. "Okay. A girl can dream, can't she?"

Yes. But not about him. He was their sworn enemy.

"Wouldn't Brendle suit you better?" Wynter asked.

"Psst. Why? Because he's Jutta?"

"Well… Yeah."

"Jutta men are too serious for me. I'm a free spirit."

Wynter smiled. It was nice to have a friend. Talking with Six about men was the closest thing to normal she'd felt in days.

"Why do you think he came back for you?" Six asked.

"I don't know. Their seer has said some strange things."

"Like what?"

"Until the wolf unites with the eagle…"

Six squeezed Wynter's waist.

"Daughters of Alrenia! What's the rest of it?"

"That's it. We got interrupted."

"Anything else?" Six asked.

Wynter hesitated. The vision of Lark and the baby came to mind. Whether it meant anything or not remained to be seen. But it felt good to talk to someone about it—finally.

"I had a dream about a baby. It was crying. The woods around us were on fire."

Six gripped Wynter by the shoulders. "You're going to marry the king and have his baby!"

Several of the men around them, including Finn, looked over, curiosity in their eyes. Wynter grimaced. Six had a voice that could travel for miles.

"Would you mind lowering your voice," Wynter said quietly.

"Sorry," Six said, grinning.

"Anyway, that's not what it means," Wynter said, mortified at Six's interpretation.

"Okay. Whatever you say."

Ten seconds later. "No wonder your spirit wolf wanted you to go back," Six said loudly.

Wynter's face flushed. What if Six was right? The thought of marrying Gideon made her stomach churn. His brooding dark eyes, his cold stare—the thought of him touching her made her shiver. Six started humming, and Wynter was left with her feelings, her fears. She needed to speak to the seer, Gotz, again and tell him about the vision the Morbid had given her. She needed to know what it meant and what the seer's strange words about the wolf uniting with the eagle *really* meant.

She glanced at the back of Gideon's shorn head. It seemed his hair was already filling in. He wouldn't be without his black locks for long.

As if he sensed her watching him, he turned and looked back. They locked eyes for a moment through the flames of the torches. A shudder ran through her. She quickly looked away.

I need to find Gotz—and soon.

40

GIDEON

"Why did you let her bring the girl?" Brendle asked, moving his torch toward Gideon.

Gideon glanced over. Brendle's posture was stiff as always, but Gideon had learned that in order to read Brendle, you must read his words. Wynter's friend was Jutta. For some reason, this irked Brendle.

"I thought you'd rather enjoy having one of your own people around."

Gideon thought he detected a small frown, but it could've just as easily been a reaction to the gnats flying about Brendle's eyes.

"You are my people," Brendle said.

"Technically, we're not."

Brendle grunted, though it was barely perceptible.

"What is your issue with Six? You can reminisce about your mother country."

Another grunt. "She will be trouble."

"Do you know her?"

"No. All Jutta women are trouble."

Gideon was intrigued. He turned around and found Wynter and Six riding several horses back. He caught Wynter staring straight at him. Her face flushed as if she had been caught steal-ing. She quickly looked away. Her stupid stunt of running away had cost him dearly. Twenty men were dead, their bodies left behind, never to return home. The grimness of his people's situation returned.

"You will train Six in combat," Gideon said.

Brendle looked over this time. "That would be a mistake."

"We'll need every able-bodied person armed and ready to fight. Valen is still a threat. He will likely come after us."

"And if I refuse?" Brendle asked.

Brendle had never refused a direct order.

"You won't," Gideon said, then he took Brendle's torch and spurred his horse forward. He needed some time alone.

41

WYNTER

When they arrived back at camp, it was late. Candles and lanterns were lit up like fireflies. Many came out of their tents looking for loved ones who hadn't returned. Wynter expected loud wails or at least anger, but there was none, just the solemn faces of those who knew death would eventually come for them too.

Finn helped her down from the horse, smirking at her as he often did, like there was some kind of inside secret she wasn't privy to. Something about him made her skin crawl. She broke from his grasp quickly and waited as he helped Six. Brendle watched from close by.

Wynter led Six to the tent she shared with Kidron.

Kidron shot out of the tent with a lantern in her hand. "Where have you been?" she asked, grabbing Wynter around the waist in a huge hug. "I was so worried."

She held the girl tight. *I should never have left.*

She pulled Kidron back and smiled. Sorry didn't seem sufficient, nor any explanation that the girl would understand, so instead Wynter looked over at Six. "This is Six. She'll be staying with us."

Kidron's eyes lit up at the sight of Six and her bristly short locks and large brown eyes. "You're Jutta, like Brendle."

"Wow. What gave it away?" Six said, rolling her eyes at Wynter. Six scooted around them both and ducked into the tent.

"I like her," Kidron said, and they followed Six into the tent.

Six plopped down on Wynter's straw pallet and began pulling off her shoes.

Kidron watched in fascination, like a child with a new puppy. "I'm Kidron," she said trying to be friendly.

"I'm zonked," Six said. She pulled a thin blanket over herself and rolled to her side.

Kidron gave Wynter a questioning look.

"She'll be in a better mood in the morning," Wynter reassured her. She stroked Kidron's silken hair. "I have to go out for a little while."

Kidron frowned. "What? You just got back."

"I won't be long. I promise."

Kidron crossed her arms in displeasure.

"Can you keep an eye on Six for me?"

Kidron scratched her cheek, studying Six's sleeping form, then nodded.

Wynter grabbed a cloak, slipped it on, and ducked out of the tent. One of Brendle's men was standing guard. She held herself as one with authority and announced that she was going to visit the seer. Without waiting for the guard to protest, she headed up the hill toward Gotz's tent. The guard followed her into the shadows, and for once she was glad for the protection. How many of the Ulun people would blame her for the deaths of their loved ones?

If I hadn't run away, people wouldn't have died.

She reminded herself she was a prisoner and owed these people nothing.

Gotz's tent was aglow, a virtual beacon of the camp when most of the other lights had been extinguished. She paused at his entrance. Strange smells seeped into the night air. Peppermint.

Sage. Something sweet. He was mumbling to himself and making quite a racket in the process.

"You might as well come in," Gotz said.

Her face flushed. She pushed back the flap and ducked inside. The tent was in a state of turmoil. Gotz had multiple candles burning, and bowls filled with powders and herbs. He was flitting from one bowl to another. Every square inch of space was full of his work, even his chairs held containers of some sort. The recess to the right side where he slept was dark.

"I'd tell you to sit, but..."

"I'm fine," she said, still taking it all in. "What is all this?"

He smiled wildly. His round face, wrinkled with age, glowed with excitement. His pale eyes sparkled. He wore a knit cap, the shoots of his white hair escaping around its edges. The robe he wore came to his ankles and was tied at the waist with a piece of hemp.

"Ah," he said catching her eye. "Experiments."

"What kind of experiments?" she asked, drawing closer.

"Oh...this and that. Medicines, mostly."

She'd forgotten for a moment why she'd come. Suddenly she felt awkward and considered leaving. Gotz stopped his mad frenzy and studied her more closely.

"I should go," she said, turning to leave.

"Something's happened," he said. It wasn't a question.

She turned to him and nodded.

"A dream?" he asked, raising his eyebrows in expectation.

"No. A vision."

He set down his mortar and pestle and narrowed his eyes. "There are no other seers here but me, and I have given you no vision."

His words made her feel anxious. Morbids were vile creatures, demons. What if Gotz didn't believe that the Morbid had given her a vision?

"Was it Kyle Semper?" Gotz asked. "He mocks me by pretending to impart visions. I'll have his neck for this one."

"No," she said quietly.

Gotz took a step toward her. "Who then?"

"The Morbid. The one that was captured in the northern forest."

"Gideon killed it because it was hurting you," Gotz murmured.

"Yes. But it was not hurting me, it was giving me a vision."

Gotz stared at her, unblinkingly, then returned to his work.

He doesn't believe me.

She grew angry. She had come here for answers, not judgment. "The woods were burning. A baby cried somewhere in the distance." Her voice was hard and determined.

Gotz stopped what he was doing and watched her.

"I ran and ran, trying to find the baby." She relaxed into the words. "There was so much smoke, I could barely breathe." She paused.

"Go on," Gotz whispered.

"Finally, I found my way to a riverbank. Lark was standing there with the crying baby. He smiled and placed it in my arms." She was no longer angry, she was sad. Tears rolled down her face. "The baby was sleeping." She swiped her tears away.

"What else?" Gotz asked.

"Lark walked away."

"And the baby?"

She shook her head. "Lark left him in my arms. He was about to tell me who the baby was when Gideon killed the Morbid and I woke up."

Gotz took off his cap and rubbed his balding head. "Did Lark say anything?" His voice sounded urgent.

"He said... He said the baby was beautiful like its mother."

Gotz's eyes widen. "Sons of Ulu."

Wynter's heart raced. "Do you know what the vision means?"

Gotz began pacing around the tent as if he had forgotten she was there. "How could I be so blind? It all makes sense."

"Please. Do you know what it means? I need to know. You said before that unless the wolf unites with the eagle…"

Gotz stopped pacing and rubbed a hand across his mouth. He seemed to be deciding how to proceed. He approached her and took her by the hands. "A child born of an Alrenian queen and an Ulun king could be the one thing that could finally unite our people. There would be no doubt of its legitimacy to the throne of Ferran."

Wynter pulled her hands from his grasp. "You think the baby is mine and Gideon's?" She shook her head. "I'm not the queen!"

Gotz seemed unaffected by her outburst. He lifted her hand with the ring. "You wear the ring. But not only that, you have the gift of healing. For all intents and purposes, you are the queen."

She snatched her hand away. "I won't marry him."

"Perhaps you will. Perhaps you won't."

"What does that mean? Will he force me?"

Gotz chuckled. "Heavens no. A marriage should be grounded in love. A false love will not unite our people."

"Then it's settled," she said. "I do not love Gideon, nor will I ever love him. He's crude, spiteful, and unfeeling."

Gorgeous. Mysterious.

"And, he's a Grunt," she added with dramatic flair.

Gotz grinned.

Flustered, Wynter spun around and fled from the tent. The last thing she would ever do was love a loveless king.

42

SIX

The sun had barely broken the horizon when Six had been rudely roused from her sleep by the butt of Brendle's spear. She'd hastily teased out her hair with her hands, wolfed down something he'd handed her that tasted like a glob of horse dung, and now she stood at the edge of camp, five feet away from him, spear in hand. He was taller than she remembered. *Really* tall. And his body was all muscle, arms, and legs. Anyone else would have marveled at his stature. Not her. He was her Ulun enemy.

Everyone has a weakness, even him.

A small group of curious Uluns had gathered around despite the early hour.

"Do you know how to use a spear?" Brendle asked.

Six detected a hint of presumption in his tone. "Yes," she lied. Her motto had always been fake it until you make it.

She crouched and twirled the spear above her head, then slapped its blunt end into the ground.

Brendle did not blink. He charged toward her, spear at his side.

She raised her spear in one hand. He was a fool to come straight at her, she couldn't miss. He was making it so easy.

As soon as he got close she lunged, ready to drive the spear into his large body, but to her surprise, he ducked under her jab, spun, and slapped her feet out from under her with the long staff of his spear, then he twirled it in his hand and placed the sharp tip of the other end at her throat.

"You're dead," he announced.

There was laughter from the small crowd, which only fueled her anger at being humiliated. She slapped Brendle's spear away, rolled to her side, sprung to her feet, and held her spear in what she best guessed to be a defensive position. Sweat rolled down her brow. She wiped it away with the back of her hand.

"Fighting begins with the legs." He tapped her ankles with the blunt end of the spear. "Feet apart."

She adjusted her feet. He walked behind her and prodded the back of her knees. "Knees bent." She crouched slightly.

"Turn sideways." He poked her in the side.

She shifted her stance sideways.

"You must be able to maintain a center balance at all times or your opponent will trip you or cause you to stumble." He circled her. She moved with him, readjusting her stance and spear.

"If you fall, you lose."

She held the tip of her spear out, using it to keep him at bay. He jabbed and lunged, teasing her with his spear. She backed away, body tense. She lurched suddenly at him, aiming high.

He dropped to one knee, spinning away from her jab, and swung his spear until it connected with the back of her knees.

She fell.

He rose. "Don't lock your knees," he spat.

She scrambled to her feet. More sweat trickled down the back of her neck. She locked eyes with him. His Jutta spirit radiated in his large brown eyes. She had the same fire inside her, and it was burning as bright as his.

"Again," he barked.

She reset her feet. She was determined to meet Brendle's challenges. Again and again, he brought her to her knees. Each time, she scrambled to her feet and tried to re-center her stance, making it stronger. And finally, when she was able to absorb the impact of his spear, he stopped.

"Good," he said.

She nodded. They now had an understanding of each other. He was her teacher. She was his student. This was the way of the Jutta.

43

—————

WYNTER

Wynter had cried herself to sleep. Her future was unsure. Her life had been stripped from her. Everything was pointing to a union with Gideon. The Morbid's vision, Gotz, even Six thought it to be true. Gideon himself had been coy about the reasons he was keeping her around. Today she would confront him and find out what his real plans were. Kidron had informed her that Six had been summoned early by Brendle for training. This angered her even more. Why was she being excluded from learning to fight? Hadn't she shown that she could be trusted with a knife? If it hadn't been for her precision knife-throwing, Gideon would have had his eyes torn out by a Morbid.

She was tired. Tired of being kept in the dark. Kidron had run off to watch Six train. The rest of the camp was busy packing up. They were moving out today. They had their Alrenian queen back.

When she came out of the tent, one of Brendle's men was nearby waiting. She sighed, grasped the folds of her dress, and walked into the camp, looking for Gideon. She had become accustomed to the stares and jeers now. They scarcely bothered her anymore. She was despised, probably more now than ever, now that men had died trying to get her back.

She held her head high and kept her chin up. The Uluns seemed to have forgotten that her people had lost a whole colony. It was hard for her to feel any of their sorrow. Maybe she never would.

After an exhausting search, she finally spotted Gideon by the horses. He had two by their reins and was leading them to a wagon where an older gentleman stood ready to help harness. Gideon was dressed in beige pants, a white shirt, and tall boots. She almost didn't recognize him now that his dark locks were gone. But she could pick out those eyes anywhere.

She took up right alongside of him. He ignored her.

"We need to talk," she said sounding like a demanding queen.

"In case you haven't noticed, we're preparing to move out, so now is not the best time." Gideon handed off the reins of one of the horses to the gentleman. The man worked on connecting the horse to the harness.

"This can't wait," she said.

When it became apparent that he wasn't going to relent to her request to talk, she continued anyway. "Why am I not allowed to train with Six?"

Gideon smiled, but kept his eyes on the other man. She'd never actually seen him smile. He almost looked *human*.

"I would think the answer would be obvious," he said with mirth in his tone.

She didn't like his flippant attitude.

"Haven't I proven myself? I saved your life. That Morbid was ready to tear your head off!"

The elderly gentleman looked over, a curious expression on his face.

Gideon took her by the arm, turning her away from the man's prying ears. He spoke softly in her ear, making the hairs on the back of her neck stand up. "You mean the knife that could have just as easily landed in my back?"

Her heart raced. Despite her hatred of Gideon, his close proximity did something to her that she couldn't explain. He made her feel something she shouldn't. The feeling was unwelcome, and it only served to fan her anger. She wrenched herself from his grasp, turning to face him. "I deserve the right to defend myself," she bellowed.

"Queens don't fight," he said through clenched teeth.

Gideon led the other horse to the wagon and began connecting it to the harness. She followed right on his heels. "You fight."

"I'm not going to get myself killed."

"No. Just Lark!" She regretted the words as soon as they'd left her mouth. Gideon had been close with his brother, and Lark's death had hurt him greatly.

Gideon tightened the harness straps on the horse, perhaps a bit too tightly. The older man climbed up to the driver's seat of the wagon. Gideon turned and looked at her this time. His gaze hardened. "Are we done here?"

She hesitated. She'd hurt him, but there were things to be discussed, and she couldn't let her slip of the tongue keep her from getting the answers she needed. The old man made a clicking noise and the horses lurched forward. The wagon rolled in the direction of camp. Soon they were alone. She could speak freely. But she struggled to find the right words. Gideon turned to leave.

"I won't marry you," she blurted out.

He stopped and turned around, scowling. "What?"

"You heard me. I won't marry you."

He put a hand on his hip and scratched the back of his neck with the other. "I don't have time for this." Once again, he turned to leave.

She charged after him, grabbing him by the arm and jerking him around. He grabbed her by both arms and pulled her close to him. He looked into her eyes, his jaw tightening. She tensed beneath his hold.

"You flatter yourself," he said bitingly. "I have no desire to marry a child." He released her.

She backed away. "Lark said I was meant for you," she said desperately.

"Foolish talk."

"Gotz—"

He held up a hand to stop her. "Gotz is a man whose time has come and gone. His words are nothing but an old man's ramblings."

"The Morbid you killed gave me a vision."

This seemed to give Gideon pause. But only for a moment. She was getting nowhere. She changed tactics.

"Why did you come back for me? Why not just let Valen kill me?"

His expression softened, but pain lingered in his eyes. If only he would trust her with the truth. She closed the distance between them and without thinking, slipped her hand into his. His palm was warm, strong. "Please," she whispered. For a brief second, he closed his fingers around hers and looked into her eyes. How long had it been since he'd let anyone get close to him? There was a man in there somewhere, one with feelings. For a moment, she felt a connection—something real.

"I'm sorry," he said softly. He released her hand and walked back toward camp.

She swayed, holding her hand against her mouth to stifle the flood of emotion that rose up inside her. She couldn't move. Then, out of the corner of her eye, she spotted the black wolf at the edge of the woods, staring at her.

44

WYNTER

ynter and Six rode in the back of an open wagon amidst supplies. Kidron sat up front with the driver, a muscular man with a large blade on his back.

"I'm telling you, I'm going to be a mighty warrior. You wait and see," Six said.

Six had talked incessantly about her training session with Brendle all morning, and whether out of jealousy or hopelessness, Wynter tired of it.

Six poked her. "Hey, what's wrong with you?"

Wynter tried not to sound contrary. "I thought you didn't care for Jutta men."

"Yeah. Well, we understand each other now."

"I'm happy for you," Wynter said without feeling.

Six scooted closer to her. "What's wrong, and don't say nothing."

"Nothing," she said, then reconsidered. "Everything." She sighed.

Six wrapped her arm around Wynter's shoulder. "I'm sorry. I shouldn't have been so caught up in myself. Kidron said you talked to Gideon this morning."

Wynter shot a look toward Kidron. She was blissfully unaware and talking the poor driver into an early grave.

"That girl. I love her, but she is one nosy little thing."

"What happened with Gideon?" Six asked.

"I confronted him about why he's keeping me here. Why he risked so much to get me back from Valen."

"And?" Six asked with increased interest.

"There was a moment where I thought we connected."

Six squealed. "And?"

"And nothing. He said nothing."

The caravan abruptly halted and shouts came from ahead. They stood up, trying to get a better view. But whatever was causing the delay was blocked by all those ahead of them.

Six grabbed Wynter's hand. "Come on."

Before Wynter could protest, they were jumping off the wagon and Six was dragging her through horses, wagons, and people. Kidron called after her.

As they got closer to the cause of the delay, the crowd became thicker, but that didn't deter Six. She shoved her way through, bringing Wynter with her. When they got to the center of the commotion, they found a woman kneeling on the ground, her long black hair hanging across her shoulders. Wynter recognized her. She was the young woman who had attended King Niko and helped Kirdon dress on the day of his funeral.

Hilran.

"My poor baby," Hilran cried. A wounded dog lay at her feet. Its eyes were open, but it wasn't moving. A man stood over the scene, nervously fingering his cap. "I'm sorry, Hilran. I truly am. She ran in front of my cart. I never saw her until it was too late."

Gideon and Brendle rode up on their horses and dismounted, taking in the spectacle. Hilran stroked the dog's head and sang to it like a small child. Gideon glanced over at Wynter but said nothing.

"She'll have to be put down," Brendle said.

Hilran looked up at Gideon, her eyes pleading. "She's all I've got."

"The dog is suffering," Gideon said kindly, but there was intimacy in the look they shared, and Wynter wondered what there was between them.

Brendle stepped forward and drew a short sword from the sheath on his back.

Wynter's heart surged. She stepped forward. "Wait. Let me try to heal the dog first."

Murmurs erupted through the crowd. Hilran rose slowly, hope in her eyes. Everyone looked to Gideon. He looked at the dog, then raised his eyes to Wynter. She tried to look confident, but the truth was, she was scared. What if she couldn't do it? She hadn't been able to heal King Niko, or Lark. She didn't know if she'd ever be able to heal anyone, much less a dog. She scanned the crowd for Gotz, but he was nowhere to be seen. She was on her own.

Gideon, though reluctant, nodded his consent. Hilran backed away from her dog. Wynter swallowed and took a step forward. She knelt and sat back on her heels. She closed her eyes for a moment.

Clear your head. You must have the desire to heal.

Gotz's words came to her as if he was speaking them right into her ear. She gently laid both hands on the dog. Almost immediately, a jolt shot up her arms, and her body seized. Muffled gasps came from the crowd, right before sound faded to nothingness.

The dog's back is broken.

How she knew this, she did not know. Only that the words were given to her.

Doubt seeped into the edges of her mind. She needed to do this. She *wanted* to do this. She pushed herself further into the dog's injury. Pain shot down her back as if it were breaking in two like a brittle branch. She grew more distant from herself as she grasped at bone and muscle and nerve. The dog jerked beneath her fingers. Someone cried out, but it was barely a whisper to her. She was hurting the dog, but she was also healing it. The lifeblood of the dog fought back—angry—ugly. Sharp and unforgiving. The pain in her back became so intense, she struggled to keep her hands on the dog. But the darkness beneath her fingers had turned gray. She was making progress. Her stomach soured, and she struggled to draw breath. A scream erupted from her throat, and she collapsed. Her vision blurred—shouts—laughter—a fuzzy image of the dog licking Hilran's face. She'd never felt such joy as she did in that moment. She closed her eyes. Someone lifted her into their arms. She knew his smell now. It was Gideon. He shouted for people to clear the way. She drifted into oblivion.

45
____

GIDEON

They traveled the rest of the day and had just stopped to make camp. Wynter still lay asleep in the back of a wagon. Needing to clear his head, Gideon walked through the woods and found a river. He had hoped for some time alone, but Gotz showed up at his side, like an unwanted shadow. His pale eyes looked troubled.

"What do you want Gotz?"

"I'm sorry about the timing, but there's something you should know about Wynter."

"I know she's not the real queen. I've known all along. As I'm sure you have, yet you failed to mention it to me."

"Not that."

He was curious now. "I'm listening."

"Wynter is dying."

"We're all dying, Gotz."

"I poured through my notes after Wynter healed the dog. Her need to recover had me concerned."

"What great revelation did you find there?" Gideon didn't know if it was fatigue talking, but he was having difficulty taking Gotz seriously.

Gotz remained nonplussed by Gideon's sarcasm. "I'm convinced that every time she heals, a part of her dies."

Gideon rubbed the back of his neck.

"This may be why you dream of a drowning queen," Gotz added.

Gideon threw his hands up. "Then what's the point of all this if she's going to die!"

"Perhaps the dream was a warning."

Gideon locked his fingers behind his head and closed his eyes.

"What will you do?" Gotz asked.

He dropped his hands and opened his eyes. "She can't be allowed to heal anymore."

"Will you tell her?"

"No." He'd been quick to answer. *Why shouldn't she know?* He couldn't answer his own question.

"As you wish." Gotz made a small bow and left him alone.

Gideon rubbed his hands over his face. He wouldn't tell her about the healing. For some reason he couldn't fathom, he didn't want to hurt her. But it was time to tell her about her ring and finding Isidor. They were in this together now, bound by circumstances. There was no more avoiding the truth.

46

WYNTER

The Ulun caravan had apparently traveled on after the healing, though Wynter was barely aware of their movements. She had been drifting in and out of sleep. Once, she had opened her eyes and seen Lark standing over her, but when she'd blinked, he was gone. *Lark is dead.*

Six and Kidron had been constantly by her side. She'd often heard them arguing over the best way to care for her, though their voices had been more like a dream.

Now that she was fully awake, the wagon she was lying in was still and empty. She pushed herself up enough to look over the edge. Brendle was a few feet away, looking down at a clearing where several fires were burning. The smell of venison, boiled cabbage, and crab apples filled the air. She could tell by the sun that it was dinner time.

Brendle turned around. He jogged to her side and lifted her out of the wagon as though he were lifting a bag of feathers. He placed her gently on her feet and she held onto his arm a brief moment to steady herself.

"How long have I been out?" she asked.

"Most of the day."

He uncorked a water bag and handed it to her. She gulped greedily.

"Did the dog—" she said, wiping her mouth.

"The dog is healed."

The news lifted her spirits despite her fatigue. She'd healed —*finally*.

"He's been worried," Brendle said.

It took a minute for Wynter to realize he meant Gideon. She handed back the water bag. "I'm fine," she said, attempting to smooth out her rumpled clothing.

"He won't allow you to heal anymore," Brendle said. "It's too dangerous."

Wynter bristled at his words. Gideon was still trying to control her. "Are you speaking for him now?"

"No. I'm explaining."

As if Gideon could be explained. "Where is he?" she asked.

"In the woods."

"Can I go to him?"

Brendle didn't speak.

"I promise not to run," she added.

He motioned with his head to the other side of the wagon. "Walk straight through, down to the stream."

Her hair was hanging in a tangled mess. She attempted to comb it out with her fingers but didn't put much hope in the outcome. She stepped into the woods and followed the cadence and vibration of the trickling water. The air carried its coolness. She touched every tree she passed, as if saying hello to old friends.

Gideon was kneeling on the bank of the small stream, sleeves rolled up. He splashed water on his face. She cleared her throat. He whipped around, his hand reaching for his sword. When he saw her, he wiped his wet face with a hand and stood. She couldn't help but notice how handsome he was when he was caught off guard and not putting on the airs of being king. She approached, stopping a few feet away from him.

"Thank you for letting me heal the dog," she said.

He ran a hand across the top of his head, wetting the top of his freshly sprouted, black hair. "It was a mistake. I shouldn't have allowed it."

"Why? Because I slept for a day? It was worth it."

Her words seemed to anger him. "No, it wasn't." He turned and faced the stream, hands on his hips.

She reached out and touched his back. His muscles tightened. *He's angry. Why?*

He spun around and grabbed her wrist. His jaw tightened, his breath coming quickly. She stifled a gasp, so intense was his gaze.

"Why do you hate me?" she asked, trying to reclaim her arm.

His grip loosened. "I don't—" He released her. "I don't hate you." He turned away from her.

"I need to heal. It's who I am," she said. This was something she understood now. She had become the queen whether she wanted to admit it or not.

"There won't be any more healings."

Her heart pounded fiercely. "Why do you care what happens to me?"

He turned back to her but said nothing.

"You can't control me," she spat. With those words, she turned and stormed back into the woods.

"Wynter!"

She ran, fighting the urge to cry. He was maddening. Loathsome. And he treated her like the dirt on the bottom of his boot.

Gideon's heavy footsteps thundered behind her. She glanced over her shoulder. He was frowning, swatting at tree limbs. She tried to pick up her pace, but fatigue slowed her steps. He caught up with her and spun her around. For a brief second they stood staring at one another, breathless and angry.

"I know you're not the real queen," Gideon said.

Wynter tried to hide her surprise. She was angry, and she wasn't quite ready to let go of it.

"I told you I wasn't the queen from the beginning," she snapped.

"I know you did. But we didn't need a dead queen. I let Lark believe I thought you were the real queen. I couldn't disappoint my people. Not when there was so much to lose."

Wynter deflated. He had used her, despite knowing the truth. "You needed a queen to get through the northern forest."

Gideon shook his head. "Not just that." His anger dissolved. He closed his eyes a brief moment and rubbed a hand through his shorn hair.

Was what she'd suspected true? Was there more to her captivity than she'd been told? Her stomach churned with fear.

"King Rodolf's oracle says the two rings of Ferran are the key to our salvation—the key to the Iron Gate of Isidor," he explained.

Wynter looked down at her ring. The eagle practically soared off its shiny surface. She only vaguely knew of the oracle and the hidden land of Isidor, but it had never been taken seriously by her people. There was some kind of secret key, but she had no idea that part of that key was her ring. Everything was starting to make sense.

"It takes us both to open the gate," he added.

She nodded, still looking at her ring.

"The healings are dangerous," he said. "What if the next time you don't recover? It might not be just the ring that's needed. It might be you."

She looked at him now. The hard façade he had worked so hard to build had dropped. For the first time, he was speaking to her as an equal, and the perpetual frown he normally wore had softened to concern. This was the first honest moment she had seen from him. The truth was—he needed her.

He reached up and slowly untied the wolf medallion from around his neck—the one that Ulun boy had given her all those years ago. He handed it to her. "This is yours, isn't it?"

She gingerly reached out and let the cold metal slide into her hand. "Yes," she said softly. It made her think of all she had lost. Her home, her mother and father. Yet, here the medallion was, once again, a little piece of home returning to her.

"Where did you get it?" he asked.

She studied his dark eyes. He wasn't angry; he was curious.

"My father was a transporter. He used to take me with him and carry me on his back when I was a small child. One day we were attacked by an Ulun boy. He was trying to steal my father's pack, but he hit the strap of my sling instead, and I fell from the trees. The boy caught me in his arms. I think he was surprised to find a baby in his arms instead of a pack. When I started crying, he removed the necklace from his neck and tied it around mine. Then he returned me to my father. He should've killed me if he had done his duty." She rubbed the medallion between her fingers. "I often wondered what became of the boy. I owe him my life."

She looked for recognition in Gideon's eyes. What if he'd been that boy? He was the right age, and he'd seemed angry when he'd seen the medallion hanging around the dead queen's neck. She wanted it to be true, because then she would know there was a heart inside his hard exterior. But his face betrayed nothing. She felt a stab of disappointment.

"You were a transporter for the queen the day she was killed?"

She nodded. "I had just gone back to work. My father had died a few weeks before."

"I'm sorry." He sounded sincere.

"What now?" she asked.

"You're the queen. We travel on to find Isidor, and together we open the gate."

"Do you really believe that Isidor is real?" she asked.

"Yes, I do."

And in that moment, she wanted to believe it too. She wanted to believe there was a land where water ran clear and the ground gave up healthy crops and wild game roamed its plains.

But not just that, she hoped Isidor would be a place that could unite Ferran, where they could once again prosper as a united kingdom.

"Okay," she said.

"Okay?" he asked, sounding confused.

"I will go willingly to help find the gate to Isidor. On two conditions."

"You're not really in the position to negotiate," he reminded her, but his tone was light.

"One. You let me learn how to fight like Six."

He raised an eyebrow but said nothing.

"Two. You let me send a messenger to my people that their Alrenian queen has made peace with the king of the Uluns, and we now seek the Iron Gate of Isidor and wish them to join us. They may not listen, but I have to try. At the very least, I need to warn them of Valen and his plans."

"You want the Alrenians to join us?"

"Yes. King Rodolf wanted a united Ferran. Don't you?"

"If it's possible, yes. I'd be open to a united kingdom, but there's the little matter of the rightful heir."

He was right, of course. This was the impasse their people had been at for years. They were on the cusp of something that could change their world forever. If Isidor existed, her people had as much right to enter its hidden gates as the Uluns did. She fidgeted with her hands, searching her mind for an answer.

Gotz approached, taking them both by surprise.

"This is a private conversation," Gideon scoffed.

"The solution you seek is very simple," Gotz said.

Gideon seemed annoyed, but Wynter wanted to hear what Gotz had to say. She looked pleadingly at Gideon. He relented with a wave of his hand.

Gotz cleared his throat and folded his hands in front of him. "King Rodolf's oracle says *he who will go forward with his whole heart will obtain what he seeks. Only do not be of two minds.* The answer has been there in the oracle the whole time. If you two were to marry, you would rule Isidor together. Any children that came from your union would be the undisputed rightful heirs to the throne."

Wynter's heart raced, and she suddenly felt very aware of Gideon's handsome face and strong arms. Her face flushed. Just that morning, she had rudely told him she would never marry him and he had called her a child.

"Marry?" she croaked, not intending to say the words aloud. Then the vision of the baby came to mind.

A baby would unite our people. My baby.

The revelation of the vision took her breath away. She held a hand to her stomach, and stars danced at the corners of her vision. Gideon looked concerned and reached out a hand to steady her. But the moment was interrupted as Brendle came tearing through the woods. He glanced at Wynter briefly, then addressed Gideon. "You'd better come see this."

47

GIDEON

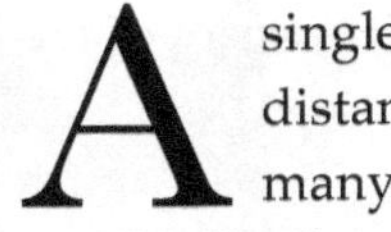single pillar of smoke rose and billowed in the distance. It was a signal meant for Gideon. "How many days behind?" Gideon asked Brendle.

"Half a day, a day at the most."

Gideon had feared that Valen might try to retaliate for the attack on his camp. He wasn't the kind of man to let things go, and he'd undoubtedly figured out it was Gideon who had rescued the queen. That alone would be enticement enough to seek Gideon out. Valen always wanted what he couldn't have.

"Valen is a vengeful man," Brendle said.

"That's why we end this now, before we get to the White Mountains."

"What do you want to do? We have the advantage in numbers now."

"No. We can't afford to lose more men. Send word to Valen that I challenge him in the court of swords."

For once, Brendle's voice betrayed his feelings. "My lord," he said, exasperated. "If you were to lose…"

The measure *was* drastic. He was risking everything, including his life, and the life of Wynter.

"Then I'd better not lose."

That should have been the end of the matter, but Brendle persisted. "Even if you kill Valen, his followers are not honorable enough to accept the judgement of the sword."

Gideon watched the smoke rising into the sky. "True enough, but I'm banking on what my father taught me about the followers of tyrants."

"And what is that, my lord?"

"That if you cut off the head of the snake, the rest of the body will wither and die."

Brendle bowed slightly. "My lord. I will make arrangements to send a messenger to Valen's camp at once."

"No. Not a messenger, send Finn."

"My lord?"

"I need a man of some importance to deliver the message so Valen will take the challenge seriously. Sending the cousin of the king will convey a certain level of authority."

Brendle let out a soft grunt of disapproval.

"If we send a simple messenger, they'll more than likely just kill him."

"As you wish, my lord," Brendle said, bowing slightly.

"Once you give Finn his instructions, gather the people. I need to tell them that a challenge has been made."

"My lord." Brendle mounted his horse and rode down to the camp.

Alone with his thoughts, Gideon contemplated what he'd just committed to—a battle to the death with Valen. But Valen was proving to be the thorn that continued to pierce his side. He needed to take care of him once and for all. But that wasn't all that was weighing heavily on his mind. When Gotz had suggested he and Wynter marry, he'd thought of his dream and Gotz's vision.

Until the wolf unites with the eagle…

If only he could see the face of the woman in his dreams. Could Wynter really be the faceless queen? She was the child he had unintentionally shot down from the trees twenty years ago.

That had to mean something, didn't it? So why hadn't he told her it was him? That he was the boy who had caught her in his arms all those years ago? He'd tied his wolf medallion around her neck, telling himself that if prophecies were real, the medallion would come back to him, and only then would he believe in visions and prophesies, and God. He had only been a kid. It was a stupid game he'd made up. Yet, the medallion had returned to him and so had Wynter.

He squeezed his temples with his fingers and gritted his teeth. He didn't have time to think on such things. Valen threatened their plans and all Gideon's energies were needed to prepare for the fight ahead. He made his way back down to the camp to announce the impending court of swords, but his mind drifted to the horrified look on Wynter's face when Gotz had suggested marriage.

48

WYNTER

Wynter stood with Kidron and Six as Gideon announced that he would face Valen in the court of swords. When Kidron explained that the fight was a way of settling a score, and it would be to the death, Wynter grew concerned. Apparently, Valen had a reputation as a great warrior. She understood the finality of a bad outcome, and so did the Ulun people. The mood in the camp quickly became solemn.

When night settled in, Gideon sent for her. Her stomach churned. Was he considering Gotz's suggestion that they marry?

Only do not be of two minds—haunting words from the oracle.

She closed her eyes. Maybe facing the threat of death had caused him to consider the union. A king husband, a baby. Her head swam with the possibilities.

Six and Kidron had insisted on fussing over her. They convinced her to wash and change her clothes, and then they plaited her long hair in an elaborate pattern. In their minds, if the king had summoned her, then it must be important. She mentioned nothing of marriage to them.

Brendle escorted her to Gideon's tent. He must have noticed

her trepidation, for she was clutching and unclutching the folds of her dress.

"I'll be right outside," he assured her.

Thunder rumbled in the distance. Rain was coming.

She nodded and ducked inside. Gideon was slouched in a chair, nursing a drink. He looked tired, weary. He didn't look up.

"You'll stay here now. I need to ensure your safety," he said without feeling.

This was far from what she had been expecting. "I prefer my own tent," she said, noticing his eyes were glassy—a clear sign that the drink he was nursing was stronger than water.

He lifted his dark gaze to her. Gone was the kindness he'd shown her earlier in the woods. His eyes were hard and unfeeling.

"This is not a negotiation."

"I see. So I'm still just your prisoner?"

He momentarily closed his eyes and rubbed a hand over his head. He stood and came to her, staring uncomfortably into her eyes. Her face flushed with heat. His breath was rank with alcohol.

"You've been drinking," she said, holding him at bay with her hand against his chest. It annoyed her that he'd chosen today to drink when the whisperings of marriage were floating about, though she supposed the fight with Valen was the true reason for his current state. The fight weighed heavily on her also. The thought of losing him upset her more than she cared to admit.

He smiled, swayed, stumbled backward. She quickly caught him under one arm, supporting him with her shoulder. "Come on. Bedtime."

"An excellent idea," he said grinning sheepishly.

She winced. He wouldn't remember this in the morning. She led him to his sheepskin pallet and knelt down with him, and then pushed him off of her. He collapsed like a sack of potatoes. His face was the most serene she'd ever seen it. Gone was the anger and the walls he kept around himself. He was just a man now—weak and vulnerable.

Could this man really be my destiny?

She removed his boots and then fished the blanket from the floor next to him and covered him. Reluctantly, she lay next to him and closed her eyes. The ground rumbled with the thunder's fury. Rain pattered softly on the tent. She was surprised to find that she felt safe being near him, and soon she fell asleep to the sounds of a steady rain and Gideon's gentle breathing. Dreams of the crying baby in the burning forest came soon after.

49

FINN

Valen snatched the note from Finn's fingers and broke the king's seal with his knife. After he'd finished reading it, he crushed it into a ball. "What is this, some kind of game?" he asked Finn.

Finn held up his hands in surrender. "I'm just the messenger."

Valen grabbed him by his coat collar and laid the cool edge of his knife at Finn's neck. Finn grimaced. Valen's breath was more offensive than the knife.

"You show your face here after letting Gideon destroy my camp?" Valen growled.

"There was no chance to warn you about the attack. If you want to blame someone, blame the petulant queen for trying to escape. Besides, Brendle didn't let me out of his sight from the minute Gideon decided to march on your camp."

Valen shoved him away. "Brendle doesn't trust you. Smart man."

"I set a few fires during the attack, but I assure you, I didn't kill anyone. I had to participate in order to maintain my cover. Our deal still stands. I keep you informed of Gideon's actions, and when the time is right, you'll make your move. One day, all of Ferran will be yours."

"And the queen? Why is she still alive? You were supposed to kill her."

"Yet you had her in your grasp and chose to lock her in a cage. So you see? The queen is not so easy to kill."

"Or maybe you're playing me, Finn? Stringing me along for your own purposes?"

Finn smiled, though he wanted to laugh at how easy it was to manipulate Valen. "If that were the case, would I have killed Lark, made it look like a failed attempt to kill the queen, and then framed my father for it? Gideon beheaded Mangus on sight. Now two of your strongest opponents have been eliminated. Although you blew the last one, you'll get a second chance with the queen soon enough."

Valen raised an eyebrow. Then he laughed. "You've managed to kill your father and your cousin? You're one sick bastard, I'll give you that," he said, ignoring the taunt.

Finn gripped the hilt of the knife at his hip, thinking how easy it would be to just draw it now and plunge it into Valen's gut. But he checked himself. Why do the job himself when Gideon was about to do it for him? Each day he was getting closer to claiming the throne of Ferran as his own.

"What is your answer to the king's challenge?" Finn asked. "Will you fight him in the court of swords? If he wins you must withdraw your pursuit. If you win, the queen will be returned to you."

Valen stroked his beard. "He thinks he can beat me, otherwise he wouldn't risk his precious Alrenian queen."

"Then he has thought foolishly. No doubt, you will be the victor." Finn plastered on a tight smile, designed to flatter. "I have no doubt that by nightfall tomorrow, you will be in possession of the queen and the throne soon after, just as we agreed upon."

This seemed to appeal to Valen's large ego. "Very well. Tell him I accept. Tomorrow at noon."

Finn bowed with a sweep of his hand.

The fool. Does he really think I'm going to help him become king?

That was the problem with great men like Gideon and Valen. They always made the mistake of valuing brawn over brains. He chuckled.

"What's so funny?" Valen barked.

"Nothing, my lord," he said, then added another stroke to Valens's ego. "I'm only thinking of Gideon's face when you run a sword through him tomorrow."

50

———

WYNTER

The next morning, Wynter woke, warm and serene. She reveled in that first moment when one's body is relaxed and the mind is still fuzzy. She rolled over, her hand touching the warm sheepskin next to her. She suddenly remembered where she was and sat up with a start, patting herself down to make sure everything was where it should be. Her clothes were intact. She sighed and pushed her hair out of her face. She scanned the tent. Gideon was gone. The edges of morning seeped through the seams of the tent. The cattle called to each other and the sheep bleated—sounds she had now become accustomed to.

There was breakfast on Gideon's table—a wooden board of fruit, cheese, and bread. She made a quick meal of it, grateful she hadn't had to face the community eating table. She blushed to think what people would think of her sleeping in Gideon's tent, not that they needed another reason to think poorly of her. Nothing had happened beyond Gideon's momentary flirtation. And that, she was sure, was the drink talking.

Gideon scared her, but at the same time she was drawn to him. It irritated her that she felt this way. She smoothed back the loose strands of her hair and ventured out of the tent. Brendle was there waiting for her.

Doesn't he ever sleep?

The camp was riddled with puddles from last night's rain. The air was muggy and thick with moisture.

Brendle eyed her rumpled attire. It was clear she'd slept in her clothes. Her face flushed with heat.

Surely Gideon has explained she'd only stayed for safety reasons.

Brendle, being the gentleman he was, quickly saved her from her awkwardness. He handed her a belt with a leather sheath that held a jewel-handled knife. She recognized it immediately.

"Gideon wants you to have it."

The gesture caught her off guard. Whether it was the stress of the past several days or the realization that Lark was truly gone, she did not know, but soft tears fell down her cheeks. It was a strange gesture on Gideon's part, to be sure, and a kindness she didn't expect. But his gift said more to her than that. It represented a token of trust.

She swatted the tears away and tried to smile. "Will you thank him for me?"

Brendle nodded, then left her. The belt would be too large for her small waist, but she wasn't without resources. She had an idea.

The camp was already bustling with activity. Most seemed to be keeping busy for the sake of keeping busy, likely to distract themselves from the impending duel between Gideon and Valen.

She took a deep breath, pushed back her shoulders, and held her countenance as a queen would—with dignity and confidence. There were whispers and stares as she made her way to the community table. Specifically, to where Hilran was currently sharing a meal with some other women. As soon as she approached, the women clammed up, eyeing her critically. Hilran's dog stood up from its position at Hilran's feet and licked Wynter's hand. It made her happy that she'd been able to heal the animal. *At least* he *likes me.*

"I'd like to speak with Hilran," she announced, rubbing the dog's bristly head.

She was hoping the fact that she had saved Hilran's dog would give her some esteem in the woman's eyes. She held her breath. The other women all looked to Hilran like children to their mother. Hilran studied Wynter suspiciously, but when the women remained seated, Hilran shot them a scowl and waved a hand for them to leave. They scattered, grabbing food as they went.

Hilran continued eating, slow and methodical. Wynter couldn't help but notice that Hilran was a beautiful woman. Feminine, yet strong. Her long, silky dark hair was tied back with a leather cord and she wore a green linen dress that complimented the intense green of her eyes.

If a woman like this couldn't capture Gideon's heart...

Wynter placed the knife and its belt on the table. "I need this altered so it will fit me."

Hilran stopped chewing and swallowed abruptly. It was clear she recognized the knife as Lark's. She stood and dusted her hands off, picking the last bits of food out of her teeth delicately with her tongue. She studied the knife without touching it.

"It was a gift from Gideon," Wynter explained. The words were out of her mouth before she realized her mistake.

Hilran studied her closely and Wynter blushed. The mention of Gideon wasn't a way of making her claim on him, but she feared Hilran would think so. If there *had* been something between Hilran and Gideon, as she had sensed, then she had just said the exact wrong thing.

"Follow me." Hilran plodded off, her dog following.

Wynter breathed a sigh of relief. She had no friends beyond Six and Kidron. And if she was going to be queen of Ferran, she needed to expand her circle beyond an Alrenian Jutta and a twelve-year-old Ulun girl.

She followed Hilran to her tent and waited. An Ulun couple walked past, then stopped and stared at her, whispering. Hilran returned with a wooden box. She caught sight of the bystanders and immediately took things in hand. "Well get on about it. There's nothing here that concerns you."

The couple looked rather put off, but scrambled away nonetheless.

"Thank you," Wynter said, relieved.

Hilran waved off her gratitude. "Give them no mind. Those two have their noses in everyone's business but their own." She then proceeded to slide open the lid of the rather refined-looking box. She gently pulled out a brown leather baldric—a leather belt worn cross-body. There was a loop at the hip for a knife, and a sheath at the back for a sword. Hilran held it out to Wynter as if it were her most precious treasure. "This was my brother's." Her eyes welled with tears. "He was barely a man—fifteen. This is all I have left of him after one of King Niko's mercenary wars —not even a body to burn."

Wynter didn't know what to say, what to do. The gift was too much. "Hilran…I…"

She pushed it into Wynter's hands. "He wasn't a big lad. It should fit you."

The leather was fine, and it smelled rich and musky. Hilran closed the now empty box. She had nothing left of her brother. It didn't feel right to accept something so precious, but a gift from the heart should never be returned. "I hope I will give him honor by wearing it," she said instead.

Hilran nodded, fighting back her emotions. Her dog nudged her hand. She smiled and rubbed his head. "If that is all, Your Majesty, I have chores to do."

"Of course." Wynter turned to leave, but then turned back. "Thank you, Hilran."

Hilran nodded and disappeared inside her tent with the empty box and her dog right at her heels.

Now Wynter understood why the dog had been so important to her. It truly was all she had left.

Wynter strapped on her new baldric and sheathed the knife

in the hip loop. It fit her well, as Hilran had said it would. She didn't have a sword—yet. But she planned on remedying that straightaway. Especially now that Gideon was about to face Valen. Who knew what would happen if Gideon lost. She wanted to be prepared no matter what the outcome.

She found Brendle and Six at the edge of camp, sparring with their spears. Six was holding her own, considering Brendle's size advantage. He was large, strong. But Six was quick, ducking and spinning away from his jabs. It was quite impressive, really. Wynter's confidence faded as she approached. She reminded herself that even though she was small, she had strong legs and arms.

I can be just as good as Six.

Brendle continued with his instruction, ignoring Wynter. She cleared her throat. They broke practice and looked at her, both breathing heavily, sweat running down their temples. Their faces glistened with their efforts.

"I'm here to train," she announced.

Six glanced at Brendle, uncertainly. Brendle wiped the sweat from his face with one hand and studied Wynter's newly acquired baldric.

She placed her hand on the grip of her knife. "A gift from Gideon."

Six grinned. "You're not going to do anything in that dress."

Six's flippancy irritated her.

"Besides, I doubt you got much sleep last night," Six added with a chuckle.

Heat rose to Wynter's face. She drew her blade, turned toward the nearest tree, set her stance, and threw the knife. The tip sunk into the tree trunk with a thud.

Six's smile disappeared.

"You'll need a sword," Brendle said.

He hastened to his horse, which was tied up nearby, and returned with a short sword. She took it and inserted it into the sheath on her back.

Brendle motioned for her to come closer. "Let us begin."

51

GIDEON

large circle of stones had been constructed the day before, forming the arena in which Gideon and Valen would fight. Last night's heavy rains had turned the scene into a mud pit. This would not stop the court of swords. It would only make it more challenging for the opponents.

Valen rode into camp with a small contingent. His shoulders were draped in black sheepskin, a large sword strapped to his back. His head was shaved, and he wore leather cuffs at his wrists. This fight could end Gideon's short reign as king, but when he had woken that morning with Wynter sleeping peacefully at his side, he'd found that he had something to fight for, and everything to lose. So with a newfound confidence, he took his place at the eastern edge of the circle. Valen removed his sheepskin and tunic, choosing to fight shirtless. No doubt this was an attempt to intimidate Gideon by exposing his large barrel chest.

Valen crossed the stone markers and stood at the western edge like a mad bull.

Gotz traipsed through the brown sludge, holding up the edges of his robe, and stood at the center of the circle. The crowd grew silent.

"Do you both submit to the judgment of the court of swords?" Gotz asked.

Gideon and Valen both nodded their assent.

Valen took two practice cuts in the air with his sword. "Sure you don't want a shield?" He sneered at Gideon.

Gideon ignored the taunt.

"I'm ready, Grunt!" Valen snarled.

Gotz lifted his eyes to the heavens. "May God's will be done." He quickly left the circle.

Gideon held his sword at the ready. As he expected, Valen immediately charged, but the mud caused him to slip, and Gideon suddenly found himself storming toward him. The fire of battle ignited inside him, and he poured it all into his sword as his drove Valen back with his fast, sweeping strokes. Their swords clashed with anger and bitterness. Gideon struck again and again, never giving Valen a chance to gain an advantage in the exchange. But Valen fought well, defending himself at times on his knees. Try as he might, Gideon couldn't break through Valen's defenses, though he had managed to drive him back to the edge of the circle more than once.

Just as Gideon gained the upper hand, his good fortune changed. He slipped. Though he recovered quickly, Valen took advantage of the stumble by taking a lightning fast lunge. Gideon sidestepped, but the tip of Valen sword drew blood from his side. Gideon deflected and rebuffed blow after blow, stepping back from Valen's advances—ones that could have easily pierced his heart.

Valen's men cheered on their champion.

Valen threw himself at Gideon, trying to bring him down into the mud. But anticipating the move, Gideon sidestepped and grazed the back of Valen's neck with his sword. Blood mixed with sweat rolled down Valen's broad back. The cheering men grew silent. This was Gideon's opportunity to end it.

Valen spun around, baring his teeth. Gideon charged, putting Valen on the defense. They were both mud-splattered and bloody, their faces glistening with sweat. Gideon cut left and right, holding the sword with both hands now. He felt Valen's fear in his desperate counterstrikes. But he finally threw off Gideon's blade and tried again to charge and drive him onto the ground. This time he succeeded and they tumbled into the mud, only Gideon managed to push him off and scramble to his feet. He stumbled backward breathing hard. Valen sprang to his feet. They stood gauging each other. Then Gideon sprinted forward and swung his sword, slashing left then right. Valen held him off.

Gideon's energy was waning; he had to end it. He slipped. Only this time, he fell to his knees. His hand and sword disappeared into the mud. Valen raised his sword for the death blow. But Gideon was ready. He came to one knee, drew his sword up through the mud, and lunged. The sword went straight through Valen's stomach.

Gideon screamed like a wild animal, letting the blade rest there, finishing its work. Then he stood and wrenched the blade from Valen's body, splaying blood across the mud. Valen fell to his knees, disbelief on his face. He clutched at his stomach, blood turning his hands red.

Panting and spent, Gideon mustered one last surge of strength and swung the sword, taking Valen's head. There was complete silence. Gideon stepped back, feeling nothing. For when a sword was in his hand, he was no longer man, he was beast.

He turned in a circle, taking in the shocked faces of his people and Valen's men. He held out his arms, though he could barely lift them. "Does anyone here dispute the court of swords?"

Valen's men looked at each other uneasily. One by one they broke off and returned to their horses, leaving almost as quickly as they had arrived.

Brendle approached and Gideon handed him his blood-drenched sword. "Make sure there's not a trace of that traitor's blood left on my sword."

"Yes, my lord."

Brendle smiled and raised the bloody sword in triumph. Cheers erupted. Gideon scanned the crowd and found Wynter. She held his gaze, but only for a moment before she turned and disappeared.

Brendle clasped a hand on Gideon's shoulder. "I believe the king has won the hearts of his people," he said as the cheers continued.

Not everybody's. Not hers.

52

WYNTER

Gideon was lying on the doctor's worktable, shirtless, barefoot, in only his long undergarment. Wynter watched as Barrow finished sewing up Gideon's side wound. He bit off the thread from the needle and tied it off. Gideon flinched, then sat up.

"You're lucky," Barrow said. "A few more inches and the blade would have pierced the liver."

Gotz was in attendance and handed Gideon a cup. He downed the contents. Barrow frowned. "Now is hardly the time for your experimental potions and tonics."

Gotz shrugged and took the empty cup from Gideon.

"You'll have to be careful," the doctor said, gathering his things and placing them into a leather pouch. "No lifting or strenuous activity." Barrow glanced at Wynter. Her face flushed. Apparently, the doctor knew of their new living arrangement. He handed her a wad of muslin. "Wrap him up. Change the dressing at least once a day. You can use some sterile egg white to help aid the healing. Send for me if the stitches open. Otherwise, he needs rest."

Barrow surveyed his work one last time, and then slung his bag across his shoulder. "Stay as long as you need to. I've got to go check on a *life-threatening* infected toe," he said with dry sarcasm.

Barrow left with his sour attitude and Wynter was glad of it. Gotz dismissed himself and they were left alone. Gideon remained seated on the table. The lantern light flickered in the humid air. Dark clouds had blackened the afternoon sky, and it had started raining again. With only the sound of soft rain on the tent, Wynter began wrapping the muslin around his waist, covering the wound. His stomach tensed a few times and he gritted his teeth, but his mind seemed somewhere else.

"What you did today was…"

"Don't say honorable," he said.

She didn't even know what she had meant to say. How did one offer comfort to a man like Gideon?

She finished the wrapping and tied off the end. She looked up and their eyes meet. There was something there she had not seen before—a brokenness. Perhaps killing did not come as easily to him as she'd thought. And though the rest of the camp was celebrating a victory, he seemed to be mourning.

She reached up and placed a hand on his cheek. He closed his eyes and took a deep breath, leaning into her hand. She'd promised not to heal, but that didn't mean she couldn't feel. So she felt for his sadness—his heartache. *You can't heal the heart.* The thought was not her own; it was the gift that spoke to her. She drew closer, pulling him into her arms. He let her, wrapping his arms around her waist, relaxing his head against her shoulder. She searched him until she found a place buried deep inside. A place of utter darkness. There was so much pain there that she felt herself stifling a sob. She found a silent scream lost in the fabric of time. Her instinct was to fight his anguish. She took all the love she had inside her—the love of her father, her mother, her grandmother—and she poured it into his dark place. His fingers dug into her waist, and suddenly the moment ended, and he was holding her at arms-length, staring at her wide-eyed and afraid. Her breath caught in her throat. She had seen something he had not wanted her to see, and she had given him love without meaning to.

He grabbed her hand and slapped it against his heart. "You can't fix this," he said between gritted teeth.

"Gideon." How did she explain that she'd only wanted to help him?

"You think you know me now?" he asked, flinging her hand away. "Think you can fix me?"

She backed away, grimacing at his unkind words. *Let it go. He's delirious.*

"So great Healer? What did you see?" His eyes were ablaze.

That was enough to ignite her anger. She was powerless to stop what came next. "Fine. You want to know what I saw?"

His look of reproach spurred her on. "I saw a sad man trying to hide his sadness with anger. You're anything but cruel and unfeeling. You feel too much and it drives you to madness. You shut down any real emotion because that would mean you'd have to care. And if you cared, you'd be vulnerable. The great King Gideon will never allow himself to be vulnerable because then everyone would see who he actually is. A coward!" She labored in her breathing as if she'd been running.

His face remained stoic, but his eyes betrayed him. She had broken through his wall, and now that she had, she felt ashamed. Echoes of her past, her father's words, raced through her mind.

Words can be like a snake bite, Wynter. Once you strike, the poison quickly does its job.

Gideon slid off the table and reached for his shirt. She moved hesitantly, reaching out to try to help him. He stayed her with his hand, managing the shirt with some difficulty. When he was done, he looked over at her. "You're right. I'm exactly what you say I am."

She opened her mouth to speak, to take it all back, to tell him that she'd said those things in anger and she hadn't meant any of it. She only wanted to *heal* him, and that had been her mistake.

You can't heal the heart.

He grabbed his boots off the floor and stuffed his feet into them. He limped toward the tent flaps.

"Gideon—" Her voice cracked with emotion.

He hesitated, his back to her, then he ducked away.

She grabbed on to the table. What had just happened? *I only wanted to comfort him.*

Her breaths came so fast that her knees started to crumble. She raced out of the tent and ran through the deserted camp. Everyone had taken cover from the rain. She was drenched in seconds. She continued running until she found an open meadow. Her shoes sank into the soft ground. She pushed herself, running as fast as she could. All she wanted to do was run away from the flood of feelings—feelings for Gideon that she shouldn't have—that he didn't want.

Out of the corner of her eye, she saw something moving in the murky distance. It was the black wolf. It was running parallel to her, matching her strides. Its presence gave her a surge of energy, and they ran together in the fading light until she could go no further. She stopped, her chest heaving, the rain dripping into her eyes. She pulled the short sword from her back and sparred with the darkness, slicing and cutting through an invisible enemy. The wolf sat twenty feet away, watching her.

When the blade became too heavy in her hand, she dropped to her knees. She looked over at the wolf. She was no longer afraid of it. It didn't seem to want to harm her. In fact, it always seemed to show up just when she needed it the most. Maybe Six was right. Maybe this was her spirit animal and it was there to help her.

She rose and lumbered toward the wolf, her sword dangling in her hand. It stood up, anticipating any sudden movements. When she was five feet away, she stopped. "What do I do, spirit wolf?" she asked as rain poured down her face. She licked the salty rain from her lips. The wolf seemed to understand; it turned and walked back toward camp. She followed.

53

WYNTER

The next morning, the air had turned bitter cold. A wool blanket and the ill-fitting shirt Lark had given Wynter on her first night was all that was between her and the unwelcome chill. The smell of last night's rain lingered on the wet clothes she had slung over a chair in the corner of the tent. She was tempted to roll back over, but Gideon was up and attempting, unsuccessfully, to put on a clean shirt.

She rose like a petulant child and ripped the shirt off of the one arm he had managed to shove into it.

"Your dressings need to be changed," she snapped. She knew she shouldn't be angry. She had said things last night that she should've never said. She'd hurt him, but he had hurt her too.

He scowled at her and attempted to snatch back the shirt. "I'll get the doc to do it."

She hid the shirt behind her back. "No. I'll tend the wound."

When he saw her resolve, he relented and sat down in a chair.

She wasn't sure how to behave after last night. But she had decided, after the encounter with the wolf, that her place was still here if she was going to help unite their people and find Isidor. She had not counted on developing feelings for Gideon, but she couldn't let that keep her from her duties as the Alrenian queen.

Feeling too scantily dressed, Wynter grabbed her cloak and put it on. She methodically unwound some clean gauze and cut away the old bandage with Lark's knife, careful not to prick Gideon with its tip. She was about to clean the dried blood around the wound with a sponge when he spoke.

"You came in late last night," he said. "Where were you?"

She hesitated. She was in no mood to talk, so she dabbed at the wound.

"I was worried," he added.

She stopped and set the sponge down. "Don't," she said looking at him.

"Don't what? We need the two rings to open the Iron Gate," he said stiffly. "You can't be out running about. It's too dangerous."

She laughed. "All I am to you is a ticket to Isidor."

He rubbed his eyes with one hand, as if her words were tiring.

"I'm sorry I've been such a burden for you," she said tersely.

Gideon bolted from his chair, startling her. "You're not—" he said between gritted teeth. He winced with pain. She steadied him with her hand. They were inches apart. The heat of his chest radiated between them. He gazed into her eyes, and she felt the same intensity between them that she'd felt last night, but she wouldn't be drawn in again only to be rejected and mocked.

She took a step back. "Perhaps you're right. Maybe Barrow should change your dressings." Without another word, she left the tent. He didn't come after her. She went to the tent Six and Kidron shared and demanded that Six give her a pair of pants to wear. From now on, she was going to do what was best for herself.

54

WYNTER

ynter rode next to Six. Gideon was a few horses ahead leading the caravan with Brendle.

"Well?" Six said.

"Well, what?" Wynter asked.

"What's up with you and Prince Charming?"

"Nothing is *up*."

"Something is. You came charging into my tent this morning demanding pants. It was pretty clear you were angry."

"I just needed pants, Six. The dress is too impractical. We're almost to the White Mountains."

"So you're angry at pants?"

Wynter sighed. Six could be relentless when she wanted information.

"We shared something last night."

"Whoa," Six said loudly. So loud, in fact, that Gideon turned in his saddle and looked back at them.

"Do you mind keeping your voice down," Wynter said quietly.

"Sorry," Six whispered. "So why are you angry? I mean... look at him. He is fine like—"

"Stop."

"Okay, okay. But I'm going to need more than that," Six said.

"There isn't any more. I tried to comfort him, he pushed me away. I'm just a means to an end for him."

"Oh. How unfortunate."

"That's one way of putting it."

Six tightened her grip on the horse's reins. "I have a good mind to go up there and tell him what I think of him."

Wynter sighed and glanced over at Six. "You'll do no such thing. Besides, I'm over it."

"Right. You really *act* like you're over it."

"Can we not talk about this anymore?"

The caravan suddenly halted, and Brendle helped Gideon dismount. She pulled her mare's reins to the left and dug her heels lightly into its side. Six followed. When they reached the lead horse, she couldn't believe what she was seeing. Just beyond them, next to the White Mountains, was a camp of hundreds of people. She and Six quickly dismounted and stood by Gideon's side.

"Valen's men?" Wynter asked.

"No. There was no way for them to get around us. The terrain would have been too difficult," Gideon said.

"I'll go and scout it out," Brendle said.

Gideon nodded and Brendle departed on his horse.

Gideon led the caravan back into the woods to keep out of sight, and they waited. The people became anxious as word spread that there was a camp of people between them and the White Mountains. The journey had been long, and no one was ready for another battle. When Brendle finally returned, his face was laced with concern. They all gathered around.

"They're Alrenians."

Six's face betrayed her shock. "They must be the survivors of the northern forest. What are they doing here?"

"There's something else," Brendle said. "I recognized one of them."

"Who?" Gideon asked.

"Our informer. The blond kid."

Wynter's stomach dropped. *Jack.* Her cousin.

Gideon rubbed the back of his head, thinking.

"Gideon, can I speak to you in private?" she asked.

He gave her a questioning look but nodded, and they stepped away. She wasted no time. "We have a small problem."

"What problem? We have their queen. They'll bend to whatever we ask of them."

She took a deep breath. "The blond informer is my cousin, Jack."

At first it didn't register, and he looked confused. Then he understood. "He told us you're the real queen, but he knows you're not. If he exposes you, you'll have no sway with the Alrenians."

She nodded.

Gideon cursed under his breath and clenched his fists. "You might have mentioned your cousin was the informer before now."

Anger swelled inside her. The heat of it burned in her cheeks. "I told you I wasn't the real queen from the beginning. It was your decision—and Lark's—to continue with this farce!"

Gideon seemed to reconsider. He ran a hand over the top of his new hair growth. "You're right. This isn't your fault."

"We can still present ourselves to the Alrenians as dual heirs to the throne. We can ask them to join us in our search for Isidor," she said.

"And if Jack exposes you?"

"Then he risks exposing himself as a traitor. I will tell them how he fed secrets to the Uluns."

Gideon stood for a moment, contemplating. "We'll send a messenger and ask their representatives to meet us halfway. They'll likely be suspicious of your *authenticity.*"

"I can convince them. I can heal their sick. No doubt they've suffered greatly from ground sickness."

He grabbed her arm, his fingers digging into her. "No. You promised me you wouldn't heal."

"I don't understand. Why?" she asked.

His grip loosened. It was clear he was struggling with something.

"Please. What is it?" she pleaded. He was scaring her. Did he know something she didn't about her healing?

"You're dying," he said releasing her.

Her heart raced. "What? No. I'm fine. I—"

"Gotz said every time the queen heals, a piece of her dies. That's why it takes you a while to recover after you heal." He said it so matter-of-factly that it took a minute to sink in.

She shook her head in disbelief and turned away, trying to hide her anxiety.

"He doesn't know how many times you can heal before you don't wake up."

She held a hand to her mouth, trying to hold back the overwhelming fear. How did she not know this? It was never spoken of among their people. It was true that the queen healed only on rare occasions, but Wynter had assumed it was because the gift of healing was reserved only for the privileged. But now that she thought of it, the queens were always young and never lived to be of old age.

Tears threatened to come, and she fought to hold them back. She would not cry in front of Gideon, not after last night. Quite unexpectedly, he wrapped his arms around her waist and pulled her to him. She turned into his embrace and clung to him, desperate for his forgiveness, for his comfort.

Is this why he keeps pushing me away? He doesn't want to lose another person he cares about?

She wondered if it could be true.

"I'm going to protect you," Gideon said into her hair.

"I know," she said. For the first time, she felt something like hope.

55

GIDEON

Once contact had been made with the Alrenians and arrangements to meet had been agreed upon, the Uluns set up a temporary camp. A tent had been hastily set up so Gideon could change into something more regal before the meeting. Tomas, his reeve, claimed to know exactly where Gideon's finer wear was, despite the fact that the camp was in flux and all Gideon's belonging were packed in wagons. But as always, Tomas' meticulous attention to detail saved the day, and he appeared with the clothes just as the tent was made ready. He'd offered to help Gideon dress, but Gideon declined. He needed a moment alone.

He grimaced as he pulled his formal high-collared white shirt over his head. His wound still ached where Valen had managed to make his mark. He slipped on his formal black coat that fell to mid-calf. The bell-shaped sleeves were trimmed in a fine gold embroidery of leaves. He fastened the coat with a silver wolf clasp that had been his father's.

I'm ready.

But would he ever feel ready to be king? This was not him. He looked down at the wolf ring—his father's ring—his ring now. He tightened the hand into a fist.

His guard pulled back the tent flap. "My lord."

Gideon cleared his head and pulled at the lapels of his coat, tightening his look. "Are we ready?"

"A visitor, my lord. Lady Hilran."

Gideon found her timing curious. They hadn't talked in months. Perhaps she wished to thank him for allowing Wynter to heal her dog.

"Should I send her away?" the guard asked.

Gideon considered. "No. Send her in." Out of habit, he ran his hands through his hair, forgetting he only had a soft covering left after shaving his head.

Hilran ducked inside. She had a blue wool cloak with fur lining draped across her arm. She curtsied, lowering her head. "My lord."

"Hilran," he said, sounding more formal than he had meant to.

She looked at him squarely, as a friend would. "I thought Wynter might be here with you. I wanted to offer my cloak for her to wear for your meeting with the Alrenians. I heard she was wearing a silk gown, and the weather is much cooler here in the north."

Heat rose to his face as he fought to maintain eye contact with her. When they were kids, they'd promised to marry when they came of age. But that was before he became heir to the throne, and before he came home from war without her brother. *Bring him home to me safely, Gideon.* He'd made more than one promise to her that he hadn't kept. They had unfinished business and they both knew it.

After holding her gaze a moment too long, he quickly stepped forward and accepted the cloak. "Thank you. I'll see that she gets it."

She smiled then turned to leave.

I can't let her leave. I need to make things right.

He gritted his teeth. "Hilran!"

She turned slowly and lowered her eyes. "We don't need to speak of these things right now," she said.

"Yes. We do." He laid the blue cloak across the back of the single chair that held his discarded clothes.

Hilran folded her hands in front of her, indicating she wished to keep the conversation formal. "Tomas has asked me to marry him," she said.

Gideon was taken aback. "But he's—"

She smiled weakly. "I know he's much older, but he's kind. And in case you haven't noticed, there aren't many men my age left for the taking."

He took a deep breath. "This is my fault. I should have…let you go…sooner."

"Maybe we both hung on longer than we should have."

"I'm sorry," he said.

She shook her head and looked down at her hands. "Don't be. I'm glad you've found the one you were meant to be with."

"What? No. I'm not—Wynter is not—"

Hilran let out a small laugh. "Gideon Glasser, I know love when I see it."

"It's not like that with her," he said bitingly.

"Yes it is," she said, relaxing into their old ways.

He tightened his hands into fists. Hilran drew closer and took him by the shoulders. "You're in love with her, you fool. Don't be such a poop-noddy."

He looked in her eyes for the old feelings between them. It would be so easy with Hilran. But when he realized he only felt friendship, his eyes widened. "Sons of Ulu," he whispered.

She dropped her hands. "Now what are you going to do about it?" she asked, smiling.

"You were always smarter than me."

"Yes."

They laughed.

"Will you forgive me?" he asked.

"On one condition," she said.

"Name it." At that point, he would have given her the world, if only to see her smile again, the way she used to before she'd lost so much.

She reached out and took his hands. "Don't just love her, Gideon. Give her your heart."

Filled with emotion, he pulled her to him, and they held each other one last time. A good-bye of sorts. "Be happy, Hilran. Tomas is a good man."

"I know," she whispered.

He gently released her and kissed her on the forehead. She made a hasty exit but turned at the last minute. "Be careful today."

Left alone, he took a deep breath and ran a hand across his mouth.

Could I really be in love with Wynter?

Was it possible? Before he could think on it further, the guard announced everyone was ready.

WYNTER

"I need to speak with Gideon," Wynter said, arriving at Gideon's tent. She was second-guessing the decision to accompany Gideon to the meeting with the Alrenians. She didn't want to risk Jack calling her out, or maybe she was just feeling reluctant to wear her dead queen's red silk dress.

The guard shifted uncomfortably. "He's otherwise engaged, Your Majesty."

"With whom?" she asked, still feeling the urgency to speak to Gideon.

The guard's face remained stoic. She huffed and pushed him aside, gently pulling open the tent flap to peek inside. Her breath caught in her throat. Gideon was embracing a woman. And not just any woman.

Hilran.

Wynter didn't need to see her face. She recognized Hilran's long black hair.

Heat rose to her face and she quickly stepped back. For a brief second, she wondered if she'd been mistaken about what she'd seen. But the embrace was not friendly, it was intimate.

She spun on her heel and raced back toward her tent. She held her hands to her churning stomach. Her head was spinning.

How could I have been so blind? He doesn't care for me, he needs me.

She was ashamed and angry that she'd allowed herself to feel something, first for Lark, and then for Gideon.

No more. From now on, I'll do my duty. I won't be put to shame again.

Wynter stormed into her tent and ripped off her cape, tossing it *at* Six instead of *to* her.

"Did you talk to Gideon?" Six asked.

"No," she said flatly. "I changed my mind."

Wynter tugged at the laces on the front of her dress with heated fervor. Six tossed the cloak to Kidron and helped Wynter undress.

Everything about what she was about to do felt wrong, but she had no choice. They had to convince the Alrenians that she was the queen and that she had made peace with the Ulun king. She didn't have the luxury of feelings anymore. She had a part to play. Gideon was obviously playing his, so she would play hers.

Of course, he tried to comfort me. He needs me.

Kidron plaited Wynter's hair, and Six rubbed berry juice on her lips and cheeks. The clothier dropped off a blue cloak lined in fur and announced that Lady Hilran had offered it for the queen's use. Her hands trembled as she accepted it.

Misunderstanding why Wynter was upset, Six tried to console her. "I'll be right at your side backing up everything you say to our people. Don't worry," she said.

Wynter turned her focus to the meeting at hand. "It's Jack, my cousin, I'm worried about."

"If he knows what's good for him, he'll keep his mouth shut. The lying thief," Six said.

"You look beautiful," Kidron said, tying the blue cloak around Wynter's neck.

"Thank you both. I couldn't have done any of this without you two."

Brendle stuck his head in. "It's time."

Kidron hugged Wynter. "Come back."

"I will, don't worry," Wynter said, smiling weakly.

Gideon was waiting outside with Lark's horse—her horse now, she had come to realize. When he saw her, his face flushed. She approached, trying to hide her fear, her hurt.

"You look—" He swallowed whatever words were meant to come next. If she had not seen his embrace with Hilran, she might have thought he considered her beautiful. But she knew better now. She went to her horse and rubbed its nose, trying to calm herself. Gideon stepped up next to her and leaned in. "After this meeting, we need to talk," he said.

Wynter nodded without looking at him. He no doubt wanted to tell her about Hilran. Thankfully, before Gideon could say more, Brendle arrived to help her up onto her horse. She needed a clear head for the meeting, not a broken heart.

Brendle, Gotz, and two other soldiers rode with Wynter, Gideon, and Six to the meeting place. She'd left her sword and knife behind. Queens didn't carry weapons.

Her heart pounded fiercely, but she held her head high and rode her horse with the confidence of a queen. The Alrenians arrived on foot with a contingent of the same number, as agreed upon. There were five men and two women in their party. Jack was with them, just as she'd feared. She avoided eye contact with him, fearful she'd be tempted to unleash her fury at his betrayal.

A man, finely built with brown hair and a beard, stepped forward, the others staying one step behind him. He was smartly dressed as one who belonged to the queen's privy council would be.

Brendle helped Wynter dismount. Gideon managed on his own, but she could tell his wound pained him. She understood that he needed to appear strong, so there would be no question as to why she hadn't healed him.

The Alrenian official spoke. "My given is Elias. I'm part of the queen's privy council from the northern forest. Why have you sought us out? Will you not be satisfied until you have slain us all?" His words were bitter and filled with hatred. He eyed Wynter up and down. His eyes rested on her ring.

Gideon took Wynter's hand and stepped forward. "I am Gideon, king of the Uluns, and this is your queen. We wish to unite our people and search for the hidden land of Isidor—the land promised to us in the last oracle of the great King Rodolf of Ferran. I regret that a faction of my people have deserted the sons of Ulu and are roaming our lands, unchecked. The attack on your colony was not my doing, and you have my deepest apologies." He bowed slightly.

Elias scowled, eyeing Gideon with contempt. "You think your words mean anything to us? What of justice?"

"I have avenged the Alrenian blood by challenging Valen in the court of swords. He lost. We come in peace and invite you to join us."

The Alrenians looked at each other, uncertainty and suspicion in their glances. Elias eyed Wynter up and down. "You present this woman wearing fine Alrenian silk and the queen's signet ring and we should just take your word for it that she's our queen?"

"I assure you, I am your queen," Wynter said. She looked at Jack.

You got me into this, you better back me up this time.

Elias huffed. "We have never seen the queen, so we can't be certain that you are who you say you are. This could all be some kind of trick. A ploy."

Wynter fought the urge to wring her hands. Gideon placed his hand at the small of her back in an attempt to ease her nervousness.

Six jumped in. "I was captured by the followers of Valen who destroyed our colony. Gideon and his men freed me and the queen from that murderer. I have seen her heal. She is our queen."

"You are Jutta?" the man asked Six, inferring that her word wasn't good enough since she wasn't Alrenian.

Six bit her tongue, but a fire burned in her eyes.

Wynter held out her hand. "Only the queen wears the ring of the eagle."

The man stepped forward, took her hand and examined her ring briefly. "We heard the queen had been captured, but you could easily be an imposter meant to fool us." He crossed his arms, closing himself off to further argument. "Lucky for you we have someone here who can identify the queen."

Wynter swallowed. *Will Jack betray me yet again?*

Elias turned and motioned Jack forward. Jack locked eyes with her. She thought she saw remorse until he spoke. "This is not the queen. She's a transporter passing herself off as the queen."

At least he didn't say I was his cousin. He's probably afraid to tarnish his good name.

The Alrenians grouped together and whispered harshly to each other. Jack continued to look at Wynter. She detected a small measure of shame, but it was clear to her now that Jack was on the side of whomever he needed to be on, family or not. Whatever reasons he had for outing her were somehow to his benefit. Exposing Jack as a traitor would be a gut reaction. Perhaps he was even counting on it. She had another idea that would make him look the fool instead.

She'd have to *prove* she was the queen. She knew what she had to do, and Gideon wasn't going to like it. But she had no other choice. She had to convince them that she was the queen.

"Are any of you ill or wounded?" she asked.

Elias turned, surprise on his face. The others looked equally taken aback.

Gideon whispered in her ear. "Don't. We'll find another way."

The man looked to his friends. They nodded. "We've lost

many to ground sickness, but the rest of us have recovered. There is one child that remains with a fever. She shows no signs of recovering."

"Take me to her," Wynter said.

Elias' face softened as the hope that she could be the real queen became a possibility. Elias looked uncertainly at Jack. Jack shifted his feet. If Wynter could heal, he would be proven a liar.

Jack backtracked immediately. "Well she looks like the transporter I knew," he said sounding unsure.

Gideon took Wynter gently by the arm and pulled her away to speak privately. "I can't let you do this."

She jerked her arm away. "You can and you will. You know this is the only way."

He gritted his teeth.

"I'll be okay. I promise," she said, softening her tone. He lifted her hand and led her back to the Alrenians.

"The Ulun seer will accompany me," Wynter announced. "That is, if it's okay with Your Majesty," she said glancing over at Gideon.

Gideon gave her a curious look. He had apparently noticed the change in her demeanor. He nodded his approval, but a small scowl appeared with it.

Elias eyed Gotz up and down, and also nodded his assent. An old man was no threat to their camp.

"If she doesn't come back safely—" Gideon said.

"You have my word," Elias said. "If she can heal like she says she can, then both she and you will have our allegiance. But if she is not the real queen as Jack has said, she will be tried as a traitor to Alrenia."

Wynter wouldn't think of the fact that she *had* to heal and that healing was killing her. She'd do what she had to do for her people and Gideon's. Besides, for the first time in her life, she could do something that could actually bring peace to Ferran.

She and Gotz left their horses and followed the Alrenians to their camp. She dared a look back at Gideon. He looked…confused?

I know, Gideon. I know about Hilran. You don't have to pretend anymore.

57

WYNTER

It was uncomfortable entering the Alrenian camp. Wynter's people looked empty and exhausted. Their faces were sunken, their clothes dirty. Huts built from tree limbs and pine boughs were serving as shelter. She was a stranger to them and was very out of place in her silk gown. She was grateful for Gotz's presence. She prayed this would not be the child's last day on this earth—nor her own.

Elias led them into one of the huts. Wynter had to bend down to enter, and even then, there was not enough head room to stand. A young girl, covered with a blanket, lay on a pallet made of leaves. Her eyes were closed, her face pale as milk. Her forehead glistened with fever.

Elias knelt next to the girl and took her hand into his. "Grace. You're going to get better now." He tenderly kissed her forehead. There was no response from the girl.

Only a father would treat the girl this way.

"She's your daughter," Wynter said.

He looked up at Wynter. The pain and drain of his daughter's sickness were written in the lines of his face.

"Can you heal her?" he asked uncertainly.

Wynter did not know if she could. She took a deep breath. "Yes."

"You will need to leave the hut," Gotz said.

Wynter expected Elias to argue, but he did not. He kissed the girl once more and left.

She knelt beside the girl. "What if I can't heal her?" she asked Gotz. "Not even I escaped the ground sickness, and I'm a healer."

"But you recovered. Most die once a fever develops."

She was scared. Her only successful healing had been a dog. This was a human, a child.

"You can do this, or we would not be here now. I believe you and Gideon will fulfill the oracle," Gotz said.

She closed her eyes. This was the precipice of her future. Everything depended on now.

She placed her hands on the child's shoulders. Immediately she was seized with pain, and her hands tightened so violently she feared she would hurt the girl. The sickness was everywhere. It was as though the girl lay in a grave, and only the last bit of dirt was needed to snuff out the remainder of her life.

This was different than before when there had been a dark place in the king to wrap herself around, or the dog where she had found and bound bone. She wasn't sure what to do, so she poured herself—her life—into the girl. The illness absorbed like a sponge—dissolving her efforts. She pushed with every fiber of her being. And when the sickness took that, she gave more.

Her whole body ached and she could barely draw breath, but she would heal this girl or die trying.

This is my fate.

Her lungs ceased, her mind faded. The intensity of the heat that was consuming her threatened to burn her alive. Then she saw his face.

Gideon.

Tears fell down her face, but her mind was far away—lost.

She was dying. She screamed, emptying herself of her last remaining breath. A flood of light poured into the girl and the sickness was consumed. Understanding she had won, she opened her eyes and smiled. But Gotz's face was aghast. She collapsed, then her world turned to darkness.

58

GIDEON

"What do you want, Gotz? Has there been any change?" Gideon asked.

"No. No change."

"Then get out."

"Holing yourself up in your tent isn't going to help her."

Gideon leapt up and swept his hand across his table, sending the food and drink that Brendle had left him crashing to the floor. "Do not presume to tell me how I should act." Gideon pointed his finger at Gotz. "You let her go too far. Now she may never wake up."

"If you were to talk to her. Maybe—"

Gideon threw his hands up. "That's your solution? I talk her back from the brink of death!"

"Love is a strong weapon."

Gideon laughed and ran a hand through his newly grown hair. "Now you think you know me? Know my heart?" The sight of Gotz sickened him. "Get out. In fact, pack your things. My father is dead. Your services are no longer needed."

Gotz's face fell. The words had hurt the way Gideon had intended them to. Gotz left without a word.

Gideon tore his tent apart.

· · ·

EARLY EVENING, when his emotions had tempered, Gideon went to the doctor's tent. Barrow was not present, but Six and Kidron were there tending to Wynter dutifully. A single tallow candle flickered on the table. It had been four days since she had healed the young girl. She lay on the white sheepskins Gideon had sent over from his tent. She had been changed into a linen night-gown. Her brown eyelashes fluttered like delicate feathers on her pale cheeks, but she had yet to open her eyes.

"Can I have a minute?" Gideon asked.

The girls left quickly. He knelt by Wynter's side and took her hand. How had he come to care for this woman?

Because she's the girl from the woods, the one I saved all those years ago.

They had a strange connection then, and they had one now. He had dismissed Gotz in his anger. He was losing everything. Only she could save him from himself. He needed her, and not just to open the Iron Gate to Isidor.

He leaned over and kissed her cool lips. "Come back to me, Wynter," he whispered. "I can't do this without you."

He left the tent, stumbling into the fading light. Brendle was waiting for him. "What's happened?" Gideon asked. He could tell by the look on Brendle's face something was wrong.

"Scouts of Valen have been spotted."

Gideon cursed under his breath. He'd hoped that with Valen gone, the rogue faction of Uluns would fracture and fold.

"I'm afraid your snake has two heads," Brendle remarked. "You've cut off one, yet one remains."

Who else had enough power to lead Valen's people into a civil war? There had been no other leader that he knew of.

"Any idea how close they are?" Gideon asked.

"I'm afraid not. But with your permission, I'll ride out tonight."

Gideon rubbed the back of his neck. "No."

Brendle bristled. "No, my lord?"

"I'll go."

Brendle shifted uncomfortably. "The risk is too great."

Gideon looked down at his ring. He slipped it off and handed it to Brendle. "Keep this for me until I return."

"And if you don't return?" Brendle asked, pocketing the ring.

"You know what to do."

The errand was foolish, but sitting around waiting for Wynter to die was driving him mad.

Gideon fetched his horse and galloped off into the darkening sky.

59

WYNTER

On the seventh day, Wynter opened her eyes. Six and Kidron were at her side, smiling and hugging each other. They helped her sit up and Kidron shoved a cup into her hands. Her tongue felt like rough tree bark. She drank a few sips and winced. It was horribly bitter.

"One of Gotz's concoctions," Kidron said.

She could barely hold her head up, but they helped her to her feet and sat her in a chair.

"How long?" Wynter asked, looking at her hands. She felt so removed from her own body that even the sight of her own hands was strange.

"Seven days," Six said.

"We thought we were going to lose you," Kidron said, tears welling in her eyes.

Wynter managed a small smile and took Kidron's hand. "I'm going to be fine." Even as she said the words, her head swooned. "How is the Alrenian girl?"

"She's perfect," Kidron said.

Wynter closed her eyes and thanked the Lord for the girl's life and for her own. After seeing how close to death this healing had brought her, she'd probably never survive another attempt.

She was filled with an overwhelming sadness. This was the same burden that the queens before her had carried.

"A lot has happened since you've been out," Six said. Her voice sounded cautious.

Wynter only wanted to hear of Gideon, but she held her tongue. There was no reason for her to ask about him, and she didn't want to appear anxious to see him.

Kidron offered Wynter the cup again. "Drink."

She took a small sip. Her stomach rumbled in protest.

"The Alrenian and Ulun people are adjusting to each other," Six said. "The healing has united them. It's a start."

"That's wonderful news," Wynter said, trying to feign interest. Had Gideon even visited her? Did he care if she lived or died?

He's with Hilran, not you. You're nothing to him.

Six and Kidron seemed to notice Wynter's uneasiness. They shared a knowing look.

"What is it?" Wynter asked, sensing bad news. Her frail heart fluttered.

"Gotz is gone," Six said, wringing her hands.

"Gone? Where?" Wynter asked.

"We don't know. He just disappeared."

The news was troubling, but not as earth-shattering as the looks on their faces. It seemed like they were hiding something. She tried to stand. "Where is Gideon?"

Kidron bit her lip and Six gently pushed Wynter back into her seat.

"Six, stop treating me like a child. Where is Gideon?" she said, urgency in her voice.

"He left a few days ago after scouts of Valen were spotted. He insisted on going alone. He hasn't come back."

Wynter's mind raced. Why would he go alone with so much at stake?

"He came to see you a few nights ago, right before he left. He asked us to leave so he could be alone with you," Six explained.

A memory, a shadow passed through Wynter's mind. She touched her lips. She remembered *something*. But what? A touch. A voice. It was too distant to grasp.

"I need to see Brendle," she said.

"Okay," Six said, "but let's get you fed and cleaned up. Your full recovery is our priority now, not Gideon's whereabouts. The people have been keeping prayer vigils by your tent day and night. They'll need the queen's leadership in Gideon's absence."

Six was right. Wynter had to focus on her duty now. Too many lives depended upon it. Still, all she could think about was Gideon.

He will come back. I have to believe he will come back.

WYNTER WAS VERY WEAK. Six and Kidron had called for a wooden tub. They scrubbed her down and washed her hair and force-fed her as much food as she could manage. By evening, she was starting to feel a bit more part of the world again. In honor of her recovery, the people, both Ulun and Alrenian, had gathered and created a feast with the meager stores that remained. She sat in a chair covered in sheepskins and watched as the people raised their cups to each other and sang old songs of Ferran around the camp fires. The smell of roasting rabbit and simmering greens permeated the air.

Gideon should be here for this. What if he never returns?

Brendle finally came to her. Kidron wrapped Hilran's blue wool cloak around Wynter's shoulders to guard against the cool night air, then she left them to speak in private.

Brendle bowed. He looked different. Tired. For the first time, she could imagine him as a boy and not the large man standing in front of her.

"What news of Gideon?" she asked, wasting no time.

"When he didn't return, I went looking for him. There was no sign of him or Valen's men."

"He'll come back," she said. The words were full of empty promise.

Brendle nodded, but his large eyes betrayed his sorrow and compassion for Wynter. "We must consider moving on through the White Mountain gorge. There are little sources of food here. We're on the last of our rations. We must find Isidor, and soon."

Finn approached and fell into a deep bow. Brendle scowled at the interruption, which Finn readily ignored. "Your Majesty, may I be the first to express my relief to see you have recovered."

"Thank you, Finn." She feigned gratitude. She was anxious to return to her conversation with Brendle.

"With the absence of Gideon…"

A knot formed in her stomach at the mention of his name.

"I'd like to offer my protection, and if God help us—" He looked to the sky and placed a hand over his heart, then looked back to her. "—Gideon fails to return, I'm ready to step up as regent for Kidron and lead our people into the White Mountains."

Wynter's face flushed. Brendle must have sensed her unease. He stepped up to Finn and looked down at him. The difference in size was striking. Wynter quickly diffused the situation before it escalated into something more.

"Thank you, Finn. I'll take your offer under…advisement."

Finn bowed once again and disappeared into the shadows of the night fires.

Wynter looked up at Brendle. He was following Finn with his eyes.

"You don't like Finn do you?" she asked.

"It's not a matter of liking. It's a matter of trusting."

"I've never heard Gideon voice any concern," she said, hoping Brendle would share more about Finn.

Brendle grunted. The tone seemed angry. "The gorge," he said, attempting to route the conversation back to business.

"How can we move forward without Gideon? We need his ring," she said.

Brendle reached two fingers into a breast pocket and pulled out Gideon's ring. He placed it in the palm of her hand. She stared at it in disbelief.

He went out alone without his ring.

Was it possible that he'd planned not to return?

A lump of emotion swelled in her throat and she tried to swallow the despair. She had to do what was right for the people of Ferran. Her people—Gideon's people—needed her.

She untied the wolf medallion from around her neck and laced Gideon's ring onto the cord. "You're right. We can't wait any longer. I should speak to the people."

"This can wait until tomorrow when you are more rested."

She shook her head. "The people have waited long enough."

Brendle bowed and dismissed himself. He collected more soldiers who then dispersed through the crowds, asking the people to gather.

Finn quickly came to her side, offering her assistance which she waved off with a hand. She rose slowly, digging for the energy to stand. The music and laughter died down and was replaced with curious grumblings as the people gathered around her.

She closed her eyes. She'd never spoken to a crowd. Now she had to speak as queen and hide the fact that she was terrified. She opened her eyes. The murmurs of the crowd died down.

"Fellow countrymen. There are no Uluns or Alrenians here tonight. Only sons and daughters of Ferran. Tomorrow we will enter the White Mountain gorge, together as a united people. There we will fulfill our destiny and enter the Iron Gate where we will find the land of peace prophesized by the great King Rodolf."

The crowd whispered fiercely to each other as she paused. Jack stood near the front, glaring at her. *You're not the queen. Not the true queen.* She could see his thoughts as if the words themselves were written on his face. Her resolve wavered. She cursed Gideon under her breath.

I'm nobody.

Her hands shook. She scanned the crowd, looking at the unsure faces.

I'm a transporter.

She watched as Jack smirked.

You won't win this one Jack.

She would never let that happen.

"Are you okay, Your Majesty?" Finn whispered in her ear.

His close proximity made her flinch, but she couldn't let Finn's awkward presence distract her. She squared her shoulders and began again, louder this time.

"As you know, your king, Lord Gideon, has left the camp to ensure that the Ulun usurpers, who have actively worked to destroy the peace that we seek, will not hinder our progress. We will pray for his safety and look for him to join us soon. So let us celebrate tonight what will be ours tomorrow."

At first the people just stared at her. Several people looked around, trying to gauge what kind of reaction they should have. Then suddenly, someone yelled out, "Isidor! Isidor!" Then others joined in until everyone was chanting and raising a fist of victory. She looked over at Jack. His smugness had turned to dismay, and she couldn't resist a small smile. He broke away and stormed off.

The moment was almost perfect except for one thing. Gideon was not at her side, Finn was. A heart wrenching emptiness filled her whole being. In that moment she knew.

I'm in love with Gideon.

She put on her bravest face and smiled for all to see. She even let Finn raise her arm in victory. She readily excused herself and returned to Gideon's tent, crying herself to sleep. The celebration continued into the night.

60

GIDEON

Gideon had kept tabs on Valen's followers for three days. They were definitely headed toward the White Mountains—toward Gideon's camp. So much for honoring the court of swords. Valen's death hadn't had the effect Gideon was hoping for. He didn't know of any other leader among them. It was as if they were being led by a ghost.

There was no reason to tarry any longer. He needed to return to his camp, but he found himself coming up with reasons to stall his efforts to return—finding water to refill his waterskin, tracking a deer that could provide much needed meat back at camp—anything to keep from having to see Wynter lying there, not knowing if she would ever wake up.

He was about to stop and make camp for one final night when he caught glimpses of flames ahead of him through the woods. He tied his horse to a tree and approached slowly, quietly, with his hip knife drawn. The element of surprise was always an advantage in these situations.

A hooded figure stoked the small fire that burned under a steaming pot. Something earthy with a hint of sweetness rose into the air. Gideon remained quiet, observing, waiting to see if there were others nearby.

The figure spoke. "You might as well join me."

The hood came down and Gideon recognized Gotz's white wisps of hair. He sighed and sheathed his knife. He sauntered up to the fire and dropped to the ground. He had banished Gotz and now he was sitting by the man's fire warming his hands. Regret wasn't a kind enemy.

Gotz dipped a spoon into the pot and tasted his dinner. "You're a long way from home."

"Valen's men are following us."

"How unfortunate," Gotz said dryly.

Gideon deserved the cold reception.

"And the queen?" Gotz asked.

"I don't know," Gideon replied.

"Ah."

"What does that mean?"

"You're still running," Gotz said.

"I'm not…running."

"Yet here you are, a king, running a soldier's errand without your ring on."

Gideon rubbed the empty place where the ring had been. Leaving it behind had just been a precaution. Or, was it more than that? Hadn't he thought of never returning? It would be so easy to be out on his own with no responsibilities.

"As long as you hold on to the hurts of the past, a part of you will always want to run," Gotz said.

Gideon wanted to get angry, but he found he didn't have the energy. "I've lost so much."

"We've all lost more than a man should. It's what you do in the face of it that matters."

"You mean like running away?"

Gotz ladled some soup into a cup and offered it to Gideon. Gideon shook his head.

Gotz sat. "Your father was a good man, but he didn't have a heart like yours."

"That's what made him great."

"No. That's what made him effective. But you, young Gideon, you are so much more than he ever was." Gotz set his cup aside.

"I don't understand. You've done nothing but admonish me for my stubbornness."

Gotz smiled a little. "It's true that you've built up some mighty big walls. But oh, if those walls were to come down. What a fine leader you would make for a new Ferran—for Isidor.

"How do I escape the past?" Gideon asked.

"I feel certain that you will figure it out."

Gotz's words frustrated him, but this was Gotz's way. He was never one to tell you directly what to do.

"Will you come back with me?" Gideon asked.

"No."

"Listen, I'm sorry—"

Gotz stopped him with a hand. "There's something left for me to do."

"What could be left?"

But Gotz did not answer.

"What if Wynter is dead?" Gideon asked.

"Rise," Gotz said, standing.

Gideon started to protest. Gotz was going to give him a vision, and he wasn't certain he wanted to see it, but he stood, just the same.

"Close your eyes," Gotz said, moving in front of him.

Gideon closed his eyes and Gotz placed his hands on Gideon's shoulders. Immediately, Gideon was sucked into darkness, then he was back on the bank of the river from his nightmare. The faceless queen from his dream was standing at the waters' edge with her back to him. He walked toward her, his heart pounding. She turned. She was no longer faceless. She beamed with joy when she saw him and held out a hand, bidding him to come to her.

Wynter!

His faceless queen was Wynter. *Come, let us begin.* He heard her voice though her lips had not moved. Then in a flash, he was back and Gotz was staring at him, the fire reflecting in his eyes.

"You knew all along." Gideon said.

Gotz nodded.

"Why couldn't I see her face…before?"

"Because you were not ready to receive it."

Gideon had dismissed the dream, dismissed Gotz's vision. But now everything was clear.

"I have to get back," he said with some urgency.

"I understand," Gotz said, nodding.

Gideon would tell Wynter how he felt about her. He would tell her he was the boy in the woods all those years ago. They would rule the new Ferran—Isidor—together. For the first time in a long time, everything made sense.

Gideon held out his hand to Gotz. "Thank you, Gotz. For everything." Gotz grasped his hand warmly, like a father to his son.

As Gideon headed back to camp, he couldn't shake the feeling that he'd never see Gotz again.

61

WYNTER

The next morning, Wynter woke to lowing of cattle and cackling of hens. The musty scent of last night's fires, mixed with the dew of morning, filled the air. Instinctively, she rolled over and placed her hand where Gideon normally slept. She expected it to be cold and was already trying to muster the strength to move on without him. But the pallet was warm.

She sprang up and scanned the tent. Everything looked the same as she'd left it last night. Hilran's blue cloak was draped across the chair. Wynter's soft shoes were on the floor next to it, precisely where she had left them. The only thing on the table was the candlestick with a tallow candle that she'd left burning. The last remnants of wax had slid onto the table.

I've imagined the warm bed.

She looked down at her bare feet. She gasped. There at the foot of the pallet was a small bundle of flowers and herbs tied together with a string. Her heart raced. Did she dare hope? She picked up the delicate bouquet and held it to her nose. She inhaled the sweet fragrance. Her spirits lifted.

She raced out of the tent, half dressed in an oversized shirt and no shoes—her braid a mess. The guard gave her a strange look but said nothing. The air was bitter cold, but she felt nothing of its scorn. She searched wantonly, grasping each face and discarding it, searching for the one she sought. Finn was standing close by, watching her. She barely noted his presence. Then she spotted him.

Gideon.

He was just on the other side of the morning cook fires. He had Jack by the neck in a casual way while he talked to Tomas and Hilran. He was laughing, smiling, shaking Tomas' hand. Her stomach dropped slightly, uncertain of what she was seeing. Was Tomas congratulating him on his pending marriage to Hilran? Before she could think on it further, Gideon turned in her direction with Jack in hand. She scrambled back into the tent and tossed the flowers carelessly onto the table. She gathered the blue cloak around her shoulders and quickly unbraided her hair. She fumbled through her things and found a brush and pulled it through her hair in an attempt to look busy and indifferent to Gideon's return.

He strode in unannounced with a red-faced Jack. He pushed Jack toward her. "I have a gift for you," he said.

Her excitement quickly fizzled.

"I'll leave you two alone," Gideon said, and exited.

That was not the homecoming she had hoped for, nevertheless, facing Jack was something that needed to be done. Especially now that the Uluns and Alrenians were preparing to enter the White Mountains together.

Jack looked around, judging her, no doubt. There was no regret in his demeanor. If anything, he held his chin defiantly. She didn't know where to begin, his betrayal ran so deep.

"I suppose you expect some kind of explanation," he said.

She laughed at the absurdity of his comment. "There's nothing you could say that would explain why you turned your back on me, not once, but twice."

He sighed. "Then why am I here?"

Her temper flared. "You're here because you're a traitor!"

Jack smiled. "This from the girl pretending to be the Alrenian queen."

She stepped up to him and spoke directly into his face. "I'm here because of you. You made me queen the minute you lied about who I was."

"I saved your life. The Uluns would have killed you had they thought you were a transporter."

She backed away. "I'm sure that's how you justified what you did. But you didn't do it for me."

He shrugged. "Believe what you want."

"Fine," she said, taking the bait. "Let's say I believe you. What about last week when you told your fellow Alrenians I wasn't the queen?"

"You shouldn't have to live a lie. I was giving you a way out."

Wynter crossed her arms. "Do you actually believe what you're saying?"

Jack remained silent.

"You know what I think," she said. "I think you were looking for *your* way out. You didn't want your new Alrenian friends to find out you're a traitor, so you outed me as a transporter, someone whose words would mean nothing. Except, you didn't count on me receiving the gift of healing, did you?"

Jack threw up his hands. "I don't know what you want me to say."

"You handed me a death sentence when you sent me to be a transporter for the queen!"

Jack's face burned bright red. "That's just foolish nonsense. You're fine."

Wynter circled Jack. He stood still and looked straight ahead, unwilling to meet her eyes.

"Did you ever wonder why our queen never lives to be of old age?"

"I never gave it much thought," he said, sounding bored.

She stopped in front of him. "Every time the queen heals, a piece of her dies."

He looked her in the eyes this time. His face flushed and he swallowed "I didn't know—"

"Is it all just foolish nonsense now, Jack?"

He ran a hand through his blond locks and looked away.

"There's only one fool here, Jack. And it's not me."

Gideon returned. "Everything okay in here?" he asked, looking back and forth between their flushed faces.

She was ready to let go of her past now. Ready to let go of the last remaining thread—Jack.

"Can I go now?" Jack asked.

Wynter folded her hands in front of her. "Oh, you can do more than that. You're hereby banished from this camp. I will give you three days rations. You will leave here and never return."

For the first time since Jack had entered the tent, he looked frightened. "You can't do that!" He looked back at Gideon.

Gideon grabbed him by the scruff of his neck, preparing to escort him from the tent. "I believe she can," he said. "Thanks to you, she's queen of Ferran now."

There was amusement in Gideon's tone. He looked at her with a new kind of respect which pleased her greatly.

Jack pulled against Gideon's grip, but he was no match for Gideon.

She stepped up to Jack. "If I ever lay eyes on you again, I will have your head."

Gideon forced Jack to his knees. "What do you say to your queen?"

Jack looked up at her, rage in his eyes. Gideon smacked him on the back of the head.

"Yes…Your Majesty," Jack muttered between gritted teeth.

Gideon jerked him to his feet and towed him by his collar out of the tent.

Wynter took a deep breath. Never had she been so bold. She felt a renewed strength and was grateful to Gideon for a chance to set things right with her cousin. She eyed the flowers on the table, then scooped them up.

He came back.

62

FINN

The Alrenian informer, Jack, was handed a pack and led out of camp by Brendle.

Curious. Finn thought. The lad had been escorted in to see the queen by Gideon. Now…this.

She's banished him. Why?

An alliance had been formed between the Uluns and Alrenians. What difference would the lad's indiscretions with the Uluns matter now? Hardly worth a banishment. A lashing perhaps.

Finn fetched his horse, then rode in a different direction than Jack as not to draw unwanted attention, then he circled back in the woods, making sure he would intersect with the informer.

He feigned a casual jaunt through the woods as he approached the boy. Jack didn't notice him at first. He walked with his head down and his shoulders slumped.

"Hello, young man," Finn said, pulling the horse to a stop.

Startled, Jack turned in circles as if he were expecting more men—an ambush perhaps.

"I wish you no harm," Finn said and dismounted.

"What do you want?" His tone sounded suspicious.

"Want?" Finn said, casually examining his fingernails. "What a strange question. After all, there is peace among us is there not?" He offered him a tight-lipped grin.

"You're Ulun," Jack said.

"Yes."

"Did you come here to kill me?"

Finn raised an eyebrow. "No. But I'm curious as to why you think I would be."

Jack shuffled his feet, then attempted to move on by stepping around Finn. Finn drew his knife and pressed it ever so lightly against Jack's neck.

"Go ahead then! Get it over with, will you?" Jack's face turned a bright shade of pink.

"Maybe I can be convinced to change my mind."

Jack remained silent. He seemed to be holding his breath, waiting for Finn to finish him. Finn withdrew his knife.

"That's it. I'm free to go?" Jack asked.

"I didn't say that," Finn said, sheathing his knife.

Jack sighed. "Fine. What can I say to convince you, oh great one, to spare the life of such a meager Alrenian as myself."

Finn laughed. "You've got spunk, kid. I'll give you that."

"I'm serious. I've got nothing of value to offer you."

"Oh, I believe you do."

Jack raised and lowered his hands, apparently tired of playing games.

"Why are you being banished?" Finn asked.

"You probably know why. I fed the Alrenian queen to the Uluns. That's why she was captured."

Finn paced a bit. "Yes, yes, but I sense that there's more to it than that."

Jack's face reddened.

I'm right. He's hiding something.

Perhaps some incentive was in order. Finn rubbed the nose of his horse. "He's a real beauty, don't you think?"

"Sure. Yeah. Can I go now?"

"It sure would make traveling a lot easier if you didn't

have to walk. You might even make it all the way back to the middle colony without getting your throat slit by the Ulun deserters."

This got Jack's attention. He was practically salivating as he looked the horse over. "I don't know how to ride."

"It's simple, really. Two minutes of instruction and you'd be riding him away."

Jack narrowed his eyes. "What's the catch?"

"No catch. Not really. I just need to know everything the queen said to you."

The color faded from Jack's face.

Finn laid a hand on the lad's shoulder and looked at him pointedly. "I assure you this will stay between you and me."

Jack glanced greedily at the horse, then nodded. Finn squeezed his shoulder. "Good decision."

"Wynter's not the real queen. She's my cousin and was a transporter for the real queen on the day of the ambush. I lied about who she was because Lark asked me to."

Adrenaline poured through Finn's veins. But he checked himself. The boy's word wasn't enough to out Wynter as an imposter. "Yet she can heal?"

"The queen gave her the gift before she died. I didn't know it was even possible to pass the gift on."

Finn considered. This was good, but still not enough. As long as she could heal, no one would dispute her as queen. His disappointment grew.

"Anything else," he said, lamenting giving up his horse.

Jack hesitated.

"Out with it!" Finn snapped, tiring of the conversation.

"She's dying."

"What?" he asked, unsure if he had heard him correctly.

"Every time she heals, a piece of her dies. Healing will ultimately kill her."

Finn held back a smile, but inside he was bursting with joy.

Oh yes, this will do nicely.

"Can I go now?" Jack asked, reaching for the reins of Finn's horse.

"One more thing," Finn said, plucking a sealed letter from inside his jacket pocket. "You're going to run into a group of Uluns on your way home."

Jack stared at the letter as if it were poisonous.

"Don't worry. This letter will give you the safe passage you desire. Without it, you'll surely be slain."

Jack snatched it from his hand and stuffed it into his pack.

Finn gave him the basics on riding and caring for the horse, and in minutes, Jack was galloping away.

Finn laid on the ground and rolled around a bit.

What a shame my horse got spooked by a snake, threw me, and ran off.

He was about to rise when he found himself staring at someone's shoes. He knew by the hem of the robe that it was not Jack. There was only one person who still wore an old-fashioned robe.

"Hello, Gotz," he said, rising to his feet. He made a show of brushing himself off. "My horse—"

"Don't bother," Gotz said.

Finn studied Gotz's face. He looked worn, like the bottom of a well-used boot. The pack he carried on his back made his hunched frame appear even smaller. It was doubtful that he saw or heard anything, but Finn couldn't be certain.

"Going back to camp?" Finn asked, subtly sliding his hand to the hilt of the blade at this hip.

"It was you all along, wasn't it?"

Finn cocked his head. "Sorry, you're going to have to be more specific."

"You're Valen's informer. I'm surprised I didn't see it sooner."

"I think you're confused, seer. Mangus was the informer." His hand tightened around his knife.

Gotz nodded. "You did a good job convincing us he was, I'll give you that. I heard your conversation with the boy."

"What do you want?" Finn asked.

"From you?" Gotz said with a laugh. "Nothing."

Finn drew his knife. "I'm sorry it has to end this way, seer."

Gotz let his pack slide off his shoulder and drop to the ground. "I'm not." He moved toward Finn, though he had no weapon.

Finn held his knife at the ready. When Gotz was a foot away, he stopped and smiled.

"What are you smiling about? You're about to die," Finn said.

"I'm smiling because I'm glad I lived to see your end."

"What are you going to do to me, old man?" Finn said mockingly, though the seer's words made him nervous.

"Oh, me," Gotz said chuckling, "I'm not going to do anything to you. But your time is coming, Finn." He paused, his eyes sparkling. "I've seen it," he whispered.

Finn plunged the knife into Gotz's gut and quickly withdrew it. Gotz lifted his eyes to the heavens with a smile still on his face, then he dropped to the ground.

Finn stared down at Gotz. He wiped the back of his hand across his mouth.

His words mean nothing.

He spat on the ground next to Gotz. "We'll see who has the last laugh, seer."

He cleaned his knife off with some leaves and headed back to camp, whistling. His web was being woven bit by bit and Gideon and Wynter were going to be the next ones to be snared by it.

63

GIDEON

"Finn lost his horse," Brendle said. "He said it got spooked and bolted."

Gideon made work of securing two skins of water to a strap that lay across his horse's neck. "Get him another one."

Brendle grunted. "Is strange, don't you think?"

Gideon stopped momentarily and glanced back at Brendle. They were preparing to enter the White Mountain gorge, the Ulun deserters were not far behind, and this was what Brendle was concerned about? "It's Finn," Gideon said as a way of explanation.

"I saw him ride off into the woods right after I escorted Jack off the premises."

"Same direction?" Gideon asked, turning around.

"No."

Gideon rubbed the back of his neck, trying to figure out what Brendle's concern was.

"He came back with no horse," Brendle said.

"And you think he gave the horse to Jack?"

Brendle's expression remained stoic.

"What purpose would giving his horse to Jack, serve?"

Gideon asked. "He's certainly not one to do anything out of the goodness of his heart."

"My point, exactly," Brendle said.

"Keep an eye on him if it will make you feel better, but I'm afraid that once we enter the gorge, Finn is going to be the least of your worries."

Brendle's jaw clenched, but he said no more. Gideon quickly changed the subject.

"I know you haven't had much time with her, but how is Wynter's sword training going?"

"She knows enough to buy herself a few minutes. Six, a little longer."

"Hopefully, it won't come to that," he said with a sigh. "If we stay ahead of Valen's men and find the Iron Gate, we can avoid a battle inside the gorge. We may have the numbers, but numbers won't mean a thing if we're trapped between the cliffs of the gorge."

Brendle showed his agreement with a small grunt and a nod, then dismissed himself.

Gideon led his horse through the myriad of Uluns and Alrenians. The wagons were going to have to be left behind. The descent into the gorge was simply too rocky and steep. From here on out, it was horses, mules, and whatever anyone could carry on their back. Tomas suggested taking only a handful of each variety of the large livestock and as many fowl as they could manage in cages. With the addition of the Alrenians, the food supply had shrunk faster than expected. Leaving some of their livestock behind meant they'd have enough food for two days.

They had two days to find Isidor.

He had hoped that Gotz would change his mind and join them, but there had been no sign of him. The final vision he had given Gideon had solidified Gideon's feelings for Wynter. He just wasn't sure how to approach her.

He spotted her at the edge of camp, rubbing down her horse

with a handful of straw. She had on a gray tunic tied at the waist and fitted, black wool pants. Her brown hair hung in a braid down her back.

She's my faceless queen.

The problem was, she'd been rather standoffish ever since he'd returned, and he took it to mean that she wasn't interested in him or being his wife. She'd unceremoniously handed him back his ring, and since then had said very little.

She cares. I know she does.

He'd felt it the night she'd tried to comfort him after his fight with Valen.

I pushed her away like an idiot.

He definitely had a lot to make up for, but her coolness would not deter him.

He came up behind her. "Are you ready, Your Majesty?"

She glanced back at him but stayed on task. "I am."

He leaned in a little closer. "I was really hoping we could talk."

He could have sworn she winced, but perhaps she'd only inhaled some straw dust.

She stopped and turned around. "We can talk after we get to Isidor."

He tried making eye contact, but she did everything she could to avoid looking at him directly.

"What I have to say is *important*," he said.

"A lot of things are important but getting to Isidor is our priority."

Her formal tone was not very encouraging. She turned and commenced scrubbing down her horse.

"Shall we ride together, at the front?" he asked.

"If you think that's best."

He tried to think of more to say, but he came up empty, so he left her to her task.

Well, that went well.

Lark was always the smooth one, always knowing what to

say. Gideon was too black-and-white and knew little of the gray area that most women lived in. He was not charming, but he thought intelligence and modest good looks would have accounted for something.

She didn't even mention the flowers I left her in the tent this morning.

His jaw tightened with frustration and a scowl returned to his face. He stormed toward Tomas to get an update on the readying of the supplies.

64

WYNTER

"Boo," a voice said in Wynter's ear, jolting her out of her thoughts. In one quick movement, she drew her short sword from the strap on her back, turned, and held the blade inches from the intruder's neck.

Six held up her hands and grinned sheepishly. "Sorry. I didn't mean to scare you."

"You didn't," she said, sliding the sword back in its place.

"What's got you on edge?"

"Really?" she scoffed. "We're getting ready to enter the White Mountains to find the Iron Gate to Isidor and hope that the two rings of Ferran will be able to open it. Why would I be on edge?"

"Okay, okay. I get it. This is not the way of Jutta. We don't… what's the word?" Six snapped her fingers. "Stress!" she exclaimed, grinning from ear to ear.

Wynter couldn't help but smile after that. Six's smile was contagious.

"See. Already you're better. Besides, with a fine man like Lord Gideon by your side…" She smiled sheepishly.

Wynter sighed. "I'm not so sure about that."

"What's the problem?"

"Her." Wynter nodded her head toward Gideon, who was talking to Tomas and Hilran.

Six followed her gaze, then sighed. "Hilran? Looks like they're talking. You know, using words to communicate."

"Is hugging also communicating?" Wynter asked.

Six raised an eyebrow. "You saw them hugging?"

Wynter nodded.

"Hmmm. I will find out what this is about," Six said, taking a step in their direction.

Wynter grabbed her by the arm. "I don't think so. This is not the way of Alrenians."

Six shrugged. "Fine. But the Jutta way is better. Oh look, there's Brendle. Got to run."

"Not a word," she yelled after her. She took a deep breath and released it slowly. Gideon glanced over at her and she abruptly turned back to tending her horse.

65

GIDEON

There was a reason why they called them the White Mountains. Many had tried to flee down into the gorge during the Great Destruction, and now the rocky descent was littered with their bones. The people had stopped trying to avoid them not long after they had started their journey. There were just too many. After a while, the bones became as commonplace as the rocks, and there was no distinguishing between the two.

Gideon had tried to converse with Wynter several times, but the difficulty of traveling over rocks kept her focused on keeping her horse upright. The whole caravan seemed to move in a slow death march. Once they were able to reach the bottom of the gorge, he estimated another day of travel to get to the area that had been named the Iron Gate.

How does one open a wall of rock?

When the sun was beginning to drop below the highest peak of the mountains, they reached the bottom of the gorge. There seemed to be a collective sigh of relief among the people, despite losing some animals and garnering a fair share of sprained ankles, bumps, and bruises.

The rocky cliffs of the White Mountains shot up to their right.

Trees towered above them to the left where a fresh spring of water flowed through a rocky basin. Tomas wasted no time creating some semblance of a camp. Tents would go up and fires would be prepared for cooking as if it were any other night.

Gideon spotted Wynter heading toward the woods and motioned for Brendle to follow her. He was still perplexed by her sudden coolness toward him. He'd thought she cared for him in some small way, but even that had evaporated. Had he realized his feelings for her too late? He couldn't help but think of the words from the oracle.

He who will go forward with his whole heart will obtain what he seeks. Only do not be of two minds, for the two rings of Ferran are the key to your salvation.

He needed to find a way to tell Wynter how he felt. Their whole future might depend on it.

66

WYNTER

Wynter wandered instinctively toward the ancient forest of cypress trees. The descent into the gorge had been difficult and stressful, and a little time in the woods was just what she needed. She crossed the river, leaping from rock to rock, and entered the majestic world of the giant trees. The aromatic evergreens rose eighty feet into the air. Their lace-like fronds sprouted from the trunks at a height no human could ever hope to reach. Walking among them made her feel impossibly small. They must have been hundreds of years old, for their trunks were as wide as two wagons. The gnarled trunks dug like fingers into the ground, feeding themselves from the world below—a world hidden from man. She closed her eyes and breathed in their resinous scent. The cypress had long been a symbol of death, but they made her feel intoxicatingly alive.

She came to an area where no trees grew but was overgrown with vine and bush. In its midst was a stone structure covered partially in vines and climbing weeds. What kind of place had this been long ago—a palace, a temple? Did servants gather cloaks and usher in visitors, or did people come to worship God among the towering trees?

She was rather taken with whole scene, for it felt like she had traveled to some long-ago place lost in the fabric of time. That's when she heard the growls, low and numerous. She remained completely still and held her breath. Goosebumps rose on her arms. She slowly turned her head to the left. There were three of them. Three thin, scraggly wolves with matted brown fur, baring their teeth. They had her in their sights and, by the look of them, they were hungry.

She gingerly removed the short sword from her back.

I'll never be able to kill all three.

But she wasn't going to go down without a fight. Her heart raced so fiercely that it pounded in her ears.

I've come all this way only to be eaten by wolves?

She scanned the area. She was certain that Brendle had followed her, but there was no sign of him. Her eyes caught movement to her right. The black wolf—*her* black wolf—appeared stealthily, proceeding in a low, deliberate crouch as it moved toward the other wolves. Her hands trembled. There were three wolves. Would the black wolf be able to keep them all at bay? She doubted it.

Her wolf suddenly bolted toward the other wolves, but the pack did not retreat. Two of them raced forward. Everything happened so fast after that. The black wolf became entangled with the two attackers. The third wolf set its sights on her, and she set hers on the vine-covered wall in front of her. She needed an advantage, and the wall was going to give it to her.

She raced for the wall, her sword in her left hand. Fear drove her. She could see the wolf coming for her out of the corner of her eye. She came in at the wall at an angle and leapt, planting her right foot against the wall several feet above the ground. She pushed off and turned, letting gravity do the rest.

Grasping her sword in both hands, she came down on the wolf as it leapt, planting the blade in the back of its neck as her feet hit the ground. She pulled her sword out and the wolf collapsed. Her breathing came fast and shallow.

The black wolf fought one wolf, then the other, as each one took its turn attacking and retreating. The two emaciated wolves had suffered several bites. There was blood around their necks and faces. Surely, they were no match for her wolf, but yet even he was injured—his right ear was wet with blood. She was so focused on the fight that she had failed to notice that Gideon had stepped into the clearing. He had a bow raised and an arrow threaded and aimed.

"Gideon!" she shouted.

The two wolves drew back and looked her way.

Gideon scowled.

"Not the black one!" she shouted.

One of the wolves broke off and came at her.

"Sons of Ulu, Wynter."

Oh no.

She crouched and readied her blade. The wolf leapt just as Gideon's arrow landed in its side. She stumbled backward, her hand resting on the wall.

The black wolf kept the last attacker at bay. Gideon placed another arrow in his bow.

"Not the black one!" she shouted again.

The two wolves attacked each other—a blood thirsty, growling blur of teeth and fur.

Gideon took aim.

What if he hits my wolf?

She couldn't let that happen. She took off running toward Gideon. He pulled back the bow, she screamed for him to stop, and he hesitated just long enough for her grab his arm.

"What are you doing?" he barked.

"Not the black one," she said breathlessly.

He didn't look happy, but he nodded and pulled back his bow. The two wolves parted, circling each other. Gideon's arrow sliced through the air and landed into the remaining brown wolf's side. It collapsed to the ground. The black wolf looked at her, then took off, disappearing into the woods.

He's saved me again — my spirit wolf.

Gideon turned to her, looking as if he was preparing to scold a small child. "You could have been killed," he said gruffly.

"I was managing just fine, thank you," she retorted.

Gideon spotted the dead wolf by the wall, then glanced at her sword. He smiled.

"What?" she asked, preparing for an argument.

"*You* killed that wolf over there?"

"Yes," she snapped. Then it dawned on her.

I killed a wolf.

She slowly raised her sword and looked at its blood-drenched blade. She laughed—the kind of laugh when you can't believe what just happened. She dropped her hand and they stood there grinning at each other.

Daughters of Alrenia. He's handsome when he smiles.

"I'm afraid to ask about the black wolf."

"I don't know. It's been following me…helping me."

He raised an eyebrow. "Helping you?"

"I know it sounds crazy. Six says it's my spirit animal."

"Your spirit animal."

"It's a Jutta thing. She says that if you see your spirit animal, you're destined for great things."

He didn't say anything. The smile had disappeared, and he seemed more contemplative.

"I'm sorry," she said. "I only wanted to see the trees."

"Do you miss home?" he asked, looking up into the canopy of cypress.

"Yes," she answered.

"If you could go back, would you?"

His question took her by surprise.

Why is he asking me this?

Did he want her to go back?

"I…" She looked down at the ring on her finger. The eagle represented her people, her life. But when she looked at Gideon, she saw another possibility. Except, they had no future together. He'd chosen Hilran. So she lied. "Yes. I would go back."

He studied her for a moment, the silence growing awkward. "We should get back and help make camp." The weight of disappointment came once again. For a moment, she had thought she'd seen something in his eyes. She had to stop hoping for there to be more between them. "Yes, we should get back."

WHEN THEY RETURNED to the camp, the people were in an uproar. Everyone was looking to the south where smoke rose into the darkening sky. Gideon headed straight for Brendle. Wynter chased after him.

"What's happened?" he asked Brendle.

"It appears that the Ulun deserters are burning the remains of our camp that we left behind—our wagons."

"They're coming for us—for me," Wynter said.

"I'll never let that happen," Gideon said without looking at her. "Brendle, start gathering the people. We can't avoid these deserters any longer." He hurried off, leaving Wynter and Brendle staring at the sky. That's when she noticed Brendle's ear was bleeding.

His *right* ear.

The same ear as the black wolf. She couldn't stop staring.

No. It's not possible.

"Brendle? What happened to your ear?" she asked, her voice trembling.

He kept his eyes on the sky. "An accident. Nothing to worry about." He walked away. Of course, it was just a coincidence. What had she been thinking—that Brendle was some kind of shapeshifter?

I need to talk to Six.

She scanned the camp and found Finn lounging by a fire, watching her. He raised a cup to her, smirking as he always did.

She was starting to think Brendle was right to be concerned about Finn. He always played the supportive cousin to Gideon, but behind the façade lay something untoward. She just couldn't quite put her finger on it. She sighed and hurried off to find Six. She finally found her by one of the fires, sharpening the tip of her spear.

"Where have you been?" Six asked.

"In the woods."

Six stood and brushed off her hands and examined her work with a look of satisfaction.

"I need to talk to you about Brendle," Wynter said. She didn't have much time. Brendle was gathering the people.

Six studied her face. "Why are you flushed?"

Wynter touched her cheek. It *was* hot. "I don't know. I was running." She didn't want to get into the fight with the wolves.

"What about Brendle?" Six said with a tilt of her head.

"Do you think it could be possible that he's…my…"

"He's your…? What?"

"Wolf. Do you think it's possible he's the black wolf?"

"Unlikely."

"But it's possible?"

Six sighed. "Legend says that sometimes when a Jutta kills an animal, he's given the animal's spirit. But—"

"So Brendle killed a wolf and took its spirit?"

"He wouldn't have *taken* it. He would have to be *given* the animal's spirit. It's a gift, like healing and prophecy. It's supposed to mean a person has been chosen."

"Chosen for what?"

"I don't know. Like I said, that part is only legend. Folklore."

Wynter nodded. Still, Brendle's ear injury seemed an unlikely coincidence, and whenever she had seen the wolf, Brendle had not been present.

A call came from the center of camp. Six grabbed her arm. "Come on, something's up."

Everyone left what they were doing and headed toward the

shouts. Before Wynter could explain to Six that Uluns had lit their old camp on fire, Six was pushing through the congregating mass and dragging Wynter along with her. They arrived at the forefront of the commotion. Gideon climbed up onto a crate. His eyes were ablaze with fury and passion. Brendle stood next to him on the ground.

"People of Ferran," he called out in a loud voice. "The Ulun deserters are coming for our queen." He looked directly at Wynter and her heart leapt. The effect he had on her was unnerving.

Six elbowed her, and Gideon turned his eyes back to the crowd.

"They mean to destroy what we seek—a united Ferran."

Shouts of anger toward the advancing Ulun deserters echoed through the crowd. Wynter looked around in awe. The people were listening, nodding.

Gideon drew his sword and held the blade out toward the people. "Some of you may think we should run. We will not run!" he shouted. "We will stand, united, as one people, and show them what we are made of."

Cheers erupted.

Gideon's jaw was taunt, his face red with determination. Wynter's heart beat rapidly.

"Do not fear," he continued. "They fight out of selfish ambition, and that will be our advantage. Because we fight for something more—for peace and unity." He held a closed fist to his heart. "So, I ask you now. Will you fight for the brotherhood of Ferran?"

There was a brief moment of silence before the sounds of swords being drawn cascaded through the crowd. Wynter pulled hers. Swords were lifted high in the air, and together the people echoed Gideon's words.

"For the brotherhood of Ferran!"

Gideon raised his sword. His body and words held the commanding presence of a king. "By the grace of the almighty

God. We will triumph!"

The people shouted as one. Gideon lowered his sword and held out his hand to Wynter. She moved forward without a thought, and he pulled her up onto the crate and lifted their clasped hands into the air.

67

SIX

Six watched as Wynter dozed off next to her by the fire. Morning would soon come, and their fates were more uncertain than ever. Gideon had given a fine speech, but reality was always something altogether different.

She slipped away and walked down to the river. A full moon glowed overhead. She found Brendle sitting on a large rock at the water's edge. The river bubbled and gushed in a soothing rhythm that spoke of peace. But its surface glowed with the eerie white reflection of the moon and uncertainty.

"It's late," Brendle said, without looking over.

"Who can sleep?" she said.

She stood next to him, trying to build the courage to say what she had come to say. The glimmering water continued its journey even in the darkness. There was no fear in its destination.

Where is it going?

Somehow it seemed to know. She wished she was that confident of her path. But that was not why she had come. She cleared her throat.

"I know you will not speak of this, but Wynter knows who— *what*—you are," Six said.

Spirit wolf.

Brendle remained silent.

"I only came to say thank you for what you will do," she continued. She had not told Wynter the truth. It was better that she didn't know. A spirit animal's duty was to ultimately sacrifice itself.

"Also—" Her throat tightened, and she had to swallow her sorrow. "Thank you for being my teacher of the spear. It has been my honor to be taught by one chosen for such greatness."

He didn't have to acknowledge the truth; the truth flowed between them. She could see it in the whites of his eyes as he lifted his face to the moon. She turned to leave.

"You, too, will find your path. God will make it so," Brendle said.

Tears pooled in her eyes and she wiped them away. Tears were not the way of the Jutta.

"How do you know if it's the right path?" she asked, turning around.

He looked at her, his eyes sparkling with the lights of the night sky. "When you get there. Only then will you realize it was the right path."

She smiled and nodded. This was the way of the Jutta.

68

GIDEON

awn came and the people were made battle ready. The elderly, and those unable to fight, were sent into the cypress forest. Gideon had insisted that Wynter stay back with Hilran. After a much-heated discussion, she had relented and stormed off. It didn't help that he was allowing Six to go to battle. But Six wasn't queen, and he needed every able hand.

They saw the Ulun deserters well before they arrived in the valley. Gideon could have taken the offensive and met them head on, but the rocky terrain would have made fighting too difficult; so they waited, and watched. They would meet their foe on solid ground with the advantage of having a clear path to retreat, if necessary. The rogue Uluns would only have a rocky climb out of the gorge to fall back on.

When the time came, Gideon called his people to make battle lines. The Alrenians insisted on being the first line of defense. They had lost a whole colony to the bloodthirsty, traitorous Uluns, and were anxious to avenge the deaths of their loved ones. The army rested their shields on the ground, the upper rims against their thighs. A mass of their biggest men with long spears were at the center of the line, their points gleaming in the early morning sun. It would be these spears that would attempt to break the center of the enemy line.

Gideon sat behind his army on his black stallion next to Brendle. The stirrings of war simmered deep within. His skin crawled with the yearning to wield his sword and draw blood. How had Gotz thought him a better man than his father?

"Where is Finn?" Brendle barked.

Gideon looked over. "With the bowmen where he'll be the most useful."

Brendle grunted. "I did not see him."

The enemy lined up across from them. Both sides hefted and overlapped their shields.

Gideon was about to call his men and women to move forward when the wall on the other side parted. Two people together on one horse rode toward them. Gideon's army moved aside to let him and Brendle through. Gideon gave his horse a light tap with his heels, then the shields closed behind them.

Heat rose to Gideon's face as he realized that it was Finn, with Kidron in the saddle in front of him, who had come to meet them. He and Brendle pulled their horses to an abrupt stop in front of Finn's horse and quickly dismounted.

"What's the meaning of this?" Gideon asked, looking at Kidron.

Kidron's face was bright red. Her hands were tied behind her back and she squirmed uncomfortably.

"Hello, Cousin," Finn said cheerfully.

"You are the informer," Brendle spat.

Gideon didn't need to hear it to know that it was true. His hand went to his sword.

Finn grinned. "Not so fast, Your Majesty. I've got a whole army ready to strike you down if you make any sudden moves."

"Do it!" Kidron yelled. "I don't care if I die."

"Hold your tongue, Kidron," Gideon barked. Every fiber of his being ached with the desire to drive his sword through Finn. How had he been so blind? He knew how. He had beheaded Mangus right in front of Finn, and ever since, he'd felt a painful guilt for doing so. Guilt had made him blind to the truth.

"What do you want?" Gideon asked.

Finn chuckled. "The queen, of course. Or should I say, the *transporter*?"

Gideon balled his hands into fists. "That's never going to happen."

Finn pulled his knife and laid it against Kidron's neck.

"I will kill you," Brendle said.

"Maybe. But Kidron will die first."

Finn rode his horse around them and addressed Gideon's people. "He's fooled you all. Can't you see? Wynter is not the queen. She never was. She's a lowly Alrenian transporter that they tried to pass off as the queen. Gideon is a liar and a murderer! He killed my father in cold blood without a trial."

Gideon clenched his teeth and turned around. His people and the Alrenians looked uncertain, whispering to each other and shifting nervously on their feet. But Elias stepped forward and said something to the people that Gideon couldn't hear, and they seemed to settle.

Finn circled back around Gideon and Brendle, looking smug. He had planted a seed of doubt in Gideon's people, threatening their plan to find Isidor.

"Fight me in the court of swords," Gideon hissed.

Finn laughed. "I'm not stupid. I know I can't beat you in a fight to the death."

Gideon drew his sword.

Finn drew the knife even closer to Kidron's neck. She whimpered and a small trickle of blood rolled down her neck.

Gideon raised his hands in the air and tossed the sword to the ground. "I'll fight you unarmed."

Sweat broke out on Finn's forehead.

Gideon unsheathed his hip knife and tossed it aside.

Finn's face paled. The horse stamped forward and back, as

Finn tried to maintain control of it as well as the knife he held at Kidron's throat.

"You are a coward," Brendle said with a grunt.

Finn turned and looked back at his army.

"And if I win?" he asked, turning back to Gideon.

"Wynter is yours. You have my word."

Finn motioned with his head toward Brendle. "He leaves and takes your weapons with him."

Gideon nodded his agreement. Brendle reluctantly gathered Gideon's weapons, but not before he repeated his earlier words. "I will kill you." He mounted his horse and returned to the battle line.

"Let Kidron go," Gideon demanded.

Finn smirked. "Fine. She's more trouble than she's worth." He shoved her off the saddle and she fell hard to the ground, unable to control the fall because of her bound hands. Finn dismounted and drew his sword.

Gideon's teeth clenched as he watched Kidron spit out a mouth full of dirt. He helped her up. She glared at Finn, then spat at his feet. Finn Chuckled.

"Go," Gideon said to Kidron.

He untied her hands and helped her up onto his horse, and she rode back to safety.

"You're a fool for not turning Wynter over," Finn said. He removed a shield from the back of his horse. "Now both of you will die."

"I should have listened to Lark. He never trusted you."

"Perhaps you should have, but as always, you underestimate those weaker than you. Pride has blinded you."

Gideon's adrenaline surged. He rushed at Finn, but Finn was ready. He slashed out with his blade. When Gideon ducked, Finn whacked him in the face with his shield and Gideon stumbled backward.

"You're pathetic," Finn said, coming toward him.

Gideon tried to outmaneuver the sword, but Finn was ready

with another shield to the face. His lip split and the blood roll down his chin.

Breathing heavily, Gideon charged, going for Finn's midsection, but Finn struck and the blade slashed across Gideon's arm, drawing more blood.

Finn taunted him. "You'll die trying to save her. And then she'll die anyway."

Gideon held his injured arm, staggered, and ran toward Finn again.

Finn blocked him with his shield, and then rammed the hilt of his blade into Gideon's side wound from his fight with Valen. Gideon screamed and blood poured from his side. He fell to his knees in pain. He pushed a hand against the flow and looked up at Finn.

"Surrender now and I'll let you live," Finn said.

"Never," he said through gritted teeth.

69

WYNTER

Wynter paced. All the people who weren't fighting had been sent into the cypress forest to wait. There was nothing that she hated more than being set aside. It didn't help that Hilran stood nearby watching her. Not only that, but Kidron was nowhere to be found. Wynter hoped that she'd just snuck off to watch the battle.

Someone called her name. She turned, looking for the source. That's when she spotted Kidron coming into the clearing, riding a horse—Gideon's horse. She ran to meet her, worried by the urgency in Kidron's voice. Hilran followed.

Why is she on Gideon's horse? Please, no.

Kidron jumped down from the horse, panting. "He's going to kill him," she said breathlessly.

Wynter's stomach dropped. "Who, Kidron?"

"Finn is going to kill Gideon." Kidron dropped her hands to her knees, trying to catch her breath.

Wynter shook her head. "You're not making any sense."

Kidron straightened and talked so fast that Wynter could scarcely follow her. "Finn is the informer! He held me hostage. He wanted Gideon to turn you over in exchange and Gideon refused. Finn announced to everyone that you're not the real queen. Now Gideon's fighting Finn without a weapon."

No. It can't be.

"You have to do something!" Kidron cried.

Within seconds, Hilran had their horses and they were racing toward the battle scene. Wynter fought the urge to cry.

He can't die.

"Hilran," Wynter said in despair as they rode in a fury.

Hilran looked over, but she had no words of comfort.

When they arrived, Wynter shouted for the people to move, and a path was quickly opened for her and Hilran to ride up to the front lines.

They came to a halt and surveyed the open field in front of them. There was Gideon on his knees, Finn standing over him. Wynter urged her horse into action and raced toward them. Finn caught sight of her and backhanded Gideon across the face with his shield. Gideon collapsed to the ground.

She screamed a gut-wrenching cry of anger and charged ahead. She pulled her sword from her back. Finn smiled as she jumped off her horse and stared at Gideon's bludgeoned body. Her heart pounded so fiercely that it ached in her chest. Gideon was trying to get to his feet, but one eye was already swollen shut. They locked eyes for one brief moment before he collapsed back to the ground.

"You're too late," Finn said, grinning. "And you know what's even better? I'll get to watch you die trying to save him."

Wynter looked from Gideon to Finn.

"That's right, Your Majesty. I know that your healing is killing you. So, let's see if you're willing to die for him." He walked toward Gideon with his sword ready to strike the death blow.

She didn't hesitate. Gideon would live, but only if she stopped Finn. She ran straight at Finn. He turned, just as she lashed out with her sword. He countered her blows with ease. Her arm burned as blow after blow from his blade struck hers.

Their swords finally locked, bringing them nose to nose.

"You do realize that this is pointless?" he boasted.

His smugness only fueled her anger. She twisted away and ducked under his slashes. She grasped her sword with both hands and absorbed another strong blow. Her arms were weakening. Her smaller sword was no match for his. He pushed her away with his shield like he was jesting with a small child.

"Surrender, and I'll make it painless." He grinned and twirled his blade in a mocking display.

She charged forward. Finn swung his blade out in a wide sweep. She slid to her knees, bending backward, holding her blade upright. Finn's blade flashed above her and struck her sword, shearing it in two.

She hurled herself to her feet, tossed aside her broken sword, and unsheathed her knife.

Finn laughed. "Really?"

She backed up. She had saved Gideon from the Morbid by throwing a knife. She could do it again.

Finn came toward her with determined, vengeful steps.

She took aim and threw the knife, but it didn't make the mark she had hoped for. It grazed Finn's ear and fell to the ground.

Finn stopped midstride. He brought his hand to his ear, then looked at the blood on his hand. His face flushed with anger. "This ends now."

Wynter stumbled backward. She was weaponless, but she wouldn't cower or beg. She closed her eyes and prayed that she'd go quickly. Then she heard Six yell. "Behind you!"

She opened her eyes and turned. The black wolf—*her* black wolf—was racing straight for them. She glanced back at Finn. His expression turned to one of sheer terror. She made eye contact with the wolf. An understanding passed between them. She stood her ground and let Finn believe the wolf would attack her first. Then, in that final moment, the wolf leapt. She ducked low to the ground and its large shadow passed above her. She twisted around and watched as Finn bared his teeth and ran his sword through the wolf, just as it landed on top of him.

"No!" Wynter screamed, scrambling to her feet.

Finn was struggling to get out from underneath the slain animal.

"Wynter!" Six's voice called out from behind her.

But Wynter was too angry and distraught to take in anything that was going on around her. She was only vaguely aware that both sides were now advancing forward with their shields up.

"Get this thing off of me!" Finn screamed.

She grabbed her dead wolf by the scruff of its neck and lifted it off of Finn's face. She glared down at Finn, ready to strangle him with her bare hands if necessary. But like manna from heaven, Six's spear landed with a thud by Wynter's feet. The beating of swords on shields echoed all around her. Soon she'd be trapped between the shield walls. She gritted her teeth and pulled the spear out of the ground. Finn cast his eyes toward the spear in her hand. His eyes widened, and in that moment she knew she had won.

"You killed my spirit wolf!" she shouted. Then she plunged the spear into Finn's throat, driving it all the way into the ground.

He desperately grabbed at his throat as his life bled out.

Feeling nothing but loss for her wolf, she drug the animal off of him. It was heavy, like a rain-soaked blanket. She fell to her knees and pulled Finn's sword from its lifeless body. Tears fell down her face. The Alrenian shield wall opened, passed her by, and then closed back again, cocooning her from the oncoming enemy Uluns. She let herself her be dragged back toward safety. She searched through the melee and caught a glimpse of Gideon being carried back.

The shield walls collided, and the war cries began.

70

WYNTER

Wynter was in shock and nothing seemed to register. The battlefield was littered with bodies from each side, but the united Alrenians and Uluns had claimed victory in the end. They searched the field for survivors like they were harvesting a garden. The remnants of Finn's army had retreated back up the rocky climb out of the gorge.

Wynter walked back to camp in a silent stupor with Six at her side. Though Finn had outed her as a transporter and not the queen, it didn't seem to have affected the people in the way Finn had intended it to. If anything, they looked at her with more respect than they had before. Perhaps it was because she had slain the traitor in their midst. But their newfound admiration was lost on her. There was no glory, just sadness.

Back at the camp, Tomas searched tirelessly for Brendle. Brendle was indeed her spirit wolf. She didn't need Six to tell her it was so. It was Brendle's eyes she'd seen in that last moment before the wolf leapt.

Gideon was taken to his tent to be treated by Barrow. He was in no condition to continue their journey through the gorge. And with food growing scarce, hunting and gathering parties were quickly sent out. Wild goats had been spotted in the cliffs, and there was fresh sorrel and dandelion growing in the forest.

On Wynter's request, Elias and some of the other Alrenians helped take the wolf into the cypress forest for burial. She and Six watched as a hole was dug.

"You knew all along, didn't you?" Wynter asked.

"Yes," Six said quietly.

Wynter turned to her friend. "Why did you lie to me?"

"I didn't lie. I said it was unlikely he was your wolf."

Fresh tears came. "But you knew…"

"You are not Jutta," Six snapped, as if that explained it all.

Wynter brushed away her tears. "He was my friend. If I had known…"

Six's expression softened. "If you'd known who he was, *what* he was, he would have left, and then he would've never been able to fulfill his purpose."

Wynter stared at the wolf's body. His fur was wet with blood. "He said once that God had put him here, so he had to wait and see what God's purpose was for him. He's been protecting me this whole time. I've been his purpose. I don't understand how that can be."

Six reached out and took her hand. "This is the way of the Jutta. You can honor him by accepting his sacrifice."

This was Six's way of telling her that she wouldn't be able to understand. Somehow, that made sense to her. Brendle had only done what he was called to do. But it was humbling to think that he would give his life for her. But hadn't she been willing to give hers for Gideon when she attacked Finn?

Sacrifice *was* love.

As soon as the wolf had been laid in the grave, and the last shovel of dirt was thrown upon it, Wynter thanked the men and said a silent prayer. Afterward, she turned and made her way to the river to wash away the blood of her wolf, and of Finn. It was time to see Gideon.

He was lying on his pallet, unconscious, stripped to the

waist. Hilran was on her knees, cleaning him with a sponge. Barrow pushed past Wynter on his way out and mumbled instructions, but she was in no condition to absorb anything he said.

"Where have you been?" Hilran asked gruffly.

"We had to bury—" She didn't finish the sentence. Hilran would never understand. "I'm sorry," she said instead.

Hilran rose and handed Wynter the sponge and bowl of water.

"Keep a close eye on him. I'm going to go forage for some dittany for his wounds and mix a tincture. I'll be back in the morning."

"Aren't you staying?" Wynter asked.

Hilran gave her a puzzled look. "Why would I stay? I'm sure you can manage." She quickly ducked out.

Why is Hilran pretending she doesn't have a relationship with Gideon? Especially now.

Wynter set the bowl and sponge on the table. Gideon slept, breathing softly despite the noises of celebration going on outside. She sat down beside him. His right eye was swollen and purple. His lip had been split open and was puffy. He had multiple bruises across his chest. The wound he had suffered in the fight with Valen had been reopened, and a small amount of blood seeped through the new bandage.

He did this for me.

She quickly reminded herself that he did it for her ring.

She lay down next to him, touched his swollen eye with her fingers, and closed her eyes. The wound was angry and raw. The blood pooled beneath her fingers, and she pushed it away with her power to heal. She told herself she'd only help a little. Just enough for him to be able to open his eye. She moved to his lip and let her fingers graze the cut. Soon she was asleep.

71

GIDEON

"How long has she been out?" Hilran asked.

"I don't know. You tell me." Gideon's voice sounded like gravel. His throat was sore from all his contusions. He winced as Hilran dabbed ointment on his facial wounds.

"It's been since yesterday afternoon then," Hilran said.

Gideon looked over at Wynter. He was surprised that he could see out of his right eye. It was only half opened, but it was open.

"I'm surprised your eye has healed so quickly," Hilran said, as if reading his mind.

He had a sneaking feeling that Wynter had something to do with the speedy recovery, despite her promise to him that she wouldn't heal.

Hilran proceeded to tell him everything that had happened after he'd been beaten unconscious yesterday. She went into minute detail about how Wynter had stopped Finn from killing Gideon by attacking Finn—fighting the good fight up until she lost her weapons. Then a black wolf had appeared and gone for Finn, giving her that split second she'd needed to grab Six's spear and kill Finn. As an afterthought, she mentioned that Brendle hadn't been seen since the battle.

He wouldn't have believed the story about the wolf had he not witnessed firsthand its connection to Wynter—her spirt wolf she had called it.

"Are you certain the battlefield was checked for Brendle's body?" he asked, more concerned about his right-hand man than a wild wolf.

"Yes. No sign of him." She dabbed ointment on his lip.

He didn't really believe that Brendle would have been among the dead. He'd never seen a soldier more capable. But he was a little surprised by Brendle's disappearance. Gideon had always told him he was free to go anytime—return to his people. But whenever Gideon mentioned that Brendle was free to return home, Brendle always said he would stay until he'd fulfilled God's purpose.

How did Brendle determine God's purpose for his life?

Gideon was still trying to figure out his own.

He hadn't realized he'd been staring at Wynter until Hilran asked, "Have you told her yet?

"Told her what?" he mumbled.

Hilran sighed. "That you're in love with her." She put the ointment aside.

When Gideon didn't say anything, she gathered her things. "Get dressed. Tomas has got the camp in a packing frenzy. He'll be coming for your tent soon." He heard her mumble "*Men*" on her way out.

He stood with a grimace and tried to get his arms into a shirt, but it was too painful. Between the bruised ribs and his reopened wound, he was lucky just to stand. He groaned louder than he'd meant to and Wynter stirred. He lowered himself back into the chair, wincing quietly with the effort.

"Gideon," Wynter said, sitting up.

He looked over and his breath caught in his throat. She'd never looked more beautiful. Her face was flushed and wrinkled from sleep, and her hair hung loosely around her shoulders. Her shirt had slid off of one shoulder.

He swallowed and quickly looked away.

She hurried to his side and examined his right eye. She bent down, drawing in close, and lowered his bottom lip with her thumb.

"Ouch," he said, pulling her hand away.

She straightened. "Sorry," she said, cringing. "You look so much better than yesterday."

He gave her a curious look.

"You know what I mean."

He didn't ask her if she had healed him. He didn't want to know.

Her standing there now, fussing over him, made him long for her all the more. Before he knew what he was doing, he reached out and took her hand. She stiffened in his grasp. He lifted his eyes to hers. "Thank you for what you did."

"I couldn't let you die," she said softly.

"You would give your life for mine?" he asked.

"We need each other, don't we? For Isidor?"

He kissed the top of her hand, letting his lips stay longer than he should have. She moved closer and pulled him to her. He wrapped his arms around her, resting his head against her stomach. She cradled his head in her arms and they held each other for the briefest of moments. Then Tomas poked his head in and announced that he was ready to pack up Gideon's tent.

72

WYNTER

Wynter rode behind Gideon and Elias as they led their people through the gorge. With Brendle now gone, Gideon had appointed Elias as his new lieutenant. It was the first real sign that Gideon was working toward a united people.

The trail was a dusty path of small rocks that skirted alongside the river. Small sycamore trees grew at the river's edge on the other side. All of this was nestled between cliffs on both sides of them that soared into the sky so high that no man could ever reach their tops. The rock face itself was layer upon layer of variegated gray and yellow. And despite the harshness of something so impermeable, green vegetation had mocked the unyielding home by growing between the cracks and crevices. Even the eagles soaring above them had found sanctuary in the undisturbed, imperishable nature. And knowing that the symbol of her people flew above her gave her a new peace. For the legend was that the eagle soared so high, it kissed the face of God.

The people were uncharacteristically quiet, and the time passed in a slow rhythm of feet and hooves grating against tiny gravel. Everyone seemed to be feeling the significance of what their journey meant—the fulfilling of the oracle of King Rodolf, or the end of their very existence. The mood was as somber as their unspoken thoughts.

The way eventually became so narrow that there was only six feet between the cliffs. Those on horses dismounted and led the horses by their reins. Wynter could almost touch both sides with her hands. The river was now a trickle beneath their feet, and Wynter's soft leather shoes quickly became nothing more than a flimsy barrier between her and the river's rocky bottom. They were like trapped animals in a fortress of rock. Her heart raced with anticipation.

Gideon finally halted the caravan and called her forward. She handed Six her horse's reins and gave Kidron a reassuring smile, though she was feeling just the opposite. Elias moved his horse and Gideon's aside to let her pass.

Gideon held out a hand to her and said, "Watch your step."

She didn't realize until she had stepped up next to him that their path had come to a dead end. The water beneath their feet was falling into a giant hole below them that was completely surrounded by the cliff walls, forming a perfect circle. There was a single ledge of rock approximately two feet wide just to their right, and the small path on that ledge led to the mouth of a giant carved head in the rock face. The prehistoric carving had hollow eye openings and a large forehead. Where its mouth should have been was a gaping hole that looked like an entrance to some kind of cave. A stream of water fell from the opened mouth.

"Daughters of Alrenia," she said. If anyone were to fall into the watery pit below, there would be no escape.

She looked at Gideon. "You think the Iron Gate is in that cave?" she asked.

"There's only one way to find out."

Panic rose inside her. Gideon seemed to sense her trepidation. "We're in this together, right?" He squeezed her hand.

She nodded.

Gideon called back for a torch, and an unlit one was quickly prepared and sent forward. He stepped out onto the ledge with a grimace and offered her his hand. She wished she would have been able to heal more of him and not just his eye and lip. But her days of healing were passing as quickly as they had come.

She followed closely behind him, their hands intertwined in a death grip. She tried not to look down and had to fight her desire to turn and run back to safety. She stopped suddenly, unable to move forward.

Gideon turned, confusion on his face. "What's wrong?" he asked.

She released his hand and pressed her back to the wall. "I'm scared," she said, looking up to the sky above them.

He moved in front of her and gently took her by the shoulders. "I'm not going to let anything happen to you, I promise."

She dared to look him in the eyes. Those dark eyes that she had once feared, now brought her comfort.

"What if I can't open the Iron Gate because I'm not the real queen?"

He bent down so that he was eye to eye with her. His grip tightened. "You are the queen." He gathered her hand and lifted it so she could see her ring. "God has put this ring on your finger. After everything we've been through to get here, do you still doubt he has made it so?"

She thought of Brendle and how he'd found himself somewhere he was never meant to be. He'd never questioned why; he only waited for God to show him his purpose. Brendle had done his part, and now she had to do hers.

She looked down at the ring. The eagle was a symbol of her people, a token of trust. It was time for her to honor that trust and honor Brendle's sacrifice.

She lifted her eyes to Gideon's. "You're right. I'm queen."

He smiled at her. "A fierce one at that," he said cocking an eyebrow.

Heat rose to her face. She wasn't used to compliments. She

thought of their embrace earlier that morning, but once again reminded herself, *He's with Hilran.*

She refocused. "I'm ready," she said firmly.

Her took her hand again and they treaded carefully, sticking as close to the cliff wall as possible. The rock ledge was dry, but as soon as they got to the mouth of the cave, they had to step into the water to enter.

"Be careful," Gideon said as he stepped forward.

The water was ice cold, and a chill ran up her arms. Within seconds, she could no longer feel her toes. She was grateful that the water only came up to her ankles.

The cave was pitch black even though the afternoon sun was at their backs. She held the torch as Gideon lit it with his flint and steel, and they waited until their eyes adjusted. He took the torch and held it out as they turned in a slow circle, surveying the cave, looking for the gate. Wynter's stomach dropped as the light of the torch came to stop on the back wall. There was no gate. Every wall was solid rock.

"It has to be here," Gideon said under his breath.

He trudged forward, grunting as the water became deeper. She watched as he reached the back wall and felt along the surface, pushing, prodding, looking for anything that might trigger the opening of a passage. That's when she heard a soft humming sound coming from above. Her heart pounded so fiercely that she could scarcely draw a breath. The last time she'd heard that sound, she and Gideon had been standing on a bridge in the northern forest.

She lifted her eyes to the ceiling. There, pulsing like a giant heart, was a hive of Morbids. A lump formed in her throat. If that hive woke, she and Gideon would be overrun in minutes. Any attempt at retreat would certainly be in vain. The whole camp was hemmed in between the narrow walls of the gorge.

This is bad. This is real bad.

Gideon finally turned toward her, looking exasperated. She silently pointed up. He must've seen the terror in her eyes. His face went slack. He slowly lifted the torch and peered up. He gritted his teeth and made his way back to her as quietly as possible, and they scampered out of the cave.

They stood a moment near the entrance of the cave, talking in hushed tones.

"No wonder no one ever found the Iron Gate," Gideon said, bitterly. "We have no choice now but to leave."

"We can't leave." She had no idea how they were going to get past a hive of Morbids. And even if they did, there was still no sign of the Iron Gate.

Gideon ran a hand through his short hair and sighed.

"I know it sounds crazy, but there has to be a way." Wynter wasn't convinced of anything she was saying, but one of them had to be optimistic.

Gideon pointed at the cave. "The only thing in that cave is a death sentence."

Her mind raced. *Do not be of two minds.* The words from Rodolf's oracle played over and over in her head until something stuck—something completely crazy.

"The Morbids," she said, searching for words.

Gideon furrowed his brow.

"The Morbids never tried to hurt me when they chased us through the trees."

"Your point?" he asked, sounding skeptical.

"In fact," she said, "the only one that ever got near me gave me a vision."

"I don't like where this is going, Wynter."

"Maybe all they've ever wanted to do is help the queen." She gazed at him with hopeful eyes.

Gideon shook his head. "No. Absolutely not."

"In the vision the Morbid gave me, I leave the world of destruction and step into a new place."

Gideon's face flushed. "What? You never mentioned this before."

She had all but discarded the vision. But now…

"What else was in this vison?" he asked.

She swallowed. Did she dare mention the baby? What would be the point?

"We need to leave here, *now*," he said.

"Lark was there too, Gideon. The vision has to mean something."

Gideon's jaw worked back and forth, and a scowl returned to his face. She had to get through to him.

"I believe the Morbids will show me where the Iron Gate is."

He studied her face. "You're serious, aren't you?"

She was sensing that he was about to pull his giant ego out of his pocket. "Of course, I am," she barked.

"Your stubbornness is going to get us killed."

"You're calling me stubborn?" she retorted. "That's a joke."

"We're leaving," he demanded. The king had spoken.

She planted her feet and crossed her arms.

He took a deep breath through his nose. "If I have to, I'll carry you out of here."

She laughed. "Not with those bruised ribs, you won't."

His face turned bright red. He could no more carry her than he could a bucket of water.

She took his hand. "You're going to have to trust someone sooner or later."

He looked in her eyes. She could see that he was struggling with himself—his need to control everything. But she also knew that he wouldn't abandon her.

"Okay," he finally said, but his face remained uncertain. "What's the *plan*?"

"I'll go in and wake up the hive."

He took a deep breath and blew it out, then scratched his forehead. "Then what?" he asked.

"I wait."

Gideon rubbed his eyes with his fingers. She pulled at his arm. "This will work."

He nodded, but there was doubt in his eyes. He handed her the torch.

She had turned and taken two steps toward the entrance when he grabbed her by the arm. "What?" she snapped, spinning around. But his face was anything but angry.

"There's something I need to tell you."

"Now?' she asked, growing impatient.

He hesitated. "I'm the boy."

"The boy?"

"The boy in the woods. The one who shot you out of the tree twenty years ago." He reached out and lifted the wolf medallion from beneath her shirt. "I'm the one who gave you this."

She held his gaze, unable to form a response. She had always wondered about the boy but had given up on the idea that it had been Gideon. This grand revelation painted Gideon in the light of being the boy that had spared her life—someone with a heart.

"Why didn't you tell me?" she asked.

"I didn't want to admit that we've been connected almost our whole lives. That you were more than a simple transporter."

"What am I then?" she murmured, afraid to hear the answer.

"More," he said simply.

She didn't know what that meant, but it made her stomach twist into knots.

"I want to go with you into the cave," he said.

She nodded, and together they entered the cave.

73

WYNTER

The hive of Morbids above them was still asleep. How had they survived living in the gorge with so little vegetation or animal life to live off of? What she and Gideon were about to do was risky, but she had to believe that if unthreatened, the Morbids would show her where the Iron Gate was.

They waded through the shallow water to the center of the small cave and stood close together, facing each other. Gideon held the torch to the side. They locked eyes in the glow of its flame, finding courage in one another. They needed to wake up the creatures, but she didn't want to do anything to startle them for fear of creating a frenzy. She did the only thing that she could think of, she sang. It was a song from long ago, one that she remembered her mother singing to her as a small child.

O great land of Ferran
A home so bright and fair

There was a loud screech, a singular alarm to awaken the mass from their slumber. Chill bumps rose on Wynter's arms, but she kept her eyes on Gideon and he kept his on hers. They were inexplicably bound in that moment. Together they would rise or fall. Gideon gave her a reassuring nod and started the next verse. Her voice wavered, but the words came, and they sang together.

> *whose valleys doth the swallow rest*
> *And harvest comes the grain*

The creatures dropped from the ceiling, splashing into the water like a sudden hailstorm. Her whole body tightened with anticipation. They hissed and screeched. They were coming for her, the bait had been taken. Gideon's voice rang louder, encouraging her to continue to sing.

> *There is no place as grand as thee*
> *And nowhere else would I go*

The Morbids gathered at her and Gideon's ankles, climbing over each other, clamoring, reaching out with their clawed fingers to grasp a hold of her legs like impatient children. They seemed to ignore Gideon. Their tiny hands tugged and pulled, clinging to her pant legs. They had become part of her and were now hers, and she felt their unbearable burden. Gideon reached out and grasped one of her hands, reassuring her that he was there. Her voice shook as she and Gideon sang the last verse.

> *For, o the land of Ferran*
> *You're my forever home*

Everything went black.

74

GIDEON

Gideon breathed in a lungful of smoke. The woods around him were in flames. Leaves fell from the trees like wistful embers. He coughed into his sleeve. It didn't take him long to realize what was happening.

This is a vision. Sons of Ulu, Wynter was right!

"Over here," he heard her cry.

He caught sight of her just ahead and ran to catch up. She grabbed his hand and took off running.

Before he knew it, they were out of the burning woods and suddenly the air was clear and the trees were green. It was as if they'd stepped out of one world into another. A river, pure and clear, flowed in front of them. He froze and dropped Wynter's hand. She ran around like she was looking for someone, but all he could see was the river. The same river from his nightmare where he pulls the dead, faceless queen from the water. Only the queen wasn't faceless anymore. She was Wynter.

No. This can't be. I can't lose her now.

Wynter came back to him, but he kept his eyes on the river.

"This is the place from the vision the first Morbid gave me," she said.

He looked at her. "We must leave here. Now."

Wynter looked taken aback. "In case you haven't noticed, the only way to leave is back through the burning forest. I'm not sure we can die in a vision, but I don't want to find out."

She was right, of course. But he'd never felt such fear as he did in that moment.

"What's wrong?" she asked.

But before he could answer, a baby crying echoed from the burning woods behind them.

The color drained from Wynter's face.

"Wynter..." he said.

Her breathing quickened as she scanned the woods. "You're right, we have to go back. I have to find the baby."

"Baby? What baby?" he asked.

She took a step toward the woods. He grabbed her by the arm. "You're not going back in there." He was beginning to realize what was going on. He didn't understand exactly, but it seemed as though they were facing their worst fears.

She tugged against his grasp. "Let me go!" She broke free, stumbled, and raced toward the woods. He chased after her, then grabbed her around the waist and lifted her off the ground. She kicked and screamed as he pulled her away and brought her back toward the river.

"Let me go!"

"Wynter, this isn't what it seems. This isn't real."

She continued to struggle, but he kept whispering in her ear that it wasn't real until she finally calmed and stopped fighting him. He slowly released her, and she turned into his arms.

"I don't understand what's happening," she said.

The baby was still crying; the river was still flowing.

"If we can't see past our own fears, we'll never find the Iron Gate." He released her and pointed at the river. "In my dream, you drown in that river."

Wynter stared at the river. "The baby..." she whispered, glancing behind her.

"Who is this baby?" he asked.

She looked him in the eyes. "I think he's...I think he's ours."

Gideon's heart raced.

She covered her mouth with her hand and backed away. "But it can't be," she mumbled. "You're in love with Hilran."

He reached out, but she stepped back. Tears pooled in her eyes.

"Wynter. I'm not in love with Hilran."

"What?" she whispered.

"I'm in love with you." The words came with no thought. The stone had rolled away from his heart.

She shook her head. "But…"

He was about to reach for her when the ground beneath their feet shook.

75

———

WYNTER

Trees on the other side of the river toppled over with giant thuds. Gideon grabbed Wynter, and they watched in horror. The river exploded as the earth turned itself inside out. Then, out of the deep bowels of the earth, came a giant rounded stone. Hollow eyes appeared.

"Daughters of Alrenia, it's the cave," Wynter said.

The mouth rose from the ground, spilling an avalanche of dirt, rock, and river out of its gaping hole.

Gideon pulled her back as the ground splintered and cracked all around them. Then, just like that, the ground stood still.

Wynter looked behind them. The forest was no longer burning. It was a landscape of black tree trunks that stood like a memorial to death.

She was having a hard time wrapping her mind around the fact that the cave their physical bodies were currently in, was now right in front of them.

"You know that thing you said about this not being real?" Wynter said. "It sure feels real."

They separated and stared at the apparition in childlike wonder.

"We should go in? Right?" Wynter said.

Gideon went to draw his sword, but they both realized rather quickly that they were different inside the vision. They no longer had their weapons, and Gideon's wounds were gone.

Wynter took off, and he raced after her. They climbed the mound of debris that had been regurgitated by the giant head. Their hands and feet sank into the soft ground as they scrambled for the cave entrance.

Wynter arrived before he did. She waited as he grappled through the last few feet, and they once again found themselves standing at the entrance to the cave.

"Are you ready?" he asked, catching his breath.

She nodded.

Gideon motioned toward the entrance. "Let's find Isidor."

She smiled and they entered the cave together.

The first thing she did was check the ceiling. No Morbids. Not that it mattered. Back in the real world, she and Gideon were surrounded by the little beasts.

The cave was just as before. All rock walls, no exits.

"I don't get it," Gideon said. "What now?"

"We're missing something," she said.

"What?"

They split up and walked around the cave, searching.

Wynter replayed the words of the oracle in her mind.

Yet, he who will go forward with his whole heart will obtain what he seeks. Only do not be of two minds, for the two rings of Ferran are the key to your salvation.

Do not be of two minds... Do not be of two minds... They had the two rings. They were united now, they weren't of two minds. Then it hit her.

No. It can't be that simple.

She turned to find Gideon. He was running his hands along a wall on the opposite side.

"Gideon."

"Yeah," he said, without turning around.

"I think I know what to do."

She walked toward him. He stopped his search and met her in the middle of the cave.

"I'm open to ideas," he said, scanning the ceiling.

"You know that thing you said just a few minutes ago?"

He dropped his gaze to hers. It was clear he knew exactly what she meant. He seemed to be holding his breath.

"I love you, too," she said softly.

They stood there gaping at each other like a couple of awkward teenagers. Then he drew her into his arms and kissed her, and never had she felt such happiness.

THE NEXT THING SHE KNEW, they were back in the *real* cave, standing in water with Morbids all around them.

76

GIDEON

"Remind me never to fall in love while I'm trying to save the world," Gideon said, looking at the Morbids clawing at their knees.

"I couldn't agree more," Wynter said.

A blinding light suddenly illuminated the back of the cave as part of the wall broke away. The Morbids scrambled as if the light was their master, come to call them home. They all huddled in a back corner, screeching in a fever pitch.

The back wall crumbled bit by bit, letting in more and more light. It appeared as though someone were breaking through from the other side. Gideon and Wynter drew their swords and stood at the ready. But once they saw what was being revealed, their swords dropped to their sides. It was a gate. An old, worn gate, flooded with bright light, revealing nothing of what lay beyond it.

"The Iron Gate," Gideon whispered.

"It's real." Wynter said.

They looked at each other in astonishment. They sheathed their swords and moved in slowly. The Morbids had calmed and were now emitting a low humming sound.

Gideon's hands shook. If the legendary Isidor was behind

that gate, then their people would finally be able to make a new start.

He held up a hand to shade his eyes and reached out and took Wynter's hand with the other. They approached the gate together.

"Whatever happens," Wynter said.

"I know."

Gideon's heart raced when he saw the lock. It had two circular holes. Their rings *were* the key! They looked at each other expectantly and removed their rings. They placed them in the holes.

"Together," Gideon said.

Wynter nodded.

"1...2...3."

They both turned their rings inside the lock. There was a brief nothing, then a singular click. Gideon pulled Wynter back, and the gate swung open. The blinding light slowly dissipated.

"Gideon, are you seeing what I'm seeing?"

"Isidor."

They looked at each other and smiled.

77

———

WYNTER

Three weeks later

How did one describe a place untouched by man? Isidor was a land of endless hills and meadows of verdant green surrounded by higher rocky ground. The ancient forests were full of Oak, Yew, and Chestnut trees with trunks as wide as barrels and limbs as thick as a man's body. Higher up through the tree line, along rocky paths and moss-covered cliffs, there were dozens of waterfalls flowing with water as clear as crystals. And though the cool air of fall was upon them, there were still tiny blue forget-me-nots and orange globe flowers blooming all around them. How did one explain the abundance of wildlife around them—red deer, field hares, and wild horses? How did one describe the great horns of the mountain goats that roamed the mountains and plains? And when Wynter stood by the shimmering lakes of Isidor, she had no answer but that God's hand had delivered them.

Kidron barged into the tent, breaking Wynter's quiet reflection.

317

Six sighed but continued to braid Wynter's hair.

"You're not going to believe this," Kidron said breathlessly.

Wynter wasn't surprised by Kidron's outburst. Since they had settled in Isidor, Kidron had often shown up with some new discovery to share—a sighting of a rare vanilla orchid, or chasing a marmot across a field. One could spend hours exploring the new land. But today Wynter needed to focus on one thing—marrying Gideon.

"Not now," Six said gruffly.

Wynter watched with mild amusement as Six looked Kidron up and down. Kidron's hair hung in messy waves, the knees of her pants looked like she'd been crawling through tunnels like a mole.

"Why aren't you dressed? The wedding is in less than an hour," Six said, exasperated.

Wynter found it charming that Six had taken a motherly role with Kidron.

Wedding. The words seemed like a dream. But today she would marry Gideon, and they would be king and queen of the new land. They'd only just declared their love for each other a few weeks ago, and since then, they'd barely had a moment alone. Their days had been filled with decisions—where to settle, how to lay out their new city, which wood to use for the new structures, how to organize work groups. There was little time for a wedding, but Gideon had insisted that they marry as soon as possible in order to solidify their unity and rule of the people. It didn't sound very romantic, but she didn't care because when she looked into Gideon's eyes, she knew his heart belonged to her.

Kidron glared at Six. "I'm not dressed because there's not going to be a wedding!"

Wynter pushed Six's busy hands away and stood. "This isn't funny, Kidron."

"I'm not playing, I swear." She pointed outside the tent. "Hundreds of people just showed up and one of them says he's the Alrenian queen's chamberlain. He says there's not going to be a wedding until he meets with the queen."

Wynter's heart fluttered. "Daughters of Alrenia." She lowered herself into her chair.

The middle forest must have received her message about coming to Isidor and joining the Uluns. The last time she saw the queen's chamberlain was back at post 21, right before he'd told her that her job wasn't to protect the queen.

Six put a hand on her shoulder. "Don't worry," she said in typical Jutta fashion.

Wynter wished she had some of Six's Jutta optimism. The chamberlain would take one look at her and know she wasn't the real queen. It was true everyone else had accepted her as queen, but that didn't matter if the new arrivals objected to her claim. This sudden twist of events could erase all the progress they had made to unite the people of Ferran.

She stood and rolled her shoulders, trying to relax. She was in her blue woolen dress, nothing fancy by a queen's standard, but there was no time to worry about appearances. The sooner her legitimacy was addressed, the better. She wasted no time and marched out of her tent.

There were people everywhere—hundreds of Alrenians walking around, amazed by their new surroundings. She spotted Gideon talking with a man that she recognized right away—the queen's chamberlain. The man from post 21—short in stature with the pockmarked nose.

At least their conversation looked cordial. Elias stood by Gideon's side as Brendle once had, and she had a moment of wishing her spirit wolf was there to reassure her of her path.

She pulled her shoulders back and headed straight for them.

I'm the queen. I'm the queen. She fingered her gold ring with her thumb.

She cleared her throat as she arrived, and a path was made for her. The chamberlain stopped mid-sentence when she presented herself at his side.

"I'm glad to see you received my message. Welcome to Isidor." She avoided looking at Gideon for fear she would falter. She could see him staring at her curiously out of the corner of her eye.

The chamberlain squinted at her, giving her a good once over. The last time she'd seen this man she'd been disguised as a boy.

"Can I have a moment alone with the chamberlain?" Wynter said, looking around her.

Gideon responded with his trademark scowl, but reluctantly drifted away, the others following his lead.

Wynter held her head high. "I'll make this real simple for you," she said matter-of-factly. He raised an eyebrow. "The queen you remember is dead. She gave me the ring and the power to heal right before she died. I tried to return to the colony to relinquish the *gift*, but circumstances did not allow me to."

"I'm quite aware, young lady," he said coolly.

"Well then, we find ourselves at a crossroad."

"You tried to heal the Ulun king?" he asked, with a probing eye.

"Yes," she said, feeling ill at ease.

"His son?"

Daughters of Alrenia. How does he know this?

"Yes," she said softly.

"A *dog*?"

She swallowed. "Yes." It barely came out a whisper.

"You killed this traitor, Finn, who led the Ulun pigs who destroyed our northern colony?"

"That's right," she said, trying to sound more confident.

The way he had rattled off her escapades made her realize how impossible it all sounded. She flustered.

A lowly transporter takes the queen's gift, tries to heal their sworn enemies and a dog, and then kills the traitor who sought to destroy them all.

"I realize how this must look—"

He held up hand, cutting her off.

"You won't be able to heal anymore. You've wasted too much of yourself. Perhaps your children will be able to heal, perhaps they won't. It's hard to say."

She wasn't sure, but he seemed to be conceding that she was queen. "What are you saying?"

"I'm saying that healing a dog was a very foolish thing to do. You and I need to have a talk about proper behavior."

She dared a small smile. Out of everything she'd done, he thought the *dog* was the worst of it?

"And for the love of Alrenia, no more killing. Oh my, the thought of a queen wielding a spear." He rolled his eyes.

"Wait. How did you know all of that?" she asked.

He waved a dismissive hand. "That seer of yours, Gotz. He's very talkative, let me tell you."

"What? Are you sure?" Wynter scanned the crowds, looking for him.

"We found him in the woods with a nasty stab wound. I'm surprised he survived. But now that I've gotten to know him, I'd say stubbornness is what has kept him alive."

"I should go see him," Wynter said, feeling a sudden euphoria.

"He's fine. I assure you. Though he didn't much like being carried here on a stretcher. And he refused to wear anything but that ridiculous robe of his."

"Thank you," she said. This was more than she could have hoped for on her wedding day. Gotz was more like family to Gideon than he cared to admit.

"Truthfully, we needed a guide," he said with a thin smile.

"Regardless," she said smiling, "he's very important to me and Gideon."

He stopped his tirade and examined her clothes. "Oh no," he said shaking a finger. "No. This will not do. Absolutely not." He lifted his arm and snapped his fingers. "Portia!" A girl standing not too far away came to attention. "Bring the queen's wardrobe!"

He spun Wynter around, taking her by the arm, and led her back toward her tent. "If there's going to be a wedding, I'm going to make sure you're dressed properly for it."

She couldn't help but be amused. "Of course, whatever you think. But I should probably know your name if you're going to be my chamberlain."

"My given is Warin, Your Majesty."

"Nice to meet you, Warin."

In time, he would learn that his new queen carried a sword and would likely be in pants more often than a dress, but for now she'd humor him and let him think he was in charge. Today was her wedding day, and perhaps she did need that perfect dress, if only for a day.

78

GIDEON

Gideon knelt down next to Gotz's stretcher. "You have no idea how glad I am to see you."

"Bah," Gotz said, holding up a hand. "Help me up. The Alrenians treated me like an invalid. I would have been perfectly fine to walk on my own."

He grimaced as Gideon pulled him to a sitting position.

"You've never been a good patient. You probably complained the whole way here," Gideon said.

Gotz gave him a wry smile. "Who's the seer here? You or me?"

Gideon grinned.

"Come on," Gotz said, waving a hand. "Get me up."

Gideon grabbed him under the arm and helped him stand. Gotz made a myriad of faces in an attempt to disguise his pain.

Once standing, Gotz smoothed out his robe, then looked Gideon over like he hadn't seen him in ages. "I knew you'd find Isidor."

"Did you *see* it?" Gideon asked, wondering if perhaps Gotz had seen it in a vison.

Gotz shook his head. "No. I didn't have to." His look turned contemplative. "But I am sorry I didn't see Finn for who he was."

"Even seers aren't perfect."

Gotz smiled weakly. "I suppose that's true." He raised a finger. "However, I did *see* that snake Finn's end. I only wish I had been there to witness it."

"I wish I could say I saw it, but I was unconscious."

Gotz's eyes sparkled. "She's quite the woman, that Wynter."

Gideon smiled. "Yes, she is."

"And I hear there's a wedding today?"

Gideon rubbed the back of his neck and squinted at him with one eye. "I suppose this is where you say I told you so?"

"No," Gotz said with tenderness in his eyes. "This is where I ask if I can do the honors?"

The offer hit Gideon in a way he didn't expect. A lump formed in his throat, and for a minute, he couldn't speak. Gotz had been more like a father to him than his own king father. He clasped Gotz gently by the shoulder. "I wouldn't have it any other way."

Gotz patted Gideon's hand and nodded. A newfound respect passed between them. "Now then," Gotz said, eyeing Gideon's brown pants and white shirt. "Is that what you're wearing?"

He looked down. "What?"

Gotz rolled his eyes. "Trust me, that chamberlain, Warin, will have Wynter in gossamer wings if he can manage it. I think your dress shirt and jacket are in order."

Gideon smiled and held up his hands in surrender. "Okay."

Chaos had ensued around them with the arrival of the new Alrenians. Tomas and Hilran, who were married on the first night in Isidor, were running around trying to bring some semblance of order back to the base camp. But Gideon felt strangely calm. He and Gotz headed toward his tent.

"Has she told you about the vision of the baby yet?"

Gideon glanced over at him and scowled. "Not now, Gotz," he said gruffly.

But Gotz was all smiles. And inside, Gideon was smiling too.

79

WYNTER

"Let us begin," Gotz said.

Wynter and Gideon stood face-to-face under the bronze and gold leaves of a cherry tree. Kidron stood just behind Wynter, holding a small bouquet of wildflowers. Her wardrobe of clean pants and white shirt was an arguable compromise.

Gideon was more handsome than she'd ever seen him. Perhaps it was because he was smiling. He wore his white shirt with the high collar, his knee-length jacket, and his father's sliver wolf clasp on his lapel. Wynter had humored her new chamberlain, Warin, by wearing a white gown of silk with embroidered leaves that snaked across her shoulder and down to the hem. Six had removed the braiding after she saw the dress, and now Wynter's hair hung in loose waves around her shoulders.

Eager whispers of their people resounded through the air, but she kept her eyes on Gideon for fear she would faint.

Gideon held out his hand with the wolf ring, palm down.

"Place your hand upon his," Gotz instructed Wynter.

She raised her shaking hand with the eagle ring and placed it on Gideon's. Her head swooned.

Gotz removed a lariat from around his neck and wrapped it

around their wrists. He lifted his eyes to the heavens and raised a hand. "Before the eyes of God do we now ask that he bind these two together as man and wife. Let nothing come between their sacred bond."

He lowered his hand and looked at Gideon. "Gideon. Do you promise to honor God's sacred sacrament?"

"I do."

Gideon sounded sure, and it helped squelch her anxiety.

"Wynter. Do you promise to honor God's sacred sacrament?"

"I do," she said, smiling.

Gotz raised his hands to the sky, and looking up, said, "May these two lives, now bound as one, be at the service of the one and only God and the earthly kingdom of his mighty hand. Amen."

He unwound the cord around their wrists and kissed Gideon on the cheek. "Give this kiss to your wife to seal your marriage."

Gideon looked at her, and she could scarcely breathe. They both seem to understand as they stood there looking at each other that this was the moment they would start their lives together, and nothing, not even death, would ever destroy the love they had come to feel for each other.

He gently pulled her close to him. She willed herself not to shake. He placed his hands on her face and his forehead on hers. "I love you," he whispered. She wrapped her fingers around his wrists and smiled, willing herself not to cry. The people cheered them on, laughing.

"Kiss her already, you fool!"

"Hurry before she changes her mind!"

But their calls faded away as Gideon kissed her. Not only was she Gideon's wife, she was the Queen of Ferran and of Isidor. Their lives had always been inexplicably intertwined, and now fate had finally bound them. If she ever grew old, and time had forgotten all of this, she would start her story at the place where she and Gideon had first met...the day she fell from the trees. And no one would scarcely believe it.

ACKNOWLEDGMENTS

I owe a heartfelt thanks to my Blue Ink editors, Amanda and Stephanie. They took my imperfect manuscript and challenged me to do better. Without their hours and hours of editing and proofing, The King's Oracle would not be the story it is now. Also, thank you to Christa, who has kindly edited some of my short stories whenever I've asked. You three make me a better writer. For that, I'm deeply grateful.

ABOUT THE AUTHOR

Sherry Torgent is an award-winning YA author. Her novel Dandelion on Fire won the 2016 Benjamin Franklin IBPA gold medal for teen fiction, and her novel The Curse of Viola was a 2016 Foreward Indies Book of the Year Finalist in teen fiction. Her books are creative, fast-paced, young adult novels with supernatural elements that are known to keep her readers turning the pages late into the night.

When she's not writing, she serves as the Publishing Manager for Blue Ink Press. She lives in Raleigh, NC with her husband and mini-schnauzer, Opal.

www.sherrytorgent.com
www.blueinkpress.com